Brenda,

Thank you for buying these books. We know that Shane will benefit from your generous nature and now from buying these books.

CIRCLES OF HUMANITY

by Jack Richardson

CIRCLES OF INFLUENCE SERIES

BOOK 2

I hope you enjoy them

Love Jack.

Acknowledgements:

I would like to thank a few people for their support with this project:

Gerd Altmann for the photograph on the cover.

Connie Braithwaite for an overabundance of editing.

Catherine Leipciger for her insightful and critically valuable
professional assessment.

Victoria Ross for her technical support and patience.

To my sons, Ryan and Tyler for their brilliant insights and constant
support.

My wife Carol, for pretty much everything that can be imagined.

Hello, my name is Dan Wilson. If you just finished reading Circles of Influence, you will remember that I am Cayley Wilson's father and after years of estrangement, we now have a wonderful relationship. It was Cayley who motivated me to guide you through what you are about to read. Circles of Humanity is a direct continuation of the book Circles of Influence, but it's a bit more complicated than that. In fact, I think you had better sit down for this next bit of information because complicated is a massive understatement. When Cayley left the island and started her new life, it was October 2018 and I was fifty-one years old. The Circles of Humanity story begins in October 2058 and I am.....well, I'm dead.

I warned you to sit down. Now just in case you are science fiction adverse, please hear me out. I can communicate with you because a couple of years before I passed away, Cayley paid to have a cranial download of my brain so we could continue to be connected after my death. Still too much science fiction for you? Let me remind you it's

2058. A lot of technology happens in forty years. Personal computers seemed like science fiction in the 1940s. Fortunately, a lot of other things have occurred over the past four decades and that is why Circles of Humanity exists. You see, my daughter and her friends, Julie Peters and Adam Stapleton, are pretty much running the world today. I hate to brag, but I can't wait for you to find out what they have accomplished. I know I'm biased, but it's really rather remarkable. We will get into the relationship between Circles of Influence and Circles of Humanity soon enough, but first you are going to take a trip to Western China where our story begins. Safe travels, I'll be back soon.

Chapter 1
October 28, 2058.
Lilian, China.

The ancient cast-iron pot began to steam as the water absorbed the last remnants of heat to be afforded by the final licks of the coal-fired flames to be witnessed on that night. The aged couple had neither the luxury nor the need to keep the fire burning any longer. They had survived far colder nights than this. The warm tea would provide the necessary energy to get them from their fragile wooden rocking chairs to the yak skin covered mattress, the hardness of which matched the long life they had survived together. Life had not been easy in this remote area of China where each day was a challenge, but it was life and it was cause for extreme contentment. They had raised their son who had, in turn, done the same in his modest hut eighty-five meters away. Their grandson had been chosen for university and was now working in America. He regularly sent money, but they already had everything they required; food and pride. He would get his unspent money back some day. They sat together, reading by the light of the oil lamp as another day of their eighty-second year of life which, like the fire, would soon be extinguished.

They didn't hear the sound of the door opening but rather felt a slight draft. Almost in unison, gloved hands covered their mouths and noses. They could see uniforms but before long they could see nothing at all. An hour or two later she opened her eyes to darkness. She had no idea she was alone at that moment. She couldn't see the note, warning her not to tell anyone what happened or she would never see her husband again. Eighty-five meters away her son and his wife slept soundly, until they heard the scream.

Chapter 2
November 3, 2058. Hanoi, Vietnam.

  The silver light of the full harvest moon ineffectively watch-guarded the chaos far below as it illuminated the actions of anarchy occurring far too clearly. The scene was reminiscent of a vintage black and white movie where medieval villagers, brandishing torches and pitchforks, made futile attempts to unleash their fury on the King's army, only to be slaughtered mercilessly in defeat.

  Now, centuries later in the fall of 2058, this passionate release of futility was doomed to create casualties unlike anything that had occurred in over a decade. The scarcity of effective weapons in support of the mortal fears of the rioters led to their predetermined demise at the hands of the shocked yet effective Public Guard. Their goal was to subdue rather than defeat the attacking mob and thankfully there had been no fatalities, so far.

Chapter 3
November 3, 2058. Trenton, USA.

Cayley Wilson watched in horror at the scene spreading out around her in real-time accuracy on the high definition screens of her work station. The three hundred and twenty degrees of three-dimensional Global-Com live video placed her in the centre of the action. Cayley's stomach crawled as the persistent Vietnamese citizens forged to their ultimate defeat. Given the determined escalation of irrationality that had been growing in the media over the past days, she really shouldn't have been surprised at what she was remotely witnessing, but she couldn't help it. Violence was so unnecessary and archaic, yet this was really happening and had been expanding exponentially as eruptions were surfacing around the globe. Groups of emotionally charged people were utilizing irrational actions to make a statement. She shook her head at the futility of the crusade she was witnessing and began to survey her thoughts as to what she might be able to do to minimize the tragedy and help restore calm. She needed to talk with Julie Peters, who she knew was already up to her neck in problems. They would have to resolve this crisis quickly before it trended out of control.

Her attention was drawn to a monitor on her right where she noticed a man attacking the guards with what looked like a relic, US Army-issue handgun. A shielded guard waited as long as he could before firing a taser weapon at his attacker who immediately reacted in a convulsing display of defeat. Cayley was transfixed on the man's eyes as they transformed from those of a cornered beast ready to fight his way out of danger to those of a paralyzed addict completely devoid of focus.

In the background of this horrific scene, Cayley recognized the tranquility of the Lake of the Returned Sword in the heart of the 'Old City' of Hanoi. Twenty years ago, when physical travel was still commonplace, she and her husband had been to the exact spot while visiting her good friend Hai Nguyen. Closing her eyes, she could restore the sense of calm and pastoral comfort provided them as they shared a few quiet hours walking with him along the shoreline of the beautiful, urban lake. The seemingly permanent, low-lying fog still clung to the surface of the water and tenderly wrapped the massive banyan trees as they silently stood witness to a century or two of human tragedies and triumphs. Cayley soberly laughed at the rationalization that what she called fog was the residue from the burning of soft, peaty coal used for cooking and warmth. The 'fog' which existed today was the co-mingling of pollutants still residing in the core of many of the larger cities of the still developing world. She had 'cyber-visited' this wonderful place many times since being there with Hai. In times of stress, when she needed to collect her thoughts and seek her own inner counsel, the hazy obscurity of this lakeside retreat would transport her mind and encourage her mental clarity.

Cayley was tempted to 'cyber-visit' there now in order to better understand what was happening but seeing one of her favourite places on earth being savaged by the events of the night almost made her sick to her stomach. She could also see Hai's family, who had recently contacted her with the news that he was missing and had been for a few days. His family had been growing frantic, fearing the worst, and had reached out to her in search of some sort of solution to their concerns about his well-being.

It wasn't as if she didn't already have enough to worry about but she and Hai had been introduced nearly thirty-five years earlier as members of the initial Circles of Humanity beta test group. She thought of him as her little brother and would do whatever she could to find out what had happened to him, but this was not the right time.

The press of a button shut down the entire three hundred and twenty degrees of monitors surrounding her, the contents of which were increasingly irritating and depressing. She needed to disengage for a while for the sake of her own sanity.

Cayley rose from her ridiculously, comfortable chair, strode the five short meters to her living room and then absently hung a right and entered her pristine, stainless steel kitchen. 'I really should cook more,' she thought to herself, noticing her spotless underused appliances. 'When Jermaine and Claire come home for Thanksgiving next week I'll make a meal,' she decided. 'Hopefully I remember how.'

She dispensed a soda and lime while she consciously planned her day which had already gone off the rails. It looked like her agenda would bear no resemblance to what she had thought she would do that day. The weather in late October was supposed to have been one of the rewards for her decision to relocate herself and her two children to the east coast about five years earlier, just after her husband died. The firestorm of colours provided by the pervasive vegetation this time of year was not to be missed, but once again it looked like her walk through the nearby park would have to wait for another day. 'Well, if I can't get out in real life, I will take a half hour hike along the Appalachian Trail at some point this afternoon,' she promised herself. Immediately she felt better about another day of fighting fires and attempting to apply reason to the emotions of those who relied on her to get things done.

She took ten laps of blood circulating exercise around her relatively tiny apartment and then settled back down at her command centre. Cayley carefully positioned her headset and turned her focus to the primary monitor where her thoughts began to accumulate in front of her eyes.

She watched as the priority list of things to do that day manifested itself on the screen. Number one was to call Julie to see how they are making out with the Population Consensus report being developed. A visual image of her best friend, the way Julie looked the last time they had spoken, appeared on the monitor along with a notation that it was currently only six in the morning in Seattle and Julie was currently offline for personal activities, which hopefully meant sleep. A transcript of their most recent discussions began to populate themselves along with a list of their individual agreed to courses of action. Checking her own list of tasks, Cayley was happy to see she had fulfilled her specific assignments. Primarily her role was to provide communication and develop strategic alliances between the Circles of Influence divisions and their end users. They included virtually every significant government and corporation around the globe. It still amazed her how the world had become unified within her lifetime. Had it not been for the seeds of reason and humanity that were planted and nurtured over the past four decades by her dear friends Adam and Julie, she could not even imagine how devastatingly different the world could be by now. They had not only salvaged her own life but had also positively reshaped society as a whole. They had begun by utilizing education and support through the Circles of Influence (COI) website to help her turn her life around, along with millions of other individuals. Adam had created an online version of the exercise they went through on the island where they sat in a circle and listened to and supported each other. She had used that part of the website many times over the years as she worked to straighten out her life.

Then Adam and Julie sparked a revolution of feelings and thought that spread around the world in a collective marriage of technology and humanity. The tool they used was called Circles of Humanity (COH) where groups of twenty-five diverse individuals from around the globe were brought together through understanding and acceptance. Cayley reflected back to when she participated in one of the first COH beta test groups. Unlike the reality of falling deeply in love with your infant baby the moment you see it for the first time, the COH process took years. Coming to know, accept, trust and eventually care for the other twenty-four individuals as you would with your most trusted friends and family took time. Fortunately it had been time well spent and the reality was it had gradually developed into the most natural thing in the world. Humans are wired genetically to love and to be loved despite our disturbing history of warring and treachery. When innocent humans are subjected to a society run by fear and powerful divisive forces, they unknowingly become transformed into something far less than they are meant to be and society as a whole is victimized. Circles of Humanity revealed our commonalities and allowed us to see beyond what we had been conditioned to see. We learned how to view others acceptingly with our hearts instead of conditionally with our brains. As the concept became scalable, hundreds, then thousands, and now hundreds of millions of groups of twenty-five people have come to exist and experience the reality of what humanity is capable of. One result of this amalgamation of six billion people into a connected and unified entity has been the growing impossibility for traditional corporate, religious and political powers to continue to control the human spirit by keeping people separate, suppressed and at odds with each other. The tipping point came when the technology was developed to allow the positive human spirit from each individual group to be captured and combined with each of the other groups. The positive energy from each group was overlain on those of millions of other groups like synchronous wavelengths in physics and music. The destructive interference, or noise, which exists when wavelengths are out of synch was eliminated when the entire population was finally brought into unison. The constructive energy of harmony is able to be fed back to each individual as a feelings and knowledge-based feedback loop of positivity.

* * * * * * *

I am sorry to interrupt the story, but I believe those last two sentences are very critical when it comes to understanding how much things have changed in the past forty years. I have an analogy that may cement a vision in your mind as to what has been accomplished. Close your eyes and imagine you have gone to the philharmonic. You arrive early and as you become seated, you are greeting by the orchestra as they are warming up. Sixty professional musicians, all on their own agenda are preparing for the performance. The confusion of squeals and squawks make you want to cover your ears and run for the exits. This is reminiscent of our society back in my day when everyone, independent of their skills and motives, was participating in a segmented society on their own agendas. Many of those people were talented, well-meaning individuals seeking to make progress for their faction of society. The problem was that, as with the orchestra, every effort was at odds with those of a separate person or group which was focused on their specific purpose. What was missing in both examples was a commonality of purpose. The orchestra, under the direction of their Maestro, or conductor, produces music that can bring you to tears in your enjoyment of their combined talent. Our global society, in the same vein produced destructive chaos as a result of each societal group being at odds in search of progressing their distinct desires. Fortunately, Adam Stapleton became a global conductor of humanity who was able to align society and allow the voice of the people to speak in harmony.

****

    Cayley had no idea how any of Adam's achievements were accomplished on a technical level, but when she wore her cranial cap and interacted with her COH group, she could feel the overwhelmingly inclusive and positive energy of all of humanity coursing through her .

When she was released from prison forty years earlier, five months shy of her twenty-fourth birthday, Cayley had found herself immersed in a world where her contemporaries used their cell phones and computers as wireless umbilical cords connecting them with the rest of the world. There were Facebook, Instagram, Twitter and Snapchat accounts, dating sites and on and on. She remembered feeling like an alien as she worked her way back into mainstream society. Her father, whom she lived with at first, was no help. He was as tech savvy as a platypus. It wasn't that she had never owned a cell phone before but a phone without friends is kind of like a steering wheel without a car. She could remember deciding at the time her priority would be to add people to her life and hope the technology would eventually come to her. Looking at the space shuttle-like workspace that surrounded her, it was clear her plan had worked.

'Thank God,' Cayley may have spoken aloud as the connective feelings of societal warmth and support flowed through her, courtesy of the collective database of humanity her headset was delivering to her limbic system. It empowered her to act and think positively, in synch with billions of other souls around the world with whom she was inextricably connected. She closed her eyes, savouring the energy and reassurance that the images of Hanoi were an outlier to the existing and pervasive positivity in the world. She had to believe the Hanoi riots were not representative of a growing existence of negativity and they would be able to successfully combat the current social unrest through the power of collective reason and support.

"Cayley, do you have a moment?" a familiar voice interrupted her moment of recharge. It was Manuel Rosales, who was able to access her due to his priority status. She recognized the smooth Latino voice of her colleague who was the Chairman of the Global Council, arguably the most powerful person on earth. Cayley opened her eyes and examined the image of the man who was her most important client but who was more like a reciprocally respectful friend. He looked tired. His eyes were red and puffy and his usually perfectly groomed, thick, black hair was uncommonly tussled haphazardly across his furrowed forehead. She decided to accept his invitation to communicate and instantly saw the relieved expression on his weary face as her image came available to him in his office in Buenos Aires.

"Have you been up all night, Manuel?" Cayley inquired.

"You don't look all that refreshed yourself this morning," he replied with a smile.

"Yeah, lots going on. What can I do for you this fine morning?"

"I was just wondering what progress is being made on the population consensus document. We really need to mainstream the presentation as of yesterday. People are going crazy with misinformation and we're losing control of this thing. The riots are growing in scale and intensity."

"I know, Manuel and I don't think they are being generated organically. The unrest is occurring contrary to the existing societal approval trends. It seems like the demonstrations are being manipulated. I just wish I knew where it is coming from," Cayley responded candidly.

"When you figure it out, I better be the first person you call. You do know you work for me, don't you?"

"Everyone works for you, Manuel, but the truth is you have no idea what you would ever do without me," Cayley countered with a sweet smile which, at sixty-three years of age, had still retained some positive effect.

"That may well be true, but this is serious. We need the people to understand they have nothing to fear and they need to know it right away. Someone is going to get killed out there."

"I am extremely cognizant of that fact, Manuel, and believe me, we are doing our best. I will be speaking with Julie in a couple of hours. I think they are pretty much ready to roll out the final manuscript. I trust you want to review it before it goes out?"

"Absolutely. I'm sure it will be great but just for my own peace of mind, I want to see it first."

"Of course. As our most important, not to mention favourite, customer, you will be the first to see it. I'll keep you posted. Is there anything else I can help you with?"

"Let's just deal with one crisis at a time."

"All right. You know where to find me if anything else comes up."

"When was the last time you went out, Cayley?" Manuel softened, now that the business had been taken care of. They were friends after all.

"Do you mean out as in sunshine and fresh air or are you asking about my dating schedule?"

"I meant any face-to-face interaction with a human who isn't made out of pixels. I don't care if you walk around the block with a friend, go to a bar or throw a party for your colleagues, you need to have some fun with real live people once in a while."

"The kids are coming for Thanksgiving next week."

"You Americans sure do love your traditional holidays. Tell me, now since the NFL no longer exists and the Black Friday experience of shopping for things you don't need is out of vogue, do you actually talk with each other and give thanks the way your grandparents used to?"

"You're a bit too young to be talking about the good old days, Manuel," she laughed.

"Just because I am four years younger than you doesn't detract from my vast wisdom. Anyway, after you solve all of my problems, I order you to have some fun and report back to me with the details."

"Sir, yes sir! Later then," she concluded and vaporized his image from the screen as she thought about his suggestion to have fun. It was an interesting concept she should consider. There was no way she could be best friends with a top-notch psychologist for forty years and not understand the complexity of abstract concepts like fun and happiness. Cayley understood that her logical conscious brain was the master of her reality, but she felt she had managed to build a fair degree of balance into her life. The demands she had put on herself a decade earlier when she agreed to the request of Adam Stapleton and took on the job of the Circles of Influence Government Liaison Manager, were well balanced by her personal life. 'Well, sometimes they are,' she backtracked, acknowledging the existing reality. Hers truly was a job filled with unreasonable demands and challenges but the knowledge and feelings that rewarded her almost every day kept her completely satiated with rewards. She was immensely proud of what they were achieving. Maybe she had been drinking the company Kool-Aid but she couldn't even imagine the kind of world that would have been left to her children, and hopefully some day grandchildren, had COI not transformed the collective morality and purpose of most of the earth's nine billion citizens. Once Adam's COI website became the cornerstone of human growth, he and Julie went to work on positively shaping the progress of our young people by developing a psychologically driven scholastic curriculum for six to eighteen year olds within the framework of Circles of Education (COE). Since then, three decades of young people have successfully survived puberty and reached adulthood armed with self-esteem, positive moral values and an understanding of who they are. They have been provided with the understanding of how each person can positively affect the lives of others and the results have been remarkable. This change included her own two children, Jermaine and Claire, who Cayley freely admitted were amazing.

****

What do you think of my sixty-three-year-old daughter now? Rather impressive don't you think? She has come a long way, but the platypus remark was definitely uncalled for. Anyway, you may be having a bit of difficulty adjusting to life forty years in the future. It's kind of like the Rip Van Winkle effect where you have just awoken to a totally new reality. Don't feel bad if you struggle with some of the concepts at first. I lived through it and I struggled with the changes all the way. The important thing for you to remember is that, as humans, we are all products of our environment. Think of putting a bright shiny penny into a pool of water. Before long, it transforms into a dull corroded disc because it has absorbed all of the elements from the water. Now compare the penny to a newborn baby. It enters the world defined by its ancestral genetics and then gradually absorbs the elements from its surroundings. Like the penny, it changes uniquely depending on what it is exposed to. Cayley's psychologist friends refer to this as 'nurture'. You are born based on your biological genetics ('nature') and then you transform based on your surroundings. You learn to think, feel and evolve depending on what and who you are surrounded by. What I am trying to help you understand is that, because you have not evolved through the past forty years, you may not relate to some of the realities of what is to be your future. Some things you read in this book will just seem wrong to you. I suggest you keep an open mind and think beyond yourself. We are all limited by our own personal frames of reference. They define how we think and feel about things and restrict other possibilities. Close your eyes and imagine having been born a hundred years before or after your actual birthdate. Or perhaps consider having been born on the same day but into a completely different circumstance. Imagine that your gender, race, religion and socioeconomic situation is different from the one you are currently living. You may be able to relate to some of the variables of these new realities but your perceptions will be controlled by your actual present day circumstances. Let's say you imagined being born in a cardboard shelter in the slums of Mumbai in the year 2030. You are a baby girl with eight siblings and a mother. Immediately, the actual 'you' feels sorry for the future, alternative 'you,' knowing that your life expectancy will be short and your life will be defined by a meagre existence at best. The thing is, this future little baby 'you' doesn't know any of it. She has no understanding of anything besides her reality. She has no reason to be sad or pessimistic about her life. There is no reason for her to expect and create anything other than happiness. That, my friends, is the power of perspective. Okay, now back to the story.

Chapter 4
November 3, 2058. Trenton/Seattle, USA.

"Julie, good morning. I hope I didn't wake you," Cayley cringed, as it seemed clear she had. Julie Peters was her best friend even though they lived five thousand kilometres and three time zones apart.

"You did, but it's okay. If you decide to live on the West Coast, you need to be a morning person. I'm starting to get accustomed to six hours of sleep a night."

"I'm really sorry."

"It was a late night. I got on a roll finishing off the new program. I suppose that's what you are calling about."

"Well, yes, and to see how you are doing."

"Nice try. Actually I was looking forward to your call. We have basically wrapped up the next segment, but I wanted to check on a few things."

"Okay, fire away."

"Well, as I understand it my mandate was to initiate a philosophical discussion designed to allow the Circles of Humanity groups to understand and explore their feelings about such topics as mortality, quality of life, spirituality, and life after death. And then we are to create a statistical analysis of the relative importance of the varying responses. Am I right so far?" Julie tried to clarify.

"That's pretty much it. You make it sound so easy."

"Trust me, Cayley, there was nothing easy about it. It's no problem for me to facilitate a discussion process, but turning thoughts and feelings into numbers is never easy. Any exercise in statistics is so easy to inadvertently manipulate that it is common to do so without even realizing it. Controlling the output is easy but preventing yourself from doing so unintentionally is really hard."

"I couldn't agree more, and it's something we have to be so careful about. In the past, people used surveys and statistics to manufacture the answers they wanted. How they worded a question would dictate the answer they received. With enough forethought you could devise a result to convincingly support any agenda. I would have expected our current method of recording brain wave activity would be more clear cut and accurate."

"Well, yes and no. We are more clearly able to understand the thoughts and feelings the brain is processing, but it still doesn't take into account the clarity or truth of what is triggering the response. That can still be manipulated. All we can do is to strive for clear 'cause and effect' relationships where a specific reaction can be related to a single trigger. It sounds simple enough, but when you are dealing with complex intangible topics involving death and spirituality, it can get a little tricky," Julie explained.

"No doubt," Cayley agreed, "I am still blown away by how it all works."

"As a participant in your Circles of Humanity group you've had lots of experience when it comes to the interactive process. How would you describe the feelings you experience when your group is creating a positive synchronicity while discussing an emotional issue?" Julie asked.

"Well, you know how it is when you get creeped-out by something and chills run through you?"

"Yeah."

"Well, it's like the opposite of that," Cayley tried to explain. "You feel a warmth as it grows and moves through you. You feel uncontrollably good and positive. But when the conversation is strained due to any sort of conflicting discussion you get a feeling of uneasiness. Sometimes when it happens I take off my headset so that I'm not so consumed by the intensity of it all."

"You probably shouldn't do that. It will affect the feedback we receive and skew the data."

"Maybe so, but it can be hard to handle the negativity."

"I know, Cayley, but that is the point of the whole thing. It encourages the group to collectively overcome negativity through support and understanding."

"I know, and believe me, when the group is connected and communicating about something that gets us excited and in sync, it's a wonderful thing."

"It's called humanity and it is a wonderful thing," Julie confirmed. "Anyway, if we can get down to business, one thing I need to do is to confirm that the population statistics we were provided with are accurate and each of the plans being recommended are exactly as described."

"Of course they are! Credibility is the cornerstone of what Circles of Humanity is all about. That is the precise reason the public can trust us. We have never had an ulterior motive, bias or mandate other than helping everyone understand the truth about themselves and the world they live in. For centuries, the public had been lied to for the sake of promoting the agendas of others. We finally have two generations of citizens who do not expect and will not accept deception, and we're not going to screw it up now," Cayley affirmed with a great deal of intensity.

"So you can trust your sources?"

"What do you mean sources? This comes straight from the Global Council. They have grown with us. We are all on the same page."

"Yeah, I know, but this is important."

"It's all important, Jules. What's with the paranoia?"

"I don't know. Maybe it's the spread of violence. People are being hurt and it's escalating. That sort of thing isn't supposed to happen any more."

"Yeah, thanks to you and Adam and your staff."

"Thanks to people," Julie corrected," who now understand and recognize the truth about what is really important."

"Which you have helped them understand. They trust you because they have no reason not to."

"And we need to stay trustworthy, Cayley. That's why I need you to be sure. Whatever we tell the public, it's paramount that it is an honest and clear message with no hidden agendas."

"Look Julie, I don't know what's fuelling the violence going around, but whatever it is needs to be stopped. What I provided to you are the straight goods, as always."

"I'm sure that's true. I just get worried sometimes. When we started all of this, it would never have occurred to me it would get so big. We're connected to more than three quarters of the people on earth. They rely on us to get this right. It wasn't so long ago people would kill for a small fraction of the influence we have. Just because we use it for the common good doesn't make it any less of a commodity than it's always been. No one group in the history of mankind has been able to speak directly to over seven billion people and actually be accepted as the voice of truth and reason. When we started this whole thing we were being branded as a cult and described as communists. We facilitated the greatest grassroots movement in the history of humankind and a lot of powerful people were swept aside in the process."

"And many of them didn't go down quietly," Cayley concurred. She understood all too well what Julie was referring to. "Just because the most recent occurrences of pre-meditated or conflict oriented deaths happened more than a decade ago, we still need to be aware of potential threats of any nature."

"It's really hard to think that way anymore, but you're right, Julie. Something is causing this current social upheaval and since we are intimately connected to the existing humanity, we are right in the thick of things."

"I'll send you my final draft to have a look at. Let me know if you see any issues with what I have put together. We'll be ready to disseminate the information in a couple of days."

"Sounds good Julie. I'll look it over as soon as you get it to me."

"I just did. I hope you like it"

"I'm sure I will."

"If you have a few more minutes, Cayley, the other thing I wanted to talk to you about relates to the inconsistencies we have been getting with our data interface with Braintrust."

"Are we going to regret the day we agreed to merge our data with them?"

"I hope not. I know it sounds like science fiction, but the reality of being able to download a person's brain onto a computer and then access the knowledge, reason, and emotionality it contains is really impressive," Julie marvelled.

"And now that we can link all of the downloads together into a kind of super think-tank, we have a database of knowledge and wisdom that keeps growing as it is being added to," Cayley agreed. "I guess we have to remember that our lives are the science fiction of our grandparents' era."

"Do you remember what year they started doing the cranial downloads?" Julie asked.

"I think they finished their testing about four years ago. I heard they downloaded their one-thousandth brain a couple of months ago."

"Adam told me he was number nine hundred and eighty-two. It was quite an honour for him to be asked to be a part of the program and have his knowledge added to the database."

"Well deserved for sure. You won't be far behind, Jules."

"Don't hold your breath. Anyway, what I wanted to talk about was my meeting with Josh Li, our Head of Information Technology. He is literally pulling his hair out because of the increasing data variances he's seeing when he does projections with data combining the COH and Braintrust data sets."

"Really, I thought the merge had gone well. It's been almost two years since we successfully merged the data, which, if I recall correctly, was your idea."

"Yeah," Julie acknowledged, "well, I'm not sure I want to take ownership of that idea the way Josh has been ranting. I saw him briefly yesterday afternoon and he isn't a happy camper."

"But it sounds so ideal. You take the raw data from all the COH groups that contain the collective desires of seven billion people, you use the algorithms from our 'Circles of Consensus' (COC) group to produce a statistical analysis of the data, and then apply the mental capability of a thousand of the brightest minds of the past two or three generations to be able to develop strategies to achieve mankind's mandates. The ultimate marriage of desire, purpose and know-how," Cayley marvelled. "It's been going really well. The Global Council is thrilled to be accurately informed about what our society wants and needs and to have been directed how best to achieve the desired results."

"Well, I'm afraid there's a 'but' coming," Julie warned her friend. "Josh told me he's almost to the point where he can't believe the Braintrust output data. He wants you to talk with them and have them run some analytics to confirm that their data isn't being corrupted somehow."

"How does he know the problems aren't originating from our systems?"

"Because it's his data base and he's already tested it five ways from Sunday."

"Maybe he's too close to see it," Cayley offered.

"Yeah, maybe, but I don't know enough to tell him that. Besides, we've spared no expense to hire the best and the brightest to ensure the problem doesn't reside with us, so we are going to have to trust them until proven otherwise."

"I know," Cayley agreed, "but I am sure the Braintrust people feel the same way."

"It only makes sense they would. Anyway, if you wouldn't mind closing the loop on this and approach them at a management level, through the Global Council, it would really help."

"Are there any specific topics of data we should ask them to investigate for their validity?"

"Maybe start with agricultural yields, Julie suggested. "One of the most important aspects of sustaining population growth is being able to feed everyone and the data seems to be showing reduced yields. If there is any foundation to the fears that our population trends are unsustainable and will have to be dealt with in some negative way, it may well be due to a lack of food. Maybe you can check with Hai Nguyen at the UN and get their raw input data so we can compare it to the Braintrust output parameters and see if there is a major discrepancy.

"I would love to, but Hai seems to be missing in action. No one has heard from him for the past few days."

"That's weird. You must be worried!"

"Definitely, but I'm sure he'll show up. Regardless, I'll get to work on your request," Cayley confirmed. "Just get Joshua settled down if you can."

"You know I can't prescribe drugs," Julie teased.

"Then support and understanding will have to do. It's your specialty, as I recall. Later, Jules."

****

Hi again. Cayley and Julie just talked about a bunch of things which would be new to you. Hopefully, I can help you get this Circles of Influence (COI) thing straight in your head. COI is the name of the non-profit company Adam Stapleton founded forty years ago and it's the name of the website he built to help individuals deal with their lives. Then Adam and Julie created Circles of Education (COE), which was designed to educate young people about themselves as humans and teach them how to fit into society. The next achievement was Circles of Humanity (COH), which designed and support-ed the groups of twenty-five people from around the world who were taught to accept and respect each other. They then developed Circles of Consensus (COC) which is the business arm of the company. It uses all of the data that accumulates from the millions of COH groups to help governments and companies understand the wants and needs of the global and regional populations. The information is then shared with Braintrust, which is a database of the collective cranial downloads from the brightest minds to create strategies on how to keep everyone happy.

In case you're wondering, my cranial download didn't make the cut. You'll be hearing a lot more about all of this in the story, but I thought it would be helpful to get them straight in your mind before we go any further. Oh, by the way, you are heading back to China now with one of Cayley's friends. Have fun, and when the time comes, don't look down!

Chapter 5
November 4, 2058. Old Town, Lijiang, China.

Hai Nguyen stopped in the middle of the intersection to get his bearings as passing pedestrians flowed around him from all angles. This seemed like the place his friend Vincent had suggested they meet. Five narrow, cobblestone streets dissected the ancient wooden buildings into irregular sectors that appeared to have been arranged in the most haphazard of possible orientations. The labyrinth of pathways meandered off as arbitrarily as the streams flowing through the area. Numerous picturesque, half-moon shaped stone bridges spanned the three tributaries of the Jinsha River that punctuated the Old Town of Lijiang in westernmost China at the foot of the Himalayan Mountains. This historic nucleus of what is now a large, bustling, modern city pays tribute to the settlement that had existed and evolved for the past twelve hundred years. It is situated at the geographical gateway to the Himalaya and the headlands of the major waterways of central and southern China. Being located on the once-famous and vital 'Silk Road' had predetermined its importance throughout the centuries.

With great relief, Hai spotted the smiling face of Vincent Wang as he appeared from around a blind corner. As longtime members of the same Circles of Humanity group, Vincent opened his arms as he closed in on his good friend for their first ever physical encounter after thirty-five years of friendship. At Hai's request, Vincent would enjoy his friend's company for a couple of nights.

"Welcome to Lijiang," Vincent proclaimed. "What do you think?"

"I think I am very happy to see you. I have been terminally lost since the moment I stepped into the old part of the city," Hai admitted.

"You and everyone else who wasn't born here. I've been living here for twenty years and I still get turned around sometimes," Vincent reassured him.

"This is fascinating. I read somewhere that this place was established in the ninth century. Is that true?"

"When you see the plumbing and the foundation of my house you will know it's true," Vincent laughed. "Assuming we can find it at all."

"Lead the way. I am so happy you invited me to stay with you so I can get acclimated to the temperature and elevation here before I head off. The air is a little warmer and thicker down by the coast."

"It is my honour to host you. It is such a treat to finally meet such a valued friend in person instead of online as we have for so long."

"The feeling is absolutely mutual," Hai confirmed as he followed Vincent through the maze. He thought it would be kind of strange meeting someone in person for the first time after sharing decades worth of emotional and intellectual intimacy. Other than Cayley, Vincent was now the only member of his COH group he had ever physically met. 'It seems pretty relaxed and natural,' he decided, as the two men talked and walked, almost in circles, completely at ease.

"You never really said what has brought you to my city."

"Well, it is kind of an extended business trip," Hai hedged his response, "but also kind of confidential so I cannot really get into it. I have been away from home for a week now, but I don't want anyone to know I am here. I hope I can count on your discretion if anyone asks."

"Anyone like who?" Vincent asked, clearly puzzled by the purpose of his friends visit.

"I don't know really. I guess just anyone who may be curious."

"Well, I'm curious and you are not telling me anything so what could I possibly divulge."

"Good, so my plan is working." Hai proclaimed, hoping the matter would be dropped.

"Then what can we talk about?" Vincent asked.

"Anything," Hai responded eagerly. "I would like to know what brought you to this part of China."

"Well, I was born near Shanghai. You know, where the air is warm and thick. The trouble was it got too thick. Besides, as you know I am a sculptor and this is one of the best known artistic centres in China."

"I have read that since tourism ended, the artisans provide the largest local economic stimulus," Hai stated. "Is that true?"

"Yes, the recent history of Lijiang over the past fifty years has been one of continued transition. It had just been a historic community in the centre of a strategically located small city. Most of the houses you see around us are a few hundred years old and have undergone numerous renovations. Around the beginning of this millennium, tourists began coming to the area, which was famous for its natural beauty and its skilled artisans. Many homes were transformed into guest houses and very good restaurants were opened. Then about thirty years ago it became a hotspot for increasingly wealthy young people who would come from universities and nearby cities to drink and party in the bars created to welcome them. Now that visitors are becoming increasingly rare, there has been a gradual transition back to a residential community but basically for poor struggling artists like myself."

They walked through a gate and Hai took in the sight of a large three-storey structure. One which apparently contained Vincent's residence and presumably his office, workshop, and gallery.

"It appears the struggle hasn't been too bad," Hai commented, based on the impressive surroundings.

"We get by," Vincent agreed with a modest smile. "Please come in and I will introduce you to my family. Maybe you can stay longer than you planned."

"I really wish I could. This place is amazing," Hai responded sincerely, but he knew his stay had to be brief. He had a lot of work to do and he was definitely on the clock. It sounded a bit like a pompous cliche he would never say aloud, but the fate of mankind may actually be depending on the outcome of his actions during the coming days.

Chapter 6
November 4, 2058. Seattle, USA.

Josh Li sat in his office pouring over the volumes of statistics flashing before his eyes on the collection of screens surrounding him. What was he missing? Normally he could do this in his sleep. Nothing could hide from him for long. The ability to identify outliers, data errors, and output irregularities were the reason he had been able to get a job with Circles of Influence and quickly progress to his current position of Senior Data Management Specialist for Circles of Consensus. His team was tasked with collecting all of the data from each of the two hundred and fifty-million Circles of Humanity groups. They attempted to recognize trends and amalgamations of how the more than six billion participants felt about their lives and the world they live in. Synthesizing such a vast amount of data took tremendous computing power but also required specialized techniques. His doctoral thesis on the Statistical Analysis of Human Emotions, completed at the Sichuan University, had prepared him well for the technical aspects of his work. It was his collaboration with Julie Peters over the past ten years that had really taught him about the psychology of human emotions. He had learned how to not only locate and identify problems with his data but to almost 'feel' when something was not as it should be and would set off his internal alarms. It was as if the data flow had a sort of body language that was calling out to him but try as he may, he couldn't interpret the current message.

"Josh, do you have a minute?" His father's voice, as it approached through his communications module, startled him as a slight shiver rolled through his body. He couldn't remember the last time his father had contacted him. Having access only through a communal system located about fifty kilometres from their home in rural China meant that their infrequent communications were always prearranged.

"What's wrong Dad?" Josh began anxiously, trying to conjure up the recollections of his best Mandarin.

"Is this a secure connection, son?"

"It is on my end, but you are on a community network there. Did you sign on with the secure setting?"

"Of course," his father responded sharply, "but can someone listen in somehow?"

"There will be no record of our conversation once we are done, but if someone wanted to listen in real time, anything is possible. What's going on?"

There was a hesitation and then finally his father spoke quietly and with guarded precision as if lowering his voice would somehow make their conversation more secure.

"Your grandfather is gone," he stated simply.

"My god. What happened? Was it his heart?"

"He was taken in the middle of the night. They warned us not to tell anyone or they would be back."

"Back for what?" Josh almost shouted in disbelief. "Taken by who?"

"Calm down Joshua. Your emotions will not help us here," his father took command with his parental tone.

"When did this happen?"

"Nearly a week ago."

"Why are you just calling me now?" Josh felt his blood pressure rising as he tried to calm himself down.

"I am not sure I should have called you at all. They said not to."

"Has there been any other contact since then, like a ransom?"

"What ransom could we pay?" His father replied.

"Well, I could…" Josh began and then paused trying to figure out how to end that sentence. Even in English, he knew he had no answer.

"I don't even know why we called but we thought you deserved to know. Now I am sorry we have worried you."

"No, you did the right thing. I will see what I can do to find him. What exactly happened?"

His father relayed his grandmother's brief account of the incident.

"Did Grandmother see what kind of uniforms they were wearing?"

"No. They are all the same to her and it all happened so quickly in the dark."

Joshua took in the scraps of useful information as his mind raced, trying to figure out what could have happened and what he could possibly do about it.

"Okay, Father, thanks for letting me know. You take care of each other and I will send a message when I know something. If anything else happens there, make sure you let me know as soon as it does."

"Okay Joshua. We will wait to hear from you," his father stated and the screen went black. Josh continued to stare blankly ahead as his mind absorbed the information he had just received. Why would anyone take his grandfather? His father was right, it couldn't be for money. They had none. Besides, it had been ten or fifteen years since he had even heard of such a thing happening. When he was young, Joshua would spend hours glued to his grandfather's side listening to his endless stories. There were tales of political dissidents who would be taken from their villages and put in isolation in remote areas of China. There were stories about large numbers of people who would be 'eliminated' because of their subversive political views, but that was almost a hundred years ago. In today's world of social and technological interconnectivity such clandestine and nefarious actions seemed impossible. Josh then thought of the work he had been doing with the upcoming population strategy meetings. He had heard rumours about people being abducted and killed, but what were the odds of his grandfather being one of those people, assuming the rumours were even true? He stared ahead blankly shaking his head. What else could it be? One thing was for sure: If the Global Council had actually sanctioned such a thing, he would get to the bottom of it. He quite literally had all the data in the world at his fingertips, and now he was more motivated than ever to use it.

Chapter 7
November 6, 2058. Leaping Tiger Gorge, Western China.

Hai had never witnessed the scale of the natural grandeur he was currently experiencing. He was slowly traversing the ancient, yet reasonably well used roadway through the narrow Leaping Tiger Gorge that served as a gateway to the Himalaya. He could imagine a giant, mythical tiger spanning the width of the gorge as it leapt from escarpment to escarpment. On numerous occasions, Hai had travelled to some of the mountain villages in northwestern Vietnam, but until this day he had no idea what a real mountain was. The majestic peaks to the west seemed so close and yet he knew from his map that the closest pinnacle was still more than fifty kilometres away. The permanently, snow-capped summits shone brightly in the sunshine as it spread across the pristine sky that backdropped the entire scene. It was at moments like this he understood the power of the earth and felt dwarfed with insignificance.

If his calculations were correct, the target of his journey should be about five kilometres ahead in the valley he hoped would soon begin to appear in front of him. He would have to be careful as he approached the mine. He needed to watch it in secrecy for a few days so he could find out what was happening in this impossibly remote site. If he could prove his suspicions, the ramifications of shutting down the suspected illegal mines would positively affect the lives of billions of people.

His first day of travel from Lijiang had been an adventure. Five hours of being jostled on a small bus along secondary roads heading into the mountains led to an additional three-hour climb along this treacherous roadway. He was happy to be on foot given the narrowness of the road and the razor's edge drop off with no railing. He chuckled as he realized he was walking along the extreme inside portion of the roadway as far away as possible from a certain death a thousand meters below. Unless he had a heart attack on the way down, which seemed likely. Fortunately, he had not encountered any vehicles moving to or from the anticipated mine while he was on this narrow portion through the gorge. He had seen two separate trucks, heading in opposite directions, about thirty minutes into his walk. But that had been in a broad part of the valley with numerous places to hide from the passing vehicles. There was no way the two trucks could meet along this stretch of the road. Hai was convinced that whoever had illegally rejuvenated the mine, which hopefully lie ahead, was scheduling the vehicle traffic through the gorge. Given he was there to investigate the mining operation for the purpose of shutting them down, he had to remain out of sight from the passing drivers. Whoever was here illegally mining rare earth elements would do whatever it took to keep their activities secret. He would have to be very careful if he wanted to get home alive.

His plan had been months in its evolution but Hai had never received the benefit of a second point of view as he was determined to maintain complete secrecy as a source of security. It was imperative that he alone could ever be punished for his pending actions. They were not only dangerous but probably illegal. For the past couple of years it had become increasingly clear to him that his family's farm land, in northern Vietnam, was being victimized by pollutants from some unknown source. Crop yields were down and diseases were on the rise. He had to be certain of the root cause of these trends before he could actually do anything about it. His position as the Southeast Asian Chair of the United Nations Food and Agriculture Agency gave him the ability to combat the issues threatening their crops. However, he respected the process too much to use his powers of authority to pursue something that may be no more than a wild goose chase or be perceived as self-serving. He could have asked countess numbers of colleagues or subordinates to undertake this reconnaissance mission, but he would rather put himself in danger than risk the lives of others. He had lived a good life and had achieved much but that didn't make his life more valuable than anyone else's. He was here because he needed to be. He just hoped, in the end, it would be worthwhile. He had studied the data from the past twenty years of crop yields along the river valleys and delta plains of the major rivers of Asia that were all sourced in the Himalayan Mountains. The Yangtze, Pearl, Mekong, and Ganges Rivers were amongst a dozen of the major fluvial arteries, along with thousands of minor tributaries, that form the lifeblood of water and nutrients supporting crops and feeding more than six billion people. All of these rivers are sourced from a relatively localized area in western China, where deep valleys and canyons had been carved into a series of north-south trending lineaments before branching off and flowing off to the sea in all directions through China, Southeast Asia and India. With roughly two-thirds of the world's population relying on these rivers for food, water, transportation, energy, and recreation, it is critical for the ecosystems to be well managed and preserved. So here he was, spending a few days off the grid beyond the remote edges of civilization along the borders of Tibet and Myanmar discretely gathering data and trying to stay alive.

As he continued his walk he began to notice a distant hum he feared was the sound of a vehicle coming his way. His eyes darted around the 360 degrees of options that may exist. Unfortunately, 180 of those degrees contained an almost vertical rock wall and the other half of his world was a wall of air giving way to a river far below that resembled a blue thread. He could tell from the distant sound he had more time than solutions. He was almost positive the truck was coming toward him from the direction he was headed so moving in that direction would shorten the narrow window he would have to devise a plan. He tried to reflect on anything he had seen but not noticed over the past few hundred metres that could provide the opportunity to become invisible. He began to run along the roadway. It would be impossible to explain why he was out on this road in the middle of nowhere. About twenty metres ahead he noticed a fracture in the rock wall that might create an opportunity. He quickly retrieved a rope from his backpack and tied a large knot at one end which he jammed down into the crevice just above the road bed. He strung the rope across the road with the other end fashioned into a loop which would soon house his foot as it would be suspended in mid-air over the edge of the cliff.

    Straining with all of his might to support the weight of himself and his pack on more than the rope, he tried to keep his free toes and fingers planted in notches in the wall. He couldn't see them but he could feel the strain in his legs and arms which were slowly beginning to go numb from a lack of blood flow. He had been in this precarious position for about four minutes already, not wanting to cut the timing too close and risk being seen. The roaring of the truck as it neared, grinding its gears in its ascent, made it clear that the vehicle was within sight. Hai hoped the top of his head was invisible to the passing driver who would be on his side of the road. His right hand burned from its tight grip on the rope. The vehicle finally clambered by and Hai decided to count to fifty before he dare attempt to climb back up his lifeline and pass over the edge of the precipice from which he was dangling. Thank God he had decided to include a rope in the list of supplies he had accumulated. As he summoned all of his remaining strength to pull himself back to safety, he wished he was in better shape. Slowly inching upward, hand over hand, with his toes and fingers desperately seeking leverage, Hai finally got one hand against the rock a few inches below the road. Not daring to look down at the terror that existed below, he bent his knees and forced the bottoms of his feet as high up against the wall as he could to increase the angle of the rope and allow his fingers the search above on the road bed. The rope had been strung through a crevice on the other side of the road and tied off with a double knot, one which he hoped was not about to release. Hai had covered the rope with gravel so as not to be seen by the approaching driver but now, the gravel was making it hard for him to grip the twelve-millimetre-diameter cord which was currently busy keeping him alive. Pushing his feet against the cliff wall while scraping through the gravel and rock with his fingernails allowed his index finger to seek a spot beneath the rope. Finally, his entire right hand, bloodied no doubt, became victorious and he felt the cord in his palm which closed like a vice and began to support more and more of his weight. Hai could hear rocks tumbling down the side of the cliff as he scampered back on to the road. He lay motionless, except for the heaving of his lungs as he strained to regain the strength to stand. Finally, he was upright and mobile, his rope coiled and slung over his head and under one arm where it would hopefully stay for the rest of the trek. He anticipated that the next truck, coming from behind him, would arrive in about forty-five minutes. There was no time to rest.

 Thirty minutes, walking at a fast pace, got him through the narrow portion of the gorge and into a highly vegetated valley providing him with all of the camouflage he would need. He could safely approach his target and set up camp as close as possible to the mine. From there he would be able to get all of the information he required to verify his suspicions. Photographs and downstream water samples would document the local mining operations. Hai's mind began to look ahead to the following week when he would monitor a different illegal mine in southern China, situated much closer to his home in Vietnam. There, his appearance and language skills were much closer to the local dialects and would allow him to pass as a local so he could try to get a job at the mine. If everything went according to plan, he would arrive home in two or three weeks with all of the data he needed and still very much alive.

Chapter 8
November 6, 2058. London, England.

"Look Spence, give me another week and I will have all of the money you need," Will Hamilton stated in a hushed but urgent tone.

"I don't understand what's taking so long. I brought this to you three weeks ago. I've got expenses I need to cover and the window is closing on this," Spencer Watt responded, maybe a bit louder than he should have given their location in the crowded restaurant. He was paranoid that anyone within earshot would notice them and overhear the details of their conversation. Simultaneously, he was a little pissed no one even seemed to notice him at all. How was that even possible? Fifteen years ago he couldn't sneeze without it becoming a headline in the tabloids. As the top-grossing movie star for as far back as anyone could remember, his actions, thoughts, and fleeting whims were of prime concern to society as a whole. His face was more recognizable than the President of the United States, and he was far better looking than any of them had been. He had ventured into the political world just because he could. He didn't really care that much about anything, other than himself of course, but since people would automatically accept his words as being relevant and at times nothing short of brilliant, it was hard not to say more. It felt pretty good being admired as much for his mind as he was for his looks and acting skills. He honestly didn't understand why everything had changed. Entertainment and sports icons had provided people with hope. They represented the kind of life normal people wanted for themselves.

"We're talking twenty-million dollars, Spence. Things aren't like they used to be when money was the primary currency, plentiful, and could buy anything and anyone. Things have changed," Will stated as he shook his head, realizing just how true the statement was.

Will had spent his life using his father's money and political connections to continue the family business. One that never had a name, a brand or a webpage. They utilized unlisted phone numbers, offshore bank accounts and backroom deals that flowed trillions of dollars to wherever they were needed to achieve the desired results. He could elect a president, overturn a political regime or 'eliminate a problem' in any number of ways. There seemed to be no limit to his capabilities or the availability of people who could be bought and paid for. But it was all in the past. Before everything changed. Before everyone changed. Maybe it was inevitable. How long did they expect that a few hundred well-placed and well-funded people could dictate the lives of the billions of others who existed, or barely existed, on the same planet? They had a great run, that's for sure. It really didn't matter if you lived in a democracy or a communist or religious state, there had always been a handful of people like him, and his father before him, who anonymously predetermined almost everything of significance.

Will looked at Spencer Watt and couldn't help but feel sorry for him. He had been a part of the so-called 'one percent,' a term that became politically relevant about the time he had been born. Basically, Spence was a nobody who was granted status and wealth for no particular reason other than the fact that it was necessary to have a buffer of visible elite between the true holders of power and the people. This sub-elite consisted of politicians, industry leaders, entertainers and sports figures. Those were the people who drew the attention of the masses away from Will's father and his contemporaries. That buffer allowed them to stay invisible while controlling everything. Individually, the one percent people, like Spencer Watt, were insignificant and interchangeable yet often fun to have around given the way society treated them. Will realized it was inevitable that their 'star' status screwed many of them up. It certainly had been the case with Spencer. His ego became so inflated he actually began to believe he was special and deserving of his status. However, over the past couple of decades, societal perceptions and values had evolved and individuals began to feel a part of a societal transformation where humans came together, after centuries of persistently successful efforts to keep them isolated and suppressed. Concepts like hero worship and distinct social classes just slowly slipped away. Individuals became focused on how they fit into a world where everyone was uniquely comparable and united on an emotional human level. People quit living as a distant subset of the rich and famous, choosing instead to maximize their own lives and relationships. They also brought this new vision and a renewed work ethic into the world of business where profits no longer formed the basis for controlling every decision. Personal drive, job satisfaction and achievement began to flourish. The symbolic red carpet had slowly but surely been torn out from beneath the collective feet of the rich, famous and powerful. Will and his family had lost immeasurable wealth and influence in the process but, as always, had maintained a lifestyle as opulent and protected as ever. People like Spencer, however, had lost their identities. The adulation and glamour they had been bathed in had gradually been reduced to indifference, a kind of rejection many of them found horrifying and impossible to accept. An artificially expanded ego is a hard thing to lose.

Will knew what Spencer was up to, and he had been tempted to reject his request at the onset when he was approached a few weeks prior to this meeting. At the age of fifty-three, Will was content to live out his life coasting along in luxury, but he had to admit he missed the adrenaline rush that accompanied the execution of a plan. It was the only thing in his life that wasn't a predictable certainty. He had his concerns about what Spencer wanted to do, and certainly his motives, but what the hell. As long as no one ever discovered he was bankrolling the whole thing, he could certainly use a bit of excitement.

"Look man, this can't wait another week. Things are moving ahead and I already spent some of my own money. I've authorized more events and they will cost another five million. I have people lined up to act on my cue, but they need to be paid."

"How much do you need up front?"

"I don't know. At least five."

"And how much of that do you have?"

"What? Money? You mean my own money that I live on? Like I said, I already spent some of mine. That can't keep happening."

"You used to make tens of millions for each movie. You must have stashed away a pretty nice nest egg."

"Well, yeah. I mean I have enough money to live on but I just have millions. This project would wipe me out, and then what? You're the one who deals with billions, even trillions."

"Dealt with."

"What?"

"Dealt with, as in the past. Things are so different now," Will tried to make his point.

"Exactly. Which is why we need to do this. We have an opportunity here to undo all of this bullshit. People need to understand. They will listen to me. We just need a few special effects to make them see the truth."

"You know that people are going to get hurt and there will probably be significant fatalities if this gets out of control."

"Since when do you care about casualties? Have these people gotten to you, too?"

"Look Spence, I said I would help you out with this, but you need to know this is a Hail Mary. There's no way you're going to get your old self back no matter how many people listen to you on this. Those days are over and you need to get used to it."

"You don't need to worry about who I am and what I want. All I want from you is forty mil," Spencer stated emphatically, frustrated by his friend's attitude.

"I remember you being a lot more charming in the past," Will commented. "I hope you are a good enough actor to make this work. I'm out of here. I'll call you when I have the money."

'What an arrogant Brit he is,' Spencer thought to himself as he watched his friend leave the restaurant. Just because William's father had gold semen, his life had been privileged from the moment he drew his first breath. There had been nothing on the planet that was beyond Will's reach or ability to attain, thanks to his ancestors who had gained and maintained the power that came hand in hand with controlling the British financial establishment. Following the stream of exclusive private schools and a business degree from Oxford, Will began to work for his father, doing whatever it is the rich and powerful do. Even though they had been friends for years of play, punctuated with the occasional business deal, Spence never felt that Will had shown him the respect he deserved. 'After all,' he reassured himself, 'I earned everything I ever got in life, unlike him!'

He glanced around the restaurant where he was surrounded by couples and groups who were collectively oblivious to the fact that he was even there. What the hell is wrong with these people? Didn't they know he was famous? He threw some cash on the table to pay the bill and stormed out.

'I'll keep going with my own goddamn money!' he decided as he tried to slam the air cushioned door and entered the moist London night. 'This is happening. Soon enough everyone will remember who I am!'

* * * * * * *

Well, you just met the bad guy in the story. I can't believe I used to pay my hard-earned money going to see his movies. I know we all used to idolize sports and movie stars but looking back at it, I can't help but wonder why. I guess it was because they were rich and their lives seemed so glamorous. Oh well, that's all in the past and I've got some good news for you. Next, you will get to go to Buenos Aires and meet my grandson, Jermaine. Yeah, his mother named after the baseball player in the first book. Jermaine's a great kid. I'd say he takes after his grandfather. Have fun in Argentina. Hasta luego.

Chapter 9
November 8, 2058. Buenos Aires, Argentina.

The towering flames provoked the night sky as their desire to shoot upwards was easily satisfied by the ready source of flammable material. The neighbouring Piramide de Maya, sitting in the heart of Buenos Aires central Plaza de Maya, reflected the firelight as its sixty-three feet of glory became completely bathed in the heat and glow of its expanding, fiery neighbour. The Statue of Liberty, perched ceremoniously atop the monument, gazed at the inferno in seeming appreciation of the symbolism of the fire and the cause it was meant to represent. The flames formed a dynamic beacon of light that had already attracted at least twenty-thousand souls, drawn like moths to the illumination.

He had laboriously set the fire and fine-tuned the message he had been given so that it would resonate with the emotionality of the local population. A skilled busker can draw hundreds of curious observers on a warm Buenos Aires night. It was only 10:00 pm, and he was concerned the timing was a bit too early for the nocturnal Argentinians who would barely be finishing their first bottles of Malbec and assortments of tapas at this early hour. Against his advice, he had been instructed about their need to get maximum media exposure on the east coast of the United States, which was only an hour behind them. To do so, he needed to literally fan the flames of unrest before the sedentary Americans were tucked into bed for the night at eleven o'clock.

He surveyed the Plaza from the window table he now occupied in a second floor bar that lined the historic square. It was the de facto centre of the city and had remained essentially unchanged for the past couple of hundred years. The plaza was free of commercial establishments with the exception of the one he currently occupied. The understated yet impressive architecture of the Cathedral Metropolitana, the Museo Nacional Historico and the Presidential Palacio all stood guard around the plaza. Dressed only in subdued accent lighting on their stone enclaves, the massive structures demonstrated their understated grandeur.

The plaza was a place he had always loved to come to, beginning when he was just a child. Throughout his life he would quietly sit and allow the impressive monuments consume his subconscious. Five centuries of life, in the city he bled for, would absorb into his being. Their collective history was one of devastation and triumph, grandeur and poverty, peace and violence. A history filled with stories of constant change amongst the pervasive and undying emotional constitutions of those who had loved and lived in this tortured nirvana.

He watched as the masses of people became energized by the fuel he had so effectively provided. It doesn't take much to get an Argentinian excited. In the glory days of football, a well timed goal was enough to have hundreds of thousands of fans carry the banners and songs of the River Plate or the Boca Juniors teams throughout the city streets. Getting his national compatriots worked up on this evening would be no problem at all. Nevertheless, he had planned the event with careful scrutiny. He set the fire himself, made the required phone call to verify any last minute orders, lit the blaze and then sought out his current position. He watched as his five associates in the plaza spread torches and propaganda over their amplified devices in order to indoctrinate the swelling mob with the message he had been provided. *'Mass genocide was being mandated by the Global Council and assuredly would soon target residents of their wonderful city.'* After all, when had Buenos Aires ever been left out of any travesty of real and tragic significance? The citizens of this glorious city had always been predetermined to deal with adversity with a hunger that defined their collective strength. It was a strength that was beginning to gain momentum. He had no idea if the message he was orchestrating was true, but the money he would be receiving was real and was all that mattered to him at the moment. His ancestors had never enjoyed the privilege of riches while living through a past measured in pesos. It seemed ironic that he would soon have more money than he would know what to do with in a society where its worth had been diminished. His payment may end up to be little more than a novelty, but at least it would be his new toy to play with.

    He began to capture video of the event. Even though the plaza already seemed saturated with humanity, he watched as a steady flow of raised fists and voices permeated the mass from Avenida de Maya and from the two diagonal streets at each of the western corners of the square. There was no human target present to absorb the focus of the frustrations his agents were feeding to the growing mob. The flames, profanities and sincere but empty threats that filled the night air merely sweated, swirled and subsidized the growing intensity of the revolt. The only Argentinian member on the Global Council, Manuel Rosales, had just travelled to Mendoza, a provincial wine capital more than a thousand kilometres away to the west. Perhaps, if at this moment, Señor Rosales was quietly sipping wine on the Paseo Sarmiento, he may be able to sense the growing energy located at the true centre of the county he calls home.

In the Plaza de Maya, a volcano of emotional fear and outrage was erupting. As he looked out over his masterpiece, he couldn't help but think he deserved some sort of a bonus. He had seen video of the riots and demonstrations that had occurred in other cities around the world over the past few days and he had to modestly admit they paled in comparison to his venture, which was becoming a work of art. He had just witnessed the collapse of a large section of scaffolding near the National Museum of History. Crowds wishing to gain a panoramic view of the proceedings had apparently overloaded the structure resulting in the collapse. Throngs of people who had been standing on the ground below were being crushed. It was hard to watch, but a few inevitable deaths was an unfortunate but necessary cost of saving millions of hypothetical lives in some pending postulation of a genocide event. At this moment, all that mattered was his ability to deliver and his benefactor was sure to be very happy with his efforts.

****

Jermaine Wilson-Cook could almost feel the heat from the flames and from the intimidating mass of people surrounding him in the Plaza de Maya. He studied the intensity of the anger and fear their collective body language portrayed. It was beyond anything he had ever witnessed. He was glad he had the ability to press a button and leave the surrounding chaos in an instant. The beauty of the Global-com Vision software was that it could take you anywhere in the world where people existed and transplant you to the centre of their collective video capture devices (VCDs). The individual feed from any existing device becomes merged with those from any number of proximal ones and a three-dimensional web of multi-sensory data takes shape on your own personal or group pod which effectively transports its occupants to the nucleus of the data. You have the ability to then migrate through the digital stream of pixels just as you would walk down a street. As long as there is data to follow, you can cyber-exist almost in real time, or in any past data sequence you wish.

As Jermaine stood in the corner of his living room surrounded by screens he was slicing his way through the crowds in the Plaza like a spirit through a maze. He had begun about thirty minutes earlier on the main boulevard of Avenida 9 de Julio, which looked as if it could have been transplanted from any major city in Europe. As he began heading east, he became transfixed by the crowds of people who were smiling, eating, drinking and enjoying the rewards of being social. He smiled at the heartfelt sounds of laughter and the sight of food being cooked and served along the sidewalk restaurants that formed a stream of glorious gluttony, suspended briefly by the cross streets. He was surprised and delighted by the synthetic smell of barbecued vegetables and meats that attacked him from all angles. He had no idea how the sense of smell could be transmitted in a cyber form but at this moment he was glad it could. He instinctively inhaled a deep breath through his nostrils and then chuckled as he realized it was his brain and memory rather than his nose providing the conduit for the amazing aromas.

He had enjoyed the seasoned odours of roasted meat before in real life, and had actually tasted it twice. Apparently, the stored memory, combined with the visual cues, created a tangible, cerebral déjà vu experience. At least that was his understanding of the dumbed down explanation he could grasp. He remembered his first experience eating meat. He was ten or eleven years old and his family went to Texas because of his father's job. The organizers had hosted a big barbecue for the sake of historical nostalgia. Above all else, he could remember the delicious odour of the food being cooked on large outdoor grills. He also remembered the taste and texture of the meat being far less impressive than the smell. Maybe his disappointment came afterwards when his mother told him he had eaten the meat of a cow, a concept his youthful consciousness had a hard time rationalizing.

Walking along the boulevard, Jermaine looked closely at the sights on both sides of the street. He could glimpse the grills in the windows containing a few morsels of browning meat amongst a sea of vegetables. He had heard that in the past, in places like Argentina and Brazil, carnivorous living was legendary.

Apparently, in 2058, they were still grasping onto the last loins of their culinary history, if for no other reason than to appeal to virtual tourists for whom the sight and smell of a t-bone steak was as rare as the Chinese Pandas used to be.

Focusing ahead, Jermaine continued to work his way down the street as his eyes and conscious thought dictated the path of his on-screen avatar. He chuckled as his view immediately swung 180 degrees as he had instinctively followed the image of a gorgeous, tall, brown-eyed, Latina woman he had noticed walking west along the street toward him. Studying her silhouette as she walked away, he found his current view every bit as captivating. Maybe he should have done his biology major in genetics rather than agriculture, he surmised, as he tried to fathom the existence of the statistically high percentage of beautiful women who seemed to be dominating the street. Despite the fact he could see and hear them, they were roughly ten thousand kilometres and about fifty-five minutes away from him. Nevertheless, it wouldn't hurt to meet a new friend, he decided, as he kept watch for another lovely Latina who looked friendly. She was sitting alone at a table for two, sipping a glass of wine that was almost depleted. Her mahogany eyes, half concealed by long, thick eyelashes penetrated the passing crowds and her subtle smile revealed her thoughts as they meandered through her range of focus. The art of observation seemed to provide her with a preoccupation that Jermaine assessed was fuelled by interest and caring rather than any sort of judgements. Just as he decided to make his approach and activate his communication setting, she focussed on her personal device and locked on his image. The smile that followed illuminated his virtual path towards her.

"Buenos nochas Señorita, me nombre es Jermaine," he introduced himself with his best Spanish prior to allowing his translator to take over.

"Carmella," she responded with her smile still fully in tact. "Please, join me if you wish."

He did, on both counts. "I'm very pleased to meet you Carmella. I am just cyber-visiting from Philadelphia and I couldn't help but notice you sitting there alone."

"Do I look like I am alone?" she replied, still smiling as she gestured to the throngs of people all around them.

"Well, not technically, I guess," Jermaine backtracked.

Her laugh was musical and not the least bit mocking. "I love to spend my evenings soaking in the energy of my people."

"And also the wine, I see," Jermaine commented, trying to match her level of enjoyment.

"But of course. Wine and social interaction are the two primary passions of all Argentinians," Carmella explained as she continued to laugh. "That is how it has always been."

"Everyone seems so happy. Is that because of the wine as well?"

"Heavens no, Jermaine. I think you have it backwards. We drink to celebrate the lives we have. All that is required is to seek the positives that exist and then celebrate them. It seems to me it would be a very sad thing to have to drink to become happy."

"Of course, you are right, Carmella."

"What brings you to my beautiful city?"

"I could say I came in search of you," Jermaine quipped, "but, in truth, meeting you is merely a very fortunate accident. I was notified there was a demonstration happening in the Plaza de Maya and I wanted to check it out."

"Yes, I see. I walked through the Plaza about an hour ago when the demonstration was just underway, but I preferred to spend my evening like this, speaking with pixel-faced American tourists."

Their simultaneous laughter generated a bond that Jermaine began to feel.

"I must have better software than you because your face is nothing short of remarkable. You will have to believe me when I tell you I look better in real life."

"I am looking at you, Jermaine, and what I believe is that your pixels are completely inconsequential to me. All I can see on my screen are your eyes, your smile, and your heart. Those things are coming through very clearly." She paused to enjoy his reaction to the feelings she had just conveyed. It was always nice to see a man blush. "Why are you interested in our little demonstration?" Carmella asked, deciding to change the direction of the conversation.

"From what I have heard, it is not so little. People are being hurt and there have been reports of a fatality."

"I can't believe you would be attracted to that, Jermaine."

"Not specifically, no, but I am very concerned about the global trend of violence that has broken out. It makes no sense to me. I can't understand what would entice people to behave in such a manner. It is kind of like discovering an entirely new species of animal."

"Perhaps, Jermaine, but that sounds very clinical and calculated. You have to allow for people's emotions to deal with the inevitable positives and negatives that come our way. We are not machines who are designed to filter out negative inputs just so we can be happy. A steady diet of positivity would become redundantly unrewarding. I believe that tears of sorrow can germinate the seeds of hope and happiness."

"How did you get to be so insightful at such a young age?" Jermaine marvelled.

"No one understands emotions like an Argentinian. We are emotional creatures who revel at the opportunity to ride the waves of our feelings. It is true that throughout yours and my brief lives there has been very little to feel negative about, but life demands balance and contrast. No artistic masterpiece can be created with a single hue of colour. It would lack interest and depth."

"Wow. I believe you are even smarter than you are beautiful. I didn't think that would be possible when I first saw you."

"And you are both sweet and naive. Go to the Plaza and witness an aspect of humanity you appear to be unaware of. Just remember, the people you see there are not different than you and me. They are merely people who have encountered a situation that speaks to a segment of their emotionality that cannot, and should not, be ignored."

Jermaine thought about what Carmella was saying. "So why didn't you stay in the Plaza?"

"I stayed long enough to understand my feelings about it. Besides, I had a date with an American that I didn't want to miss."

Her smile brought him back into the moment and then sent him on his path of discovery.

He resumed his evening stroll with a renewed and enlightened purpose as he moved east toward Plaza de Maya. He had come to Buenos Aires based on the description of the news program summary recommending this real time virtual visit. He tried to spend a couple of hours each day keeping current on what was happening in the world. Scheduling his time was the best way he could come up with to try to attain balance in his life. His days were perfectly divided into three equal parts of eight hours each . Sleeping, working and everything else. The everything else component could be a challenge. Like many of his friends, he could easily cyber-travel for the entire time. As productive and rewarding as it could be, there was still a part of him that demanded physical outdoor pursuits and direct interpersonal relationships. Meal times provided the bulk of the 'in person' time he spent. He had a large group of friends who chose to spend both lunch and dinner in the company of others and both events were highlights of his day. An after dinner run and his cyber-life dominated the remainder of his time. The Global-Com technology he was enjoying had been available for the past eight years. Before that, he would sometimes watch news reports with his parents until he became bored out of his mind. The reports would consist of watching videos clips and then being told what to think and feel about them. His mom told him once that NEWS came from the anagram of the directions on a compass suggesting that it was information from all possible angles. Over time it became referred to as WSNE, or What Seemingly Never Existed, because of its increasingly exaggerated and targeted biases.

    By the time he began to consciously use the media as a source of information rather than just entertainment, it had fortunately progressed to what he was doing now. There was a report of riots occurring in Buenos Aires so there he was, in almost real time, to see for himself what was happening. He could choose to sit in on a meeting of the Global Council Planning Committee, go to a bar in Berlin to socialize, join in on a debate on transportation ethics, or witness the birth of the nine-billionth person on earth. You can speak in real time with anyone who is willing to share his or her time with you. Anything, and everywhere, over the past eight years or so, is accessible at your fingertips, just waiting for your interest in experiencing it. There are even thousands of stationary remote VCDs in non-populated areas that provide information about their digital worlds. 'This technology is truly amazing,' Jermaine marvelled. 'You can travel the world and connect with and learn from anyone you come into contact with from the confines of your own home. There are no trains or airplanes, jet lag, passport controls or line-ups and with no cost, carbon footprint, or scheduling issues. It's no wonder hardly anyone physically travels any more.'

The gradual feel of his cyber surroundings becoming darker and more intense returned his mind to what was occurring around him. The lighthearted socializations from a few blocks back were gradually being replaced by visible stress and tension that grew as the density of the population on the pedestrian thoroughfare gained in numbers and changed in attitude. People began shouting. His translation device seamlessly stole the Spanish phrases being uttered from thousands of individual sources and re-gifted them to his ears in English, a task not easily done given some of the rich local slang profanities that were flowing through his surround sound speakers. His mother would have wanted him to activate the parental guidance version of the audio stream.

When he entered the Plaza he was astounded by the dichotomy between the impressive historical buildings and monuments and the firestorm of rebellion that defined the present moment. People were chanting anti-genocide slogans. Too many bodies were being pushed into confined areas and as a result, physical violence was breaking out where fallen waves of rioters risked being trampled by the faceless masses.

Jermaine worked his way over to the periphery of the Plaza near the Cathedral where he noticed a man who was quietly surveying the scene that was escalating around them. Locking in on the man's body, Jermaine was able to send him a communication request.

"Buenos nochas," the man spoke into his phone which contained a screen that currently featured a live view of Jermaine, "me nombre es Alfonso. Mucho gusto!"

"Good evening, Alfonso. My name is Jermaine. I'm visiting from Philadelphia and I was wondering what's going on here. Do you know how this all started and what has incited such intense emotions within these people?"

"I've been standing here watching for a couple of hours now. They are demonstrating against the genocide program they believe the Global Council is planning to undertake. They are angry and afraid."

"I thought the Council denied any plans to do that."

"Yes, they have, but it seems that these people have their doubts about the proclamation. It was kind of interesting. When I first got here there were five people with loud speakers who were playing prepared speeches that got everyone all worked up. Now that things are getting out of control, they seem to have disappeared."

"Did you hear what they were saying?"

"Yes. It was a well-worded and -orchestrated message. There were a lot of emotional references to historical, social weak points that were guaranteed to create a strong local response. We Argentinians are an emotional people and it doesn't take much to get us worked up. About thirty minutes ago a scaffolding beside the Museum collapsed and I am pretty sure there must have been casualties. There have been some emergency medical personnel over there trying to help."

"Where are the police? Shouldn't something be done?"

"Such as? What could they possibly do about this? Is it not the same in the United States now, with very small police and army contingents? Typically there isn't anything for them to do, so why have them?"

"I guess you are right, but this is out of control."

"Yes, but they will tire themselves out. Hopefully not too many people will be injured in the process."

"Do you live near here?" Jermaine asked, not wanting the conversation to end.

"East of here near the new Mercado Miserere."

"Wow, really? What's it like? One of my university thesis projects contributed to some of the design."

"Really? Well, you must have done a good job because the place is amazing."

"Thanks, but my contribution was a small fraction of one percent of the planning and labor that went into it. I can't believe that it is designed to grow and distribute enough food for six million people."

"And it will, soon. It has only been open for about a year and they say it is already at about sixty percent capacity."

"What's it like in real life? I have only seen videos and models."

"Well, you can't help but notice it. It covers more than two city blocks including the part over the Once de Septembre Estacion. It's fifty-five stories high, and kind of stands out. The dominantly glass and solar panel exterior is very nice and the fact that they grow and distribute all of our food out of there is remarkable. I can tell you for a fact that our food has never been so healthy and delicious."

"There's a lot of cutting-edge technology in that place. Have you ever been inside?"

"Only to take the elevator up to the roof-top plaza where they reconstructed the park that used to be at street level. They have flamenco dancing up there in the evenings. On a clear day you can almost make out the Andes in the west."

"Cool. I will have to visit there some night. It has been really nice visiting with you. Stay safe, Alfonso."

"I think I will head home soon. It was nice visiting with you as well, Jermaine. Adios."

After terminating the visit, Jermaine wandered around the Plaza for a few more minutes. Thanks to Alfonso, he had some insights as to what had instigated the scene around him but he was clueless as to how it would end. Just to his right, two medics were kneeling over the body of a woman who was bleeding from a large gash on her severely bruised arm. Others were trying to form a protective human shield around the three of them. The crowds continued to build and press into the Plaza which extended to the east along the water front. The contortion of humanity spread around him for as far as he could see. He had never witnessed such raw, uncontrollable emotion, especially on a scale like this. He had seen enough and decided to leave. Seconds later, following a few keystrokes, Jermaine became immersed in a blinding fury of red, like a swirling tempest, synchronized to the classical guitar music that guided the flamenco dancers. Their mesmerizing, long red skirts absorbed the glare of the gyrating spotlights that cut swaths of illumination across the dark night sky, atop one of the largest cabbage patches in the world.

Chapter 10
November 9, 2058. New York, USA.

"How do you like my set-up?" Jason Wolfe asked Claire Wilson, his new intern.

"I've never seen anything like this, and I have seen some pretty sophisticated systems at COI where my Mom works."

"Are you trying to impress me by reminding me who your mother is?"

"Uh, no. I mean I didn't mean to. Unless somehow that's a good thing, I guess."

"Well, maybe it is, but if we are going to climb your family tree, you should have picked your grandfather. We are in the media business and he was an icon in his day. I grew up reading and watching his reports. He had a great nose for the story and a really good ability to see things differently than most reporters."

"To be honest," Claire revealed, "I have a hard time associating what you are doing here with what my grandfather did."

"What 'we' are doing, you mean."

"Right, but you know what I'm talking about."

"Of course I do. Almost everything is different than it was in your grandfather's day, except for maybe the critical things like integrity and delivering honest and open news reports."

"Hasn't it always been that way?"

"Unfortunately not. The worst of it was happening before you were born, but there were some pretty dark days for the media. When I started out on my career path the media was in the business of influence. Large media conglomerates, owned by the rich and powerful, used targeted and systematic influence to manufacture societal opinions, elect governments, and promote fear as a divisive agent. Their efforts kept the general public distracted and unaware of the fact that they were all pawns in a game that was predetermined to have an outcome that would favour those in control. Big Data was being utilized at an increasing rate."

"Was it the 'one percent' that I read about in school that was in control?"

"That, too, was merely fabricated divisiveness. You must be minoring in history and not math. The one percent was a political ploy designed to create a divide between socioeconomic classes and political ideologies. Left leaning, or liberal, political parties wanted to tax the top one percent of income earners more in order to pay for the support system for the middle class and the poor."

"Wouldn't that be a good thing?"

"I suppose that would depend on whether you were part of the one percent or not. The problem is, those aren't the people that we are talking about who have most of the money and all of the power. What is one percent of seven billion?"

"Seventy-million." Claire answered after doing the calculation on her device."

"Really?" Jason smirked, expecting her to do the math in her head.

"What?" she blushed, knowing what he was referring to. "I wanted to make sure I got it right."

"Okay then, now divide that by a million."

"Seventy!" she proclaimed quickly.

"Good. That is closer to the number of people that existed in the world forty years ago who dictated pretty much everything because they controlled the global financial system, which influenced pretty much everything. The thing is, most people didn't even know who those seventy people were. We were led to believe that the politicians and the visible business leaders were in charge of things. And because most of them loved the wealth and attention that was attached, they probably came to believe it themselves."

"So what happened that changed it all to what we have today?"

"It was kind of a convergence of technology, education, and human awareness. Social media and technological advances provided the capability and your mom and her friends at COI facilitated the understanding and desire. Once people were given a taste of change, the momentum grew and the general public learned how to become self-aware and to take responsibility for making their lives better."

"It's really hard for me to imagine how things were when my mom was my age. When did it all change?"

"When has it not? Depending on where in the world you lived, and which decade you were born into, your life, and those of your peers, were unique and change has been a constant. Only the rate of change has increased."

"Is it still? I mean things are so good now that there isn't any real need to change much, is there?"

"That's an interesting question, especially given your age. There have always been people who were advantaged and those people always resisted change. On the other hand, it has commonly been young people whose idealism provided the dominant push for change as a sort of rebellion against their parents' generation and the establishment of the time. There was a huge resistance to the social changes that Circles of Influence introduced."

"Why? It has created so much good."

"Maybe so, but think of the transfer and loss of wealth and power it has created. I can guarantee you that none of the seventy people we talked about were on board and probably very few of the seventy-million who were layered in below them were particularly thrilled about potentially losing the financial security that they had worked most of their lives to attain. Adam Stapleton was accused in the mainstream media of being a cult leader, a communist, an atheist, a traitor who should be charged with treason, and many other nasty things. I have to admit that I wrote some of those articles."

"Are you kidding me? Why would you do that?"

"Partly because I was ordered to, but you have to realize that the social elite of Western society felt like it was under attack and in essence it was. It had begun even before COI became established. After centuries of a divide and conquer mentality within the powerful elite, we were essentially a diverse and segmented population who couldn't find enough common ground to create the sort of massive grass roots revolution that was required. There were the poor and starving, the disenfranchised, angry fundamentalists, and the middle class which was shrinking in the West and growing in the Third World. We had become categorized by nationality, socio-economics, religion, sexual orientation, gender, race, and political ideology. This divisiveness was peaking in the early twenty-first century, when your mother and I were roughly your age. In 2016, a fearful and frustrated slim majority voted to pull Britain out of the European Union largely over concerns around perceived immigration issues. In the United States, a President was elected who promised to bring down the Establishment and promote isolationist and protectionist ideals. These actions accentuated the social divide and served noticed to those in control that change was being demanded by those who had fared poorly under the existing system."

"So what you are saying was that people wanted change but they had no idea what it would look like."

"Pretty much, so they would jump at anything that looked like a possible improvement to what they knew wasn't working. In effect, they were running away from something they knew they didn't want, with the feint hope that things would improve. That is why when Adam Stapleton and his group began to enlighten people and help them see that the rewards of an inclusive society could be remarkable, it got noticed."

"Unfortunately Claire, our own results today have been exactly the opposite. Since this is your first day on the job, maybe we should get some actual work done. How does that sound?"

"You're the boss. What do you want me to do?"

"We are going to be following the population control storyline as we lead up to the year-end Global Council meeting. We need to synthesize all of the data into a clear and informative report that fairly presents all positions, keeps current with real time updates and demonstrates the public opinion statistics along with reasonable and preferred outcome variables."

"Is that all? And what are you going to be doing while I do all of that?" Claire asked through her broad smile.

"Make sure that you do a good job. You are a co-op student and that's why it's called education. Then, if you are lucky, you will eventually learn to be as good at this as I am."

"I will try not to disappoint you. This is a pretty high-profile topic. Why was I chosen to work on it?"

"The project wasn't chosen for you. It's my project and you work for me, so let's get started. I'm going to have you watch the show that will be airing on Sunday. It will introduce the topic of population strategies and what we will be reporting on over the next four weekly episodes. I want you to watch with a critical eye and give me your thoughts as to how we should move forward. Come find me when you are done."

With that Jason left the room and Claire turned on the program.

"Welcome to the Wolfe Pack. My name is Jason Wolfe. For the next month, leading up to and including our coverage of the Global Council annual meeting, we will be keeping you up to date with developments of their population control strategy, which highlights the agenda of programs that the 'GC' will be rolling out on December 19th. There is always suspense and anticipation leading up to these annual policy meetings and this year will be no exception. In fact, it looks like this could be a banner year when it comes to intrigue. There are few topics that we delve into that can truly be considered life and death. This year the 'GC' is planning to update its population strategy and this critical issue seems to have lit a fuse under some people. Numerous demonstrations, including some that have become deadly, have erupted around the globe. The frequency of these events has been increasing and it is unclear what, or who, has prompted them. There have also been some unsubstantiated claims of missing people in parts of China who may have been murdered. There is a growing concern that these occurrences could be the initial stages of a government mandated population control strategy.

Over the coming weeks we will seek the truth and present it as clearly and openly as possible. Our website will be updated with developments as they occur, twenty four-hours a day, and watch for my weekly Sunday night video report."

Claire watched with interest as the report unfolded with video of recent demonstrations, statistical analyses of population studies and interviews with key individuals. Finally the screen went dark and Claire sat and thought about how she would approach this story. She hadn't heard about the missing people in China. That could be anything. They would need to find out and also try to determine if the demonstrations were spontaneous or orchestrated. One obvious source of information would be from the Global Council to review their current population strategies. She couldn't believe that the GC would sanction murder. Claire considered contacting COI to see if changes in public sentiment were causing the demonstrations or if it was the other way around. There was one thing that she knew for sure. This was going to be exciting!

****

And now you have met my granddaughter, Claire. She looks just like her mother and is smart as a whip. I had the good fortune to be included in my grandchildren's lives as they were growing up, and I found it fascinating to witness their maturity as it was enhanced by the COE youth education program. When they turned eight years old, Cayley enrolled them in the program that her friends Adam and Julie designed. It was partly facilitated through their school and partly done through independent work at home and with their friends. When you and I went to school, there was nothing like that for us.

Cayley told me they learned a lot of the things that she was exposed to when she was on the island with Dr. Stapleton. Their youth education was extensive and designed to be understood by the young people as they progressed toward adulthood. By learning to understand and accept themselves at a young age, they were better equipped to deal with their peers and society as a whole. Watching the positivity and confidence that my grandchildren developed made me wonder why no one had been providing this sort of support to young people before Adam decided to do it. We all just had to figure it out by ourselves, and often we weren't all that successful.

It was critical that humans were able to evolve as I have described with Claire and Jermaine and their peers because technology was moving ahead with or without us. The need to create purposeful direction for the freight-train of technological innovation was becoming obvious, even in our day. Burgeoning technologies like the IoT (Internet of Things), Artificial Intelligence and Block-Chain Technologies that existed in the 2010s were developing potentials faster than we could understand how best to thoughtfully apply them. As you would expect, the initial applications of these technological gifts ended up being used for reasons that correlated to the state of society at the time.

During periods of global conflict in the first half of the twentieth century, nuclear research led to creating bombs rather than producing electricity. Toward the end of that century, the internet and social media were created and initially were used frivolously by large numbers of people until they finally realized the power they held. About the time Adam Stapleton was beginning to use computing technology to contribute to social progress, many other positive applications were being imagined. Some of the purposeful utilizations targeted wide-ranging societal issues such as creating cyber-currencies designed to revolutionize and limit the power of the global financial system. Social media was utilized in the '#MeToo' movement that targeted sexual predators. Once a few successes occurred, this new-found tool became invaluable as a means to facilitate change. Then it required the ongoing positive social evolution of humanity keeping pace with technology to ensure that the resulting direction of human progress was in fact socially progressive. The application of technological advances toward positivity slowly gained momentum and eventually became aligned in a worldwide movement of human achievement. A simple hammer can be used as a weapon, a paperweight or a tool of construction, depending on the mentality of the user and his societal needs. I think you are getting the idea. Anyway, I'm off for now and you're headed back to China to check up on Hai Nguyen. I have to admit, I'm getting worried about what that boy is up to. Please keep an eye on him for me.

Chapter 11
November 10, 2058. Southern China.

The sun took its time approaching the dramatic, limestone mountains as the fading light invaded the water-filled, terraced rice paddies that crept up the jagged slopes for as far as the eye could see. Nestled in his improvised blind constructed on the rim of one of those terraces, Hai momentarily forgot what it was that had taken him so far away from his home and his family. The surrounding panorama of karst topography cloaked in a light fog took his breath away. It reminded him of the beauty of life itself and how the earth had taken everything mankind had thrown at it for centuries and still managed to create such awe. As a lifelong farmer, his connection to the earth and its ability to nurture sustained life was constantly uppermost in his consciousness. From the millions of grains of rice that existed within a few meters of him to the countless single- and multi-celled organisms that were at home in the soil beneath him, the evidence of life was in abundance in all directions. Living things, that much of mankind never gave a random thought to, formed the foundation upon which humankind relied. The plants and animals that surrounded him were life itself and the glory of the vistas that rolled out in all directions was his spiritual inspiration. The profound silence defining this remote location provided space for him to notice the tiny splash of a fish-tail or the whisper of a tadpole that were witness to the bounty of organisms that shared this vibrant ecosystem wth the rice. The result of this complex juxtaposition of elements was a localized healthy abundance that fostered human survival in a single, yet multifaceted, environmental entity.

The only other noise that presented itself was a pervasive low growl that rose from the machinery being employed in the valley below where his attention was supposed to be focused. The open-pit mining site would soon become the only light source in a sea of absolute darkness once nightfall was complete. As he lay on his stomach awaiting the companionship of the approaching darkness, Hai couldn't help but acknowledge his thoughts of concern. The last stray wafts of light succumbed to the intensity of the darkness that now completely enveloped him, as he looked below at the lights of the mine that sparkled like a precious treasure. The faint lunar light provided just enough guidance to see a few feet in front of him as he shifted his weight onto his knees, took inventory of his belongings and began his descent.

Step by cautious step, serpentining his way along the levees, he spent the next couple of hours progressing like an attentive tortoise toward the target of his intended destination. The mine that he was approaching had been in existence for longer than he had been alive. His research had revealed that in the last half of the nineteen hundreds, South and Western China had been actively mined for a number of minerals including zinc and copper. It had been a productive and economically successful mine until the assays dropped around the end of the millennia. After about a decade of inactivity, an increasing interest in rare earth elements (REEs), based on the needs of a burgeoning technology industry, brought attention back to the area. Significant research was done resulting in the confirmation of the presence of significant amounts of scandium which was increasingly in demand for the production of sports equipment, mercury vapour lights and the aerospace industry. As with the mine in the Himalaya that he went to first, this one had been rejuvenated in response to the increased demand for the new-age commodity. Since the production of scandium is in the form of an oxide, which is later concentrated into a metal alloy, it is merely a by-product of mining significant amounts of host rock, much of which was radioactive. Due to environmental concerns, the mines were once again shut down. That was about thirty years ago. The location of this mine site is in the valley of a major tributary of the Li River which flows southeast from the Himalaya through Southern China and then into northern Vietnam before emptying into the South China Sea. Hai had noticed the delayed shadow effect of the toxins as they made their way through the groundwater and soil along the route of the river. When he was a boy, he could remember the stories of his grandfather and his father as they speculated as to the problems that were stifling their abilities to feed their families and sell their crops. The situation persisted for years and then, inexplicably, things began to get better. They had no idea that their change of fortunes related to the closing of this mine hundreds of kilometres away. Despite the relatively close geographic proximity, in a global sense, what happened in Southern China was a complete mystery to Hai and his family as they worked their lands. It was only his connection with a woman from America, whom he had come to know through a website his teacher had encouraged him to join, that got him involved with the Food and Agriculture Agency (FAA) of the United Nations. From that new perspective, he began to see the world as it existed beyond their extensive fields. He began to see how the world was, at the same time, so massive and yet so small. He came to understand how the complexities of society, business and politics can work at odds with each other to create a kind of organized chaos. He had never really given much thought to what happened beyond the horizon of their farmland. He was lucky that he was able to grow up with parents and grandparents. Given the tragedy of a war that ravaged their country before he was born, most others were not so fortunate. He grew up having everything he needed, and more than most. Why on earth would he look beyond their fields for anything more?

    And then Cayley Wilson happened. As one of twenty-four strangers who inexplicably, over time, became his second family, she was the one that stood out. Why she was drawn to him specifically was still a mystery to him, but perhaps, by now, he had earned the trust and respect that she had given him so early on in their relationship. At her persistent urging (damn she was stubborn), he agreed to work with the United Nations in their efforts to maximize global crop yields, organize transportation and trade and educate farmers and government decision makers about everything that they needed to know to be able to efficiently feed the nine billion people that inhabit the planet. It was never thought possible to be able to do such a thing and he knew that it wouldn't have been possible without the complete transformation that had occurred due to the efforts and influence of Cayley and her COI group.

He had laughed out loud when she initially broached the subject with him. They wanted him to head an oversight committee of eleven people who would guide the process of a complete overhaul of the agency's policies and processes. He had never been more than a hundred miles away from the town where he was born. He owned a computer but effectively was illiterate when it came to using it or any other technological device.

"How could I possibly help make changes to a system I know nothing about?" he remembered asking her. "I grow plants and raise animals. Once they leave my land, I know nothing about what happens after that. You need some kind of an expert," he tried to explain at the time. He had totally believed what he was saying to her, but then she did what Cayley always does and everything was different. She changed his mind, his life and his view of the world. He never had a view before that day. He didn't know or care what happened beyond his immediate world. As long as his family, friends, crops and animals were okay, then that was enough. Simplicity. Some days he missed that life. Some days he couldn't even believe it was possible he had lived that life. She helped him understand that because he was coming from outside of the 'system' he had no biases or agendas to infect his vision. He was free to see the truth and to act on it. She was right, which she has teased him about ever since.

Despite all of the change, turmoil, stresses and adaptations that had occurred over the past decade or so, the bottom line was that he had immense pride in what he had accomplished and contributed to. The world was better off because of him and his efforts, and the positivity of that was irrefutable. This trip was no exception and he was optimistic that the results would be positive. He was glad he had taken the time to spend the few days in the far west prior to coming here. That mine was about five times the size of this one and was upstream from the entire drainage basin of central China, which supported the lives of over a billion people. During the two days he monitored the mining activities there, he was able to witness the transport of twenty-seven truckloads of raw materials being hauled from the site. It made him wonder how the loads were merged with minerals from legitimate sites. He also was able to witness and record a release of fluids from the mine into the nearby river system. He was downstream and had taken samples that would be analyzed as soon as he returned home. If he was correct, there were nine illegal mines operating at the moment. The first one he monitored had been the largest of the nine. The one he was now presiding over was the closest to his home, which he was beginning to miss more than he would have expected. If his plan came together, he would only be home for about two weeks before his trip to New York for the United Nations annual meetings. There was a lot of work to be done before then.

Chapter 12
November 11, 2058. Cayley's Circles of Humanity Meeting.

Cayley sat and looked around her at the screens where the live images of her Circle of Humanity group were assembling. For the past thirty-some years this group of twenty-five people had assembled remotely about once every two to four weeks. What began as a curiosity had gradually transformed from a bit of a chore to what was now one of the highlights of her existence. She could still remember the strained dialogues and sessions at the beginning when this diverse group of strangers searched for commonality and understanding. The progress was slow as they were guided through a systematic evolution of self- and group-discovery. At the beginning, she had the advantage of knowing Adam and Julie who were spearheading this advancement of their Circles of Influence project. She had complete faith in the vision Adam and Julie were working toward and, as such, had no hesitation when it came to encouraging herself and the others in the group to forge ahead. They gradually inched forward toward attaining their common mission of forming a cohesive and accepting support group. The goal was to develop relationships with each other that were to become more intensely important than any of them could ever have imagined.

Now, decades later, these people were her family that she looked forward to seeing as often as possible. She couldn't imagine not having all of them in her life. They had shared so many victories, heartbreaks, laughs, discoveries and tears over the years. She would be lost without them and the support they provided to the person she had become. The changes that occurred within the group as they became a cohesive unit mirrored the growth of each of them as individuals. Cayley remembered being shocked at what she learned about herself in the process. Biases and limitations she wasn't even aware of came to the surface.

Over the years they had lost four members of their group who were at the end of their lives and one other for personal or philosophical reasons, but that led to the group welcoming five replacements. As new members joined the group, it was like celebrating a birth that brought new energy and joy to the entire circle.

When Adam first talked her into participating, Cayley was trying to grasp what she was signing up for. Psychologists seemed to love their support groups, but she was busy with her life and didn't really feel like she needed additional support for anything. She had recently graduated university and she and her new husband were up to their necks in establishing their careers. They had also just found out they were expecting their first child. Those seemed like great excuses, but once Adam and Julie were done coercing her she felt obligated. After all, she was working for them as a Circles of Influence Regional Liaison Officer, so it only made sense that she should be fully integrated into the programs they were providing. Now, with all of her cyber-family around her, she couldn't imagine not having them in her life and she realized how vastly different she would be as a person without them.

The sound of Julie's voice indicated the beginning of the program.

"Welcome everyone!" Julie began the session. Her words, were also provided in script on one of the screens for those who received information more effectively on a visual level than by auditory means. "As always we will begin by going around your circle of friends and allow everyone to greet each other on a personal level before we get into the material that we will be dealing with today. I will turn you over to your chairperson who will facilitate this part of the session. I will be back with you in a while."

Instinctively, Cayley looked over at Birget Halvarsson. She was an interesting woman from Denmark who had served as their chairperson for the last ten years. She was fifty-four years old, a mother of four and the writer of a political blog. She was a twenty-one year-old political science student when their group was formed and as with most bright young idealistic people, she was full of ideas, energy and enthusiasm. Cayley, being only about ten years older, came to think of her as the younger sister that she never had. It was amazing how so many of the people in this group had filled voids in her life, many of which she never even knew she had.

"Okay everyone, please activate your headsets and let's get started," Birget announced. Each of them took the mesh netting that contained eight cranial sensors woven into the fabric and put it on their heads like a swimming cap. The technology behind the caps had occurred about five years earlier when the COI neuroscientists figured out how to collect a person's brainwaves, combine them with those of other people and then send the combined signal back to each individual's limbic system. The result was remarkable. You were able to feel the combined emotional state of the entire group and your brain would react to it as if it were sourced within you. Another remarkable contribution to this process was the development of a program that read body language and facial expressions and collated that information into the mix. All of this technology was confined to the safety of the COH groups that had already attained a state of trust, acceptance and support. This would ensure that the technology would encounter the minimum levels of positivity required to ensure that a background of support would dominate any lesser degrees of negativity that could exist during a group interaction. Cayley had been amazed the first few times they had used the technology. She would never forget the first COH meeting after her husband died. She was an absolute mess. He had a lot of support from her children and Julie and Adam, but on days when she was alone, she just couldn't escape the painful despair. A couple of weeks later, a COH meeting was scheduled and Cayley didn't even want to attend. She didn't know how she would face this supplemental family of friends while she was so weak and vulnerable. She wanted to stay in bed the whole day, but she didn't. The meeting started with the usual sharing of personal aspects of their lives and someone who had read about her husband's death gave their condolences and asked her how she was doing. Cayley had decided that she wasn't going to bring up her loss and just fake her way through the session but there it was, out in the open. As she shared a small piece of her pain, she began to feel the love and support of the group. It was intense and overwhelming. There were none of the strained words that people awkwardly extend to those in mourning. In their place, a feeling of visceral warmth began to spread through her entire body. It wasn't just emotional empathy. It also seemed like she was receiving a new level of support through understanding and guidance. For the first time, Cayley felt that she would be okay, that she was not alone and knew that she would survive. Somehow the experience of the group, many of whom had previously lost love ones, was extended to her with a direct link to her core. Analogous to pumping drugs through an intravenous line directly into the blood stream, rather than having it slowly absorb after taking the medicine orally, this truth was not subject to being filtered by her ego or her rational brain. She immediately began to feel better as a result of experiencing the power of cranial feedback.

Now, technology allowed them to link all of the COH groups together and collate the combined positivity which effectively measures and delivers the mood of the entire planet to each individual recipient. It is remarkably reassuring to feel the commonality of mankind and to bathe in its positivity. It was in stark contrast to her early years after the island (AI) when despite the fact that her personal life was finally blossoming, she would watch the news and observe society and feel almost numb at the negativity and hopelessness that seemed to exist. Adam had talked about the nurturing influences that effect people and

Cayley couldn't help but wonder how the world could survive in such a negative global environment.

Cayley chuckled to herself when she realized that she had subconsciously used the term AI. She used to categorize her past into segments, just as Mankind had done with BC and AD referring to Before Christ and After Death. Her watershed moment was her experience on an island back in 2018 with Adam and Julie. Her life had changed and because of that, she came to define her current life accordingly. She attended University two years AI, which of course meant 'After Island'. For most people, AI meant Artificial Intelligence, which Cayley found both appropriate and humorous because before her interaction with Adam Stapleton, much of her youthful intelligence was extremely artificial.

"It has been three weeks since we last gathered as a group so who would like to go first?" Birget began to facilitate, dragging Cayley's thoughts back to forty years AI.

"I will," Ramon Hernandez spoke up. "My wife and I celebrated our sixty-seventh anniversary last week. Most of our family was at the fiesta that lasted for two days. Six of our children, twenty-four grand children, seventy-two great grandchildren and eleven great-great-grandchildren were able to attend. It was a wonderful celebration."

"Congratulations, Ramon," a number of the group chimed in almost in unison. "Give our love to Conseula," Birget added.

"No wonder everyone's talking about population programs lately," someone spoke up in a lighthearted jab at the size of Ramon's family, to the amusement of the group.

"I guess that is true," Ramon added. "Including my one hundred and forty-four descendants and spouses in our family plus the twenty-four of you, who are my other family, maybe I have more than my share of blessings in this world. But I wouldn't trade any of them, or you, for anything."

"Thanks Ramon. Why don't we continue clockwise around the group for anyone who wants to say something," Birget suggested.

"I have a new job," Maria Lagarria spoke up on cue. " I am now a logistics clerk for transportation at the new food market in Torino. I coordinate with the local growers to get their products to the market. It's really interesting and I get to deal with a lot of people from the area."

Cayley listened and observed as the group shared their latest news with each other. It was such a supportive environment that any positive news was richly celebrated, and bad news was met with sincere empathy and supported with genuine and abundant feedback. She loved getting caught up with these people and she always felt secure and whole when they were together. In this group, and the hundreds of millions of others like it, each person brought such diverse ideas, experiences and cultural characteristics to the group that its strength, as it evolved through time, was undeniably impenetrable. Once the group had been able to develop the necessary level of acceptance and trust, the ideals of support, caring and intimacy were able to flourish.

When it was Cayley's opportunity to share, having nothing except her work that was new since their last gathering, she asked if anyone had heard from Hai Nguyen lately. He had not logged in today which was very unusual. She was surprised he hadn't at least sent a notice of his absence so that no one would worry. Unfortunately, no one had heard a thing from him so Cayley made a mental note to herself to somehow find out if he was okay. In her peripheral vision she saw the notation added to her list of 'things to do' on her desktop monitor. Up until now she had been concerned, but now she was downright worried about the fate of her missing friend.

Twenty minutes later the group was finished catching up and were ready to begin the information session. Birget typed in a command and the focus was turned back to Julie's recorded voice.

"Okay, let's get started. A couple of days ago, each of you received a text of the information that I will review today, plus an agenda that we will follow for the next couple of hours. Hopefully you have all had time to familiarize yourselves with the background to our topic. Based on current records, as of about a week ago, there were nine billion, three hundred and twenty-four million, seven hundred and six thousand, nine hundred and twenty-one living humans. About eighty-thousand of these are off planet at the moment but that is nitpicking."

"The three basic components of population statistics are the birth rate, death rate and life expectancy. We will look at each of these three components individually and objectively, recognizing that many of the controls involve social, cultural, religious and regional socioeconomic conditions. Current birth rates have been holding steady at just under two hundred million newborns per year who survive child birth. Infant death rates have decreased to about one half of one percent or five deaths out of every one thousand births. The stabilized number of births is the result of a combination of factors. The increasing numbers of women in their prime, childbearing years, decreasing infant deaths and a more optimistic view of the future of society have all contributed to the occurrence of more births. These factors have been offset by an increase in birth control, family planning education and regional birth targets. As well, there seems to have been a reassessment of women's roles in society beyond being a mother and caregiver, which has led to an overall decrease in family size. It needs to be noted that there have been no instances of artificially controlling birth rates by such means as sterilization, government legislation, forced birth control or pregnancy terminations for more than a decade. At the request of the broad global population, artificial non-uterine births have been eliminated in an attempt to encourage natural child conceptions and births. Education and social programs have fostered a transition to the current reality where all women who are medically able and have the desire to give birth to one or more healthy infants are encouraged and supported to become mothers. Health and desire are the cornerstones of this initiative. Women who lack the health or social situation that would encourage them to give birth are supported with the help that they need to improve their situation. Women who do not have the desire to become mothers are being educated with respect to birth control and life skills. In the past, many women in the more developed nations who may have wanted to be mothers were burdened by social and economic stresses, which led to negative population rates in those regions. In many of the less developed regions birth rates skyrocketed due to statistical growth and a lack of birth control or prevention. In other cases the women in those regions lacked having a voice with respect to being in control of their own bodies. With the current realities we enjoy today, the vast majority of women now have their basic health and nutritional needs met and are provided social support and education. Due to these factors, the conditions are increasingly available for all women to give birth to children who will be born into an optimistic life scenario. With significant improvement in trends with respect to the facilitation of adoptions, group nurturing, single parent support, birth control and planned parenthood education, social support has never been so prevalent on a global basis. The results are beginning to show a more equitable number of births per mother on a regional basis, an overall lowering of birth rates in women under the age of twenty-five and a rebound in the number of two parent nuclear families that give birth to or raise a range of two to five children."

"A non-biological factor that also seems to be affecting birthing statistics has been the gradual migration of populations away from the urban centres and toward more rural living situations which promotes improved living conditions. People living in rural areas and smaller centres have become more likely to have larger families and they tend to be more self-reliant. It is difficult to know what all the factors are that determine the timing of when a woman or a couple decide they want to conceive a child. Unlike fifty years ago, the event is typically the result of an actual decision rather than just a biological occurrence. Unplanned or unwanted pregnancies are far less common than they were in the past."

"We will now focus on current, per capita, death rates, which in recent decades have slowly decreased. Over the past ten years the numbers have stabilized and the forward trend is for small increases in death rates. In the year 1990 the annual number of deaths was about forty-seven million people which was 0.8 percent of the population. This rose to fifty-three million by the year 2010. The numbers peaked at just over sixty-million in the year 2043, but that relates to only 0.65 percent of the almost nine billion human inhabitants of the earth at that time. Going back to 2010, you couldn't pick up a newspaper or watch the news without learning of terrorist attacks, gun violence, ethnic cleansing incidences, horrific accidents and suicides. Mankind clearly seemed to be on a downward spiral. However, if you look at the statistics related to the cause of deaths for that year you would find that these types of incidents caused less than ten percent of all deaths. In comparison, stress-related maladies such as heart disease and cancer caused approximately twenty-four million deaths which was nearly half of the total fatalities for that year. By 2030 that number had increased to thirty-four million and by 2040 it was up to forty-three million. The majority of these stress-related deaths occurred initially in the more developed world but have gradually been increasing, along with the spread of wealth, throughout the globe. Meanwhile, back in 2010, an additional thirteen million deaths were attributed to communicable diseases common in underdeveloped or what were called the 'third' world countries. These types of diseases are commonly pervasive in areas of poverty, which lack sanitation, clean water and sufficient nutrition. Thankfully these fatalities have been gradually decreasing for the past century and now account for less than ten percent of the total. The recent trends in the past fifteen years demonstrate major decreases in conflict, violent, accidental and self-imposed deaths as well as a dramatic recent decrease in stress related health issues causing death. These can be related directly to recent changes in our social beliefs and global structure. The majority of all deaths today relate to illnesses associated with aging. While still a loss, the death of a loved one who has lived a long life is easier to deal with than the loss of a child or a young person. Violent deaths, victims of war and even accidental deaths all seem so much more tragic and senseless to us as humans and these scenarios often create negative emotions such as anger and revenge which can lead to additional loss of life and an associated loss of humanity. Collectively we are all far more at peace today given the quality of the lives that we live and the nature of the deaths that exist. Depending on your spiritual or religious beliefs, as they pertain to concepts like multiple lives, there are numerous ways to emotionally approach death, which of course can come in many forms. Since the vast majority of deaths today come as a result of aging, there has been significant discussion within the COH groups about the reduction of suffering during the latter stages of life for the elderly. This discussion blends in with the third component of population statistics, which is average life expectancy. This has been increasing consistently over the past hundred years and now sits at seventy-nine years of age worldwide. This may be almost as far as we can stretch things without significant medical interventions. A healthy life lasting seventy-nine years should be considered a good thing and extending a life within a body that degenerates is not a goal our population wishes to focus on. There was significant consideration in past decades towards targeting immortality as an ideal for those whose egos and wealth made it possible. That trend has reversed in the past years. Virtually all of our current emotional and statistical feedback tells us that our aging population now desires quality of life to quantity of life. Living better is preferred to living longer. The recent technology of cranial downloads may also revolutionize how we feel about death. Surveys that have been done suggest that elderly subjects who are nearing death seem to feel that having their brain function downloaded and available for their loved ones to continue to communicate with puts them more at ease with dying. Even though they admittedly have no idea if it actually changes anything for the deceased, the concept seems to be comforting. It seems to be a condition of being human that most people, as they gradually approach an undefined death, slowly become more accepting of the inevitability of their fate. Again, this may tie back to religious beliefs and spirituality or it may simply be a by-product of being human, but overall it appears to be a concrete reality. Certainly the mourning process for the loved ones of the deceased are positively impacted by the existence of a peaceful death and the possibility of a cranial download. The charts we have assembled for you will confirm all of the ideas and statistics I have just covered and can provide you with as much detail as you need."

"So what does all of this information tell us?" Julie posed the question. "A combination of predicted future trends indicate that in twenty years the number of births will have dropped by about twenty-five percent and the number of deaths will grow by about ten percent. By extrapolating these and other observable trends out into the future, we can predict that the world population will peak in the year 2109 at about thirteen billion people and then gradually decline. This information gives us data that we can enter into our models to ensure our ability to sustain that number of people for a short time. If it is not possible, then we will determine how to offset that number either by encouraging social modifications to birth rates or to actively pursue appropriate colonization in space and subsea habitats. The good news is that we have fifty years to figure it all out."

"Thirty years ago, when the total population was around eight billion, it was thought that eleven billion was the maximum number of people the world could support, and even that was not sustainable due to fears of limitations of primary resources like clean air, water and food. Fortunately there have been a number of technological and social step-changes in how things are being done that greatly influenced those calculations and there will be new improvements we still don't know about yet."

"In today's world of unprecedented cooperation regarding the planning and implementation of global strategies, we are able to achieve far greater results while using fewer resources. Think about what a person needs to live on this earth in addition to human love and support. We need oxygen, water and food for basic survival. We also need energy and raw materials to provide the basics of clothing and shelter. For most of the history of mankind, the majority of the people on earth failed to have even these basics available to them while a small minority lived in excess. It has only been during the past decade that more than fifty percent of the people on earth enjoyed the basic necessities of a healthy existence. Even the most basic consumer items that many of us have taken for granted for a very long time were not available to half of the population. Today, however, eighty-two percent of us live above the poverty line and that number continues to increase. Collectively, in the past fifteen years we have revolutionized agriculture, water sourcing, transportation and manufacturing. There have been major advancements with clean water desalination, manufactured goods designed to last for decades rather than for a few years and with recycling initiatives. The absence of global conflicts, the ability to utilize cyber-travel and efficient public transportation, urban farms, economic reform and changing consumption practices have all combined to create an exponentially more efficient world. One where there is more of everything available to more people than ever. As these trends continue and population growth slows and eventually reverses, the world will gradually become bountiful once again. In the coming weeks, you will be provided with charts and tables that illustrate the future projections that have been developed by the various United Nations agencies for each of the categories that I just mentioned and a few others as well. I would encourage you to go through this information in as much detail as it takes for you to understand that there is no reason for the Global Council to take any steps toward any sort of strategically planned alterations to death rates. There are certainly a few areas of the world that continue to be overpopulated and where people still live in poverty but those are manageable problems that are being addressed in a logical and humane manner."

"That, my friends, concludes my presentation of the background and statistical support for this session. My hope is that the information provided will allow each of you to proceed through today's exercise with an informed and open mind."

Cayley was still amazed at how this initial concept of breaking down human barriers and forming diverse groups of acceptance had transformed from an experiment in humanity to a technological revolution where the will of the people could be heard and acted on. What a change from the political system she grew up with!

"What you will be doing today is a bit different from our usual processes," Julie continued to facilitate the process. "Typically we present you with information and then you discuss it and formulate a group consensus of thoughts and feelings which is used to set global policy. This will be the first time in the history of Circles of Humanity where we are attempting to influence you in any way. We take this very seriously because throughout the evolution of COI the only way we have been able to allow seven billion people to have complete faith in us and our mission is to have been completely void of hidden personal or organizational agendas. Our one and only focus has been to promote the ideal of encouraging the strength of humanity to flourish. Over the past thirty-five years, all of your combined personal growth has shaped society in the image of what is best for the common good of the global population. The fact that you have been able to achieve this with nothing more than our technical and psychological support is testimony to the collective power of humanity and the need for an unbiassed approach. Today we are in the midst of an unusual global occurrence. As you know, there have been violent outbursts around the world where pockets of protesters are concerned about a form of genocide being sanctioned by the Global Council to control overpopulation. Despite the fact that this is not a rational, desired or even necessary process to undertake, there is a source of negativity that has formed and is spreading and causing unrest. People have been hurt and even killed and it wouldn't be wise to leave this occurrence unchecked. This type of violence may have been commonplace in the past but certainly not in the world we have all worked to create. In some of your groups, there may be one or two individuals who have been influenced by whomever or whatever is behind this plot to undermine the existing societal processes. Fear is being utilized to spread a negative and fabricated message for some sort of personal or anarchical gain. It is the object of today's session to let those people speak, to be given the opportunity to share their concerns with the rest of you and to see what evolves from that. Just in case there is credibility to the concerns that are creating conflict and injuring and killing people, those who support the idea need to be able to broach the topic within the safe environment of a COH group. This is the perfect venue for open communication and to air your concerns. Random and orchestrated violence in our parks and plazas around the world is wrong and needs to be stopped. We have made available for you some of the audio tracks of the recorded messages being played at these demonstrations so you can try to understand the message being promoted. Many of your groups will not contain a member who shares supportive feelings or who is concerned by the threat being discussed. For those groups I would suggest that you talk about all aspects of the unrest and decide collectively if there is any merit to the concern. If the proposed fear of the Global Council using methods of planned genocide to control population growth turns out to be a significant concern of the collective, then that information will create an action plan to resolve those fears through new laws that would make such methods illegal. If, however, the fear-based message is unfounded, then the process of allowing everyone to talk about it openly will reveal that it has no basis of reality attached to it. Then the threats of violence and anarchy will have no ability to grow beyond the seeds of discontent that have begun to germinate with the localized outbreaks that have occurred. This process is about open discussion and transparency, so let's quit listening to me and get to it," Julie concluded.

"Okay, everyone, let's turn to our worksheets and begin the discussion," Birget instructed. "The first step is to determine the level of concern within our group about the proposed idea that the World Council has been, or will, utilize practices of genocide in its attempts to control population targets. Please enter the level of concern you have at this point on a scale of one to ten, with ten being the most concerned."

Everyone took a moment to consider the question and then entered their number. Once the last person had provided their input, they were all informed that the average level of concern for their group was one point seven five out of ten and that the highest anonymous individual score was a four.

"Good," Birget continued, "now we will listen to the audio tracks of the messages that the rioters are reacting to and see if that has any effect on how we feel."

They listened to four distinct yet correlated messages of fear and concern that had been broadcast in four different geographical locations designed to create a human frenzy of revolt. Cayley noticed that although the message was the same, the details were very focused toward the people who lived in the distinct regions. They preyed on historical examples of government negativity that had previously affected the people of that area. The speakers were obviously local residents of each area based on their vernacular that even the translation software couldn't eliminate. Whoever was orchestrating this had created a widespread network of participants.

"Okay," Birget spoke up after the recordings ended, " let's provide our input once again now that we have heard the concerns of those who share this message of fear."

The new numbers were entered. The highest number increased from 4 to 5 and the average increased from 1.75 to 1.91, suggesting that the recorded messages had little effect on changing anyones opinion but merely reinforced preexisting concerns.

"Good, now let's discuss how we feel about the fears that were presented. I think that we should allow whoever it was who voted four and five to speak first, if they wish, since they appear to have the greatest concerns and we want to acknowledge those fears to see if they hold up once we discuss them openly."

****

Wow. That was a lot of information to digest. Obviously, it's important because it has exposed you to Circles of Humanity. It is the title of this book, which makes it important that you understand exactly what COH is. I've had it explained to me by the people who developed it and I was part of my own group for nearly twenty years, so hopefully I can answer any questions you have without getting too technical. In a nutshell, the groups are a way to get exposure to people different from you so that you can discover that they aren't all that different from you. How often do you get a chance to sit down with a thirty-three-year-old mother of ten from Senegal and actually understand what her life is like, what's important to her, what she believes in, what her goals in life are? Best of all, though learning all of this, you have the opportunity to become one of her best friends. That is what humanity creates when you are given the opportunity to connect with people who are different from you. My Circles of Humanity group changed the way I looked at people and I hope you get to experience your own group some day.

    I think I should also comment on all of the information that Julie presented to the groups. You, and I in my younger years, were told many things designed to help you perceive the world around you in certain ways. As a former member of the media, I can assure you that much of what we were told were lies, designed to serve the needs and desires of someone other than you. This is not always done in a malicious manner because often it is second hand information that is *passed along as presumed knowledge. The existing biases are not even realized or consistent after the process of dissemination begins.*

Nevertheless, the question of where we would go to for the truth was problematic. When you can't definitely trust anyone, how is it possible to progress in a rational manner? That is what Circles of Influence provided and the results have been remarkable.

Chapter 13
November 11, 2058. Spencer Watt's Circles of Humanity Meeting.

Spencer looked at the numbers as his mind sorted through the various approaches he could take. 'Goddamn COI!' Everything with them was so rational and open. How was he supposed to turn society against the establishment that consisted of them, Braintrust and the Global Council when they already have everyone believing that they are the epitome of good and openness? He was glad he had decided to deactivate his headset so that the rest of his group couldn't detect his negativity. He understood how it was important in group building to generate trust. Understanding the thoughts and feeling the emotions of the rest of the group was critical to the process. There was no way he could deceive them while being interconnected.

His first step would be to influence his COH group. He had decided to enter a 3.5 out of 10 in the initial round of input so as to introduce concern but not put a target on himself. He had invested too much time and money into this project to screw it up here. He had facilitated and partially bankrolled twelve separate demonstrations that would be ongoing throughout the coming weeks leading up to the critical year-end meetings. Over a million people would be directly exposed to his message of fear. Yes, people had been hurt, and a couple killed so far, but that was a necessary price to pay to gain exposure. When this was all done with, he would finally regain his rightful status as someone who is admired and listened to. Maybe with this dedicated meeting, COI had inadvertently provided him with the perfect timing to come out of the shadows and become the face of the revolution. He could be a moral leader whose apparent goal is to save the people of the world from the hidden practices of this global establishment. He would openly defy the existing power structure which has been manipulating them all through COH propaganda. Sessions like the one being held today had gradually led to a global acceptance of change. 'Society as a whole may be better off as a result of their actions, but I'm certainly not. Now is the time for me to act!'

After his group listened to the four recordings that he had broadly designed, Spencer entered a 10. It would appear to all that he had been somewhat concerned initially and was now convinced that there was a serious problem. A champion had been born and he would lead the way forward against the lies and deceit of the existing system. He would convince his COH group and then go public. He had joined COH years ago when his celebrity status began to wane. These groups had incubated the cornerstones of a new human dynamic by focusing on the individual as a subset of the collective. Previously there had been a tiered system with leaders and followers. Western society, and increasingly the developing nations, had bought into the ideology of wealth and fame as the goal of the individual. They had idolized deserving people like him who served as leaders and role models who demonstrated lifestyles that were the envy and motivation for all. Then, as COI encouraged society to see things differently, everything slowly seeped away. People became self-motivated, connected and fulfilled through their own lives and relationships. In the process, he and others like him had become irrelevant and that was unacceptable. Soon, once his plan was executed, they would once again see his value. He would come back more visibly and influential than ever.

"I will admit that following the recent events of violence, I expected that those involved were just radicals looking for attention and blaming the government," Spencer began delivering his prepared speech to his COH group. He was asked to go first because of his high initial input score and he would take full advantage of his opportunity to influence them. "It appears that some people are still brought up that way. Then I began to consider some of the things they were saying and I began to wonder about the validity of what they are warning us about. In preparation for today's meeting, I went back and 'visited' a couple of the demonstration sites in order to get first-hand knowledge of what the people were saying and what they were afraid of. Listening to these recordings today, and applying them to my personal experiences with the government structure that currently exists, I am becoming convinced that these voices from the dark actually represent the light. They are warning us about a truth that we can no longer see because of the indoctrination we have all been systematically subjected to. Earlier in my career, I chose to allow my social image to be used to fight for good causes, against the greedy and power-hungry politicians and corporations. I became very good at identifying those who needed to be stopped. Now I see that same enemy in its more sophisticated entity that we know as COI and Braintrust. They control us and they control the Global Council. They form a very small elite who use their self-serving ideas and psychobabble to indoctrinate us all into their program of dominance. Just think about the introduction to today's session. They told us what to think and believe and now they are using this mock display of apparent openness and transparency to promote their agenda. They say they are encouraging us to look at all sides of this issue to make us believe that they are only looking for the truth, knowing that we have been programmed to believe them. Today's meetings have been designed to shut down the few brave souls who are still willing to speak out against them and seek the real truth. As of this moment, I pledge to be one of those brave souls who will not be intimidated or influenced. I would hope that each one of us finds the courage to look beyond what has been forced on us and look to the truth."

Spencer looked around him at the screens that held the images of the other twenty-four members of his COH group. He searched their eyes and observed their body language for signs that he had gotten through to them. For the past ten years, he had come to know each of these people intimately and, as much as he was willing to allow, they had become linked to him. If he couldn't get these people on board with his sincere display of deceit, he wouldn't have a chance with society as a whole. He had to use what he knew about them to exploit their personal weaknesses.

Chapter 14
November 11, 2058. Seattle, USA.

Julie sat with her technical staff, analyzing the data that comprised the public reactions to the program that was unfolding as it wrapped around the globe. Given the complex distribution of time zones, COH sessions were typically held at a common time where the majority of the members could participate during normal waking hours. Given that most of the people in the world live in China and India, an early evening time for them was the most convenient. They could 'attend' their COH meeting beginning between five and eight p.m. When it is seven pm in Beijing, it is noon in Berlin, so Europeans and Africans were available for an hour or two over an improvised lunch hour. On the east coast of North America it would be six a.m. so an early morning meeting before normal work or school hours was practical. It was only the poor individuals such as those in western North America, Hawaii and the South Pacific nations like New Zealand who had to disrupt their normal sleep patterns to attend their COH meetings.

Julie tried to rub the last particles of sleep out of her eyes as she sat in front of the myriad of display screens and tried to comprehend what the data was showing. She was a psychologist, not a data analyst, and after all, it was only four forty-five in the morning and she had been up since two. Thank God her speech to the groups had been pre-recorded.

The first series of data inputs were beginning to arrive and they looked positive. On average the concern levels were at about one point five out of ten and the highest was around two. Individually there were a few high scores, but they were statistically insignificant according to her technical group. Unfortunately, as a psychologist, she understood that a small number of vocal and motivated fringe players, extremists or fundamentalists could generate social widespread unrest and violence. As the expression goes, it only takes one rotten apple to spoil the whole case.

Thirty minutes later, after each of the groups had a chance to listen to the audio tracks, the input data was only marginally different. There were a few more high numbers than before the audio but the overall averages were fundamentally unchanged. Now all they could do was wait. It was Julie's hope and expectation that once the groups had a chance to discuss the issues and share how they felt about it all, common sense would prevail and the existing concerns would be eliminated. The emotion-based, coalesced feedback data would be calibrated and she would know if they had been successful in their attempt to combat the growing negativity. Julie expected the group discussions to vary in length between thirty to sixty minutes. Typically, in a group of twenty-five people, there would be five or six members who would do most of the talking. If dissenting views existed, there would tend to be one or two spokespersons from each viewpoint and eventually a resolution or compromise in position would occur. On occasion, people will be willing to listen but simply agree to disagree. Given the history and emotionally close-knit nature of these COH groups, any existing polarizing attitudes that may exist would already be well understood. Individual discussions would occur much more effectively given the intimacy of the group and the predominant desire to achieve respectful understanding rather than conflict. All of this should typically be wrapped up in under an hour depending on the skill set of the group leaders and how well they facilitate the discussions.

Julie sat, slumped down in her chair, looking out the window at the darkness thinking about absolutely nothing at all. Maybe a nap this afternoon would be in order assuming that the results of the current session doesn't put the rest of her work day into a tail spin. The sound of her phone sounded grotesquely inappropriate given the restful semi-comatose state she was attempting to maintain.

"Yeah," she murmured.

"Julie, did I wake you?" Adam Stapleton voiced his concern.

"Why does everyone ask me that question?"

"Thoughtfulness maybe, or perhaps concern."

"Or maybe because they call me at the ungodliest of hours."

"Maybe you should move from Seattle to London. It rains there all of the time too. You would feel right at home."

"I was thinking more like the Canary Islands." Julie pondered an image of stress free sunshine and beaches.

"All of those birds singing would drive me crazy, but I can see how that might suit you," Adam considered. "You have always come across like a cheerful little bird with a happy song."

"I'm pretty sure that people live in the Canary Islands, Adam. Not just birds."

"Actually, I know someone there. I could introduce you," he offered.

"How about we leave that for now and talk about what you are calling about."

"Sounds good. It's just that I'm wearing holes in my floorboards pacing back and forth waiting to hear how the session is going. It would be easier if we were in COH groups of our own so that we could get a sense of the reactions to this. Cayley is so lucky that we decided she should participate in the program."

"We are participating, Adam, just from a different perspective. We agreed it would be better for us to be able to develop the program without the bias of belonging to a specific group. We need to be able to view things from a higher level, one step removed from the participants. Psychologists don't participate in their support groups, they facilitate them and that is what we are doing."

"I know, I know. Sometimes it's hard to wait and easy to worry. For the first time ever, we are trying to push an agenda of faith in the system and in the Global Council. We don't push agendas. That has always been our steadfast rule. We point out truths and realities about people and situations and then allow them to figure things out for themselves and within their groups."

"We are under attack, Adam. The whole system is and it is our duty to point out the existing truths so that people won't be manipulated. This is just a subtle variation to our normal process."

Adam knew that he agreed with Julie. "Then why am I so worried?" he asked rhetorically.

"Because you can't control this and maybe because you're not happy you have retired." Julie answered the question anyway.

"I didn't retire, I just promoted you into my role as the head of Psychological Resources and CEO of Circles of Influence. I am still the Chairman of the Board, so I am still the boss."

"Whatever makes you happy, Adam. I just want you to relax and reap the rewards of everything you have achieved."

"But what if that all comes tumbling down. I don't know what's going on out there, but social unrest like this hasn't been seen for almost two decades. Somebody is up to something and it needs to be dealt with."

"And that is exactly what we are doing. Never before has there been a means to connect directly to the hearts and brains of seven billion people with unified clarity and truth. At the end of the day, the strength of those people will prove to be impenetrable to any negative attempts to manipulate them. After centuries of divisive manipulation aimed at delivering wealth and power to a selective few, you figured out how to align virtually all of the people on the face of the earth together based on their one true commonality. That, of course, is their humanity. Corporations, religions, governments and the media no longer have the ability to bias and control large groups of people for self-serving purposes. Everything has changed and you started it all. It's time for you to relax and remind yourself what you have achieved. You have given your life to that vision. Now you can 'travel' the globe witnessing your achievements."

"Maybe in an hour from now when we begin to see how today went," Adam cautioned. "Was it good that we ensured that no one could 'visit' a COH session?"

"You mean no one including us?" Julie clarified his point. "We get the feedback we need without prying into the personal and confidential discussions. People wouldn't be as open and honest with each other if they weren't assured absolute privacy."

"I know, but sometimes it would be nice."

"Just relax, Adam, and have faith in what we have built. I will let you know how it went as soon as we get our feedback." Julie ordered her friend.

"Alright."

"Oh, by the way, congratulations on being selected as a Braintrust donor. That's quite an accomplishment," Julie offered.

"I think that it means I am getting old and they want to salvage whatever is left of my brain before it turns to mush."

"Gee, a pre-eminent behavioural psychologist who doesn't even know how to take a compliment. How sad is that?"

"You're right Julie, I should know better and yes, I was very honoured to have been considered, although some of the latest rumours floating around give me a bit of concern."

"What rumours?"

"There has been concern that some of the Braintrust data has been experiencing some significant glitches. It has been suggested that as the donors pass on, their souls become uneasy because their brain functions are still remotely active on a computer system. Somehow their spirit haunts the downloaded brain causing it to function erratically, or something to that effect."

"Wow! Do you believe that scenario is at all possible?"

"I believe in the energy of the human spirit. Does that end when a person physically dies? Even a Braintrust donor like me isn't smart enough to know such things. I do know enough not to discount any possibilities when it comes to the human brain and the thoughts and emotions it controls."

"Fair enough. If they really are having problems with Braintrust, no matter what the cause, we need to be concerned about that. Our systems are now connected to theirs and we certainly don't want our databases and programs compromised. Cayley and I talked about it and we are trying to close the loop on some of the data to see what we can find. Hopefully we can put it all to bed at our next internal meeting just after Thanksgiving. We will deal with it then."

"Good idea. I gotta go but please let me know when you hear how the session went."

"You will be the first one I talk to." Julie ended the call fully cognizant of how that man had impacted virtually every aspect of her life. From the day of the first undergrad course she had taken from him up to the present day, she had followed in his footsteps as he revolutionized the world. She was so proud of her contributions to that vision and to what they had all accomplished. They were like pioneers in the field of applied behavioural psychology. They had developed a program that allowed people to understand and utilize the positive aspects of their humanity so they could grow together and create a world where individual and societal self-actualization was the new 'Rich and Famous'. People had finally come to realize what factors are involved in creating a lasting state of happiness and fulfillment. Big bank accounts, luxury items, fame and power have been replaced by relationships, personal fulfillment, positive self-image, health and purpose. Finally, people have figured it out. Once it was understood that by providing everyone with the basic needs in life as a condition of being human, they could then live their lives in the upper categories of Maslow's Hierarchy of Needs and become capable of so much more. The traditional methods of defining the value of a person changed and with that their capabilities and understanding of themselves and the lives they were leading, changed accordingly. People learned that they wanted to contribute to society, not for an ever-increasing paycheque but for the feeling of achievement it gave them. Having a bigger house than other people or any of the other traditional status symbols became irrelevant because finally people realized that long-term happiness was not tied to those things.

"We are starting to get some feedback data," the chief technician spoke up effectively bringing Julie's thoughts back to their purpose for being there. They sat in silence and studied the story that was beginning to unfold in front of their eyes. Streams of raw data associated with graphs and charts became increasingly populated . She had never been much of a computer person. In university, she had to take some statistics courses and had developed an aptitude for understanding trends and probabilities, which helped her interpret what she was seeing. Over the next couple of hours, it became clear that the majority of the group discussions that were just winding up had helped calm people's concerns about any disbelief that they may have had about the Global Council and its motivations surrounding genocide. The overall levels of concern dropped by almost forty-five percent to a level of just over one out of ten, which meant that the issue was basically resolved. It is only reasonable for any free thinking person to maintain a low level of concern about a wide variety of issues because that is a healthy approach to most things. Studying the data for variables and anomalies, she noticed that there were a few groups that maintained or even increased their overall scores meaning that the group discussion had intensified the concerns of the group as a whole. This would most likely mean that one or two influential persons within the group had strong opinions that they were vocal about and were able to influence a broader portion of the group. Julie asked for a detailed report on these anomalies so that she could study them more closely. There was a normal logarithmic distribution of data points showing the number of groups in each range dropping off as the variance from the norm increased. Out of the two hundred and eighty-six million groups, there were only seven hundred and forty-seven that more than doubled their concern level. That's about three in a million. Thirty-nine groups got to four and a half or higher and seven groups made it above five. Standing alone was a single group that registered at almost seven out of ten. They pulled out the details of that group and found that on the original data input there was nothing anomalous. The highest input was a three and a half and overall they came in just below two. On the second input the average was still just over two but an individual input of ten appeared. Following the group discussion, whoever that person was that submitted a score of ten had apparently been able to sway the group to his or her way of thinking as the overall level of concern increased three hundred and fifty percent, which is an impressive feat.

"Can you give me a list of names of the members of that group?" Julie asked instantly wishing that the data inputs had not been anonymous.

"Can you also pull the names of the people from the other six groups that scored above a five and look at those overall group scores so we can compare them all."

The data soon found its way to the screens and Julie closely studied the faces, names and numbers, not really sure what she was looking for. None of the other groups showed the scenario of a single person promoting the change of opinion. They all had a few individuals with consistently moderate to high scores in the three to five range that increased slightly through the process and brought the rest of the group up with them. It seemed unlikely there were any strategic alliances in play here but it would be wise to make sure.

Looking back at the names of the twenty-five people from the most anomalous group, Julie asked aloud if any of them were recognizable for any reason.

"Yeah," one of the technicians blurted out. "Spencer Watt! I used to watch all of his movies. I didn't know he was still alive."

"It looks like he is very much alive and there's a four percent chance that he has a bee in his bonnet. Thanks everyone for doing such a good job this morning. Once you have finished submitting your reports, you can take the rest of the day off. You've earned it. I'll be at home if anyone needs me."

Julie stretched in an attempt to relax her body that had spent too much time in front of computers over the past couple of weeks. It looked like it had all been worth it, but this anomalous group bothered her. She tried to recollect what she could about Spencer Watt. He had been a very famous movie star who became a political activist, using his star status to become a voice for a variety of causes. He was widely idolized in the era when that was a thing. These days he was just another person and she had no idea what kind of person he was. She left the room trying to convince herself that there was nothing to be worried about.

"What negative effect could a single person create?" she asked herself. Unfortunately, she knew the true answer to that question.

Chapter 15
November 12, 2058. Southern China.

The dawn had always been Hai's favourite time of the day but more so after spending the night in a comfortable bed rather than on a mound of soil. Still, the night had been productive. He had managed to get close enough to the mine to hear the workers who were out and about the site. It wasn't so much the content of what was being said that was of interest but more so the dialect of the workers. If he was hoping to pass himself off as a local Chinese migrant worker, he had to sound like one. For the past few months, he had been studying local languages, practicing and memorizing words, phrases, slang expressions and intonation. His native Vietnamese wasn't that different from what he was expecting to hear, but the subtleties were what would give him away. He was relieved to discover that what he had been listening to during the night was pretty close to what he felt comfortable with speaking. He had spent the last couple of hours entering into mental conversations with the people he was listening to and getting used to the typical banter. He also identified individuals he may want to target, based on their apparent knowledge and his perception of their attitudes toward their jobs. The frontline workers in any project usually understand more about what is happening than their supervisors and management do. On top of that they are typically not prone to just stating the 'company line' as middle managers had become famous for.

Hai finally decided it was time to head back to his base where he would try to get some sleep and observe the mine for another day before showing up at the gate of the mine the following afternoon pleading for a job. If he was granted access to the mine, it hopefully would provide him with the opportunity to get enough concrete information to find out if he was sitting next to the source of pollution that had been slowly destroying the crops downstream. After six months of planning, this was actually about to happen, but only if he could talk his way into a job. Given that he would only be compensated by room and board and a pitifully small wage that would be insignificant to all concerned, he was hopeful they would see additional unexpected help as a good thing. He hoped his forged documents would be sufficient for their needs assuming they did let him through the gate. After all of his preparation, he was excited by the reality that his plan was about to unfold. At the same time he was terrified of the potential danger he was exposing himself to.

Chapter 16
November 12, 2058.
New York City, USA.

"For those of you who don't know me, my name is Spencer Watt. I have spent much of my life in the public eye and have tried to make it my business to fight against those who chose to commit crimes against society. Decades ago, I fought against poverty, corruption and the destruction of our environment. Today, I find it necessary to speak up because the people who are responsible for our well-being are abusing that power by planning to murder large segments of our global society in the name of progress. They will tell you that their plans for population control are non-threatening, but they are lying to us. I have it on good authority that over the past year there have been incidents of elderly people being taken from their homes and disappearing. We must stop them before it is too late and I am dedicating my resources and efforts to lead you all in a concerted effort to make them stop before more innocent people are sacrificed. We will be organizing continuing demonstrations worldwide to ensure that we get their attention. Please log onto our website and check for information and events that will be taking place near you. You can also volunteer to organize a demonstration in order to make sure that your voices are heard. We look forward to your support. Together we can preserve the valuable lives of all of the world's citizens. Thank you for listening and I look forward to working with all of you."

The camera feed ended with his still handsome face staring into the lens.

"That went well," he stated confidently to no one in particular. "Will, are you still there?"

"Yeah, right here." Will turned his image back toward the screen, which had been off because he had been on a call with a colleague and he knew how much Spencer hated it when he wasn't the single focus of others. "So that's what you are going to be spending my money on?"

"It's my money, Will, you just found it for me."

"Semantics, I guess. So do you really believe all of that stuff that you are saying about people getting murdered?" Will knew the answer to the question but asked anyway.

"Of course not," Spencer stated bluntly after ensuring that the call was in privacy mode. "Those do-gooders in the Global Congress wouldn't think of it, but that shouldn't get in the way of a good revolution."

"With a visible leader like you to protect the hypothetically endangered."

"Look, this may all be trumped up, but these people have taken everything from us."

"So what are you looking for in return? What do you want this revolution of yours to achieve?" Will was curious. "Do you want to become the head of the Global Council or something?"

"Oh God no, I don't want a job, although it would be nice to be asked. Maybe I could be a highly paid consultant whose opinions are valued."

"So let me get this clear, you want to get millions of people to believe in something you know isn't true. What happens when they find out you made it up?"

"You really don't get it do you. When the Global Council develops their plan to do whatever it was that they were already going to do, and they don't kill people in the process, then I will take credit for the positive result. I will say that it is occurring because we demanded it. We will be heroes."

"We?"

"Sure, Will. That is if you want to add your name to this."

"So, you, then. We spend tons of money and effort to get people worked up, angry and even killed so that the Council will do what they were planning to do all along but you will get credit for it. That's your plan? No altruism, no profit, just personal glory?"

"It sends the message that the people are watching and they have to pay attention to us."

"Have you never heard of COH where the voices of seven billion people are heard on a daily basis?"

"I think the pertinent thing here is that now they have heard of me!"Spencer stated defiantly.

Chapter 17
November 13, 2058. Southern China.

As he approached the guarded gate to the mine site, Hai began to make out the warnings that were posted in large characters on a number of signs beside the entrance. No Trespassing, All Visitors Must Report to the Security Station, Danger, Open Pit and everything else short of 'Beware of Dog'. When he was about fifty meters away, an armed man stepped out of a small gatehouse and focused his attention singularly on Hai. Fortunately, the man's rifle wasn't aimed at him. Not yet at least. It was strange to even see a firearm being used for what it was originally designed.

'They are obviously taking their security very seriously,' Hai thought to himself.

"Good afternoon sir," he spoke nervously in his best local dialect. "I am here in search of a job. I am healthy, strong and a good worker."

"Papers!" the guard demanded.

Hai reached into his trouser pockets and presented his forged, purposely wrinkled and worn identity papers verifying that he was a Chinese citizen from the local autonomous region.

The guard grunted, took the papers and handed them to his associate who was still sitting at a tiny desk in the gatehouse.

Hai knew that this was a pointless exercise in optics since they had no way to authenticate the document. Even though he could see that they had a computer, there was no database of registered citizens in these remote regions of the country. Nevertheless, the other guard, who appeared to be the more senior of the two, took great care in displaying a false air of security and importance. What they could discern is if this person had ever been on site before as a worker. Seemingly satisfied, the guard picked up his phone and made a call. A few of his words were followed by his silence, as he was either waiting for or listening to an answer as to the likelihood of this stranger securing employment.

Attempting to stay calm, Hai tried to exude a sense of desperation, which they would expect from a local migrant hoping to improve his life. Despite the fact that years ago, throughout the world, essentially every person was guaranteed the basic necessities of survival and comfort, there were still remote areas like this where the logistics and capability to provide those goods and services were severely hampered. The result was that there were still people, like the one he was pretending to be, who needed to scrounge for non-sanctioned employment. Working at places like this undocumented mine being run by a company needing to stay off of the radar of the local, state and international authorities.

He stood in the heat, sweating through his shirt, nervously waiting to find out if he would be allowed inside the mine where he hoped to find evidence of the illegal actions that were poisoning the millions of hectares of land downstream from this location. Finally, a third man approached the gate from the inside. Speaking through the confining wire, he began firing questions at Hai. In essence it was an impromptu interview, interrogation and negotiation all mixed into one. Finally satisfied, he signalled the guard and an opening was made available. Twenty minutes and one signature later, Hai was preparing to begin his first twelve-hour shift. He hoped that he would be able to survive the job conditions long enough to find out what he needed to know.

Chapter 18
November 13, 2058. Trenton, USA.

"Hi, Dad." Cayley opened the conversation as her father's image appeared on the screen in front of her. That was the part that simultaneously made her feel nostalgic and just a little bit creeped out. She couldn't help but marvel at the technology that allowed her to 'speak' with her father who had died eight months earlier. He may not have been Braintrust material, but thanks to her ability to pay for it and for his willingness to comply, she had arranged for his cranial download as soon as the process became available to the public.

The authenticity of his image and voice being synchronized with his cranial download data conjured up concepts of ghosts and spirits, but it seemed so real that it gradually kind of felt normal. She had been doing this every two or three weeks since the download had occurred, even before he had passed away. It served as an easy and convenient way to pick his brain on things without bothering him at odd hours of the day or night without stressing him. Now that he was gone, she was just thankful for the continued connection. Her father even said that he was better able to accept his approaching death knowing that he would live on in this way. She wondered how he felt about it now, if in fact there was still a 'he' to 'feel' anything.

"Hello, Cayley. How's my little princess doing?"

"Fighting dragons it seems like. There's so much going on and most of it seems pretty bad."

"It sounds like you need to take a few deep breaths and refocus. You and your friends have done great things. In the beginning, I thought it was just a naive vision of some sort of nirvana that would end up wasting your time and money. Thankfully I never told you that at the time, and I'm not too proud to admit how wrong I was. So, what dragon are you are going to slay this week?"

"It's actually a person, his name is Spencer Watt."

"I always liked him. Good actor. He kind of got a little full of himself at the end when he started using his stage as a platform, but he's not the first celebrity to have a huge ego. I didn't know he was still alive. What's he up to?"

"I think he is trying to prove to everyone that he is very much alive and wants to regain his fame. He is trying to be a modern day revolutionary figure. He's waging a war against the Global Council and us by claiming that they are planning to control future population numbers through some sort of nefarious methods."

"Nefarious huh? It sounds like an animal from Sesame Street."

"I think that was Snuffleupagus, Dad. He is talking about things like genocide and making up all sorts of lies just to get in the spotlight."

"Are you sure they are lies? It wouldn't be the first time you know."

"Trust me, Dad, none of it is true. Not that they would even consider such a thing, but if they were, I would know about it."

"If I was planning to do something like that, I wouldn't tell anyone. I'm just saying."

"You actually think the Global Council would consider killing people directly or indirectly to control population? As far as we've come and with everything you've seen, you actually believe that could happen?"

"I've seen worse things in my life. I would imagine the young people today couldn't even imagine that such a thing could be possible but for those of us who have seen more, well, it opens the door to imagining the unimaginable. Maybe you are too close to it. Maybe you just don't want to believe in the possibility of such things."

"So what do you think I should do?"

"What I used to do in my career as a journalist. Investigate with an open mind and find the truth. Once you have that, you can report the facts. Hopefully, for you, they are what you are expecting."

Cayley sat and thought about his insights and advice. She knew he was right. They couldn't just say that Spencer Watt was lying. They had to find the truth, which would speak for itself. He was trying to start a fight and she was reacting emotionally which was probably the response that he was looking for. All they needed to do was to continue with the process that had been working so well: develop a population strategy, get the support of the people with whatever modifications they request and implement it. It would be business as usual.

"Are you still there, Cayley?"

"Yes, Dad. Sorry I was just thinking."

"No need to apologize for that my dear."

"Dad, are you happy?" Cayley asked hesitantly, aware of the time and space limitations of what she was delving into but wanting to understand more than she did now that he had passed on.

"Ever since that day, forty years ago in the courtroom, when we were reunited my princess."

Cayley smiled and decided to let it go for now.

"Me too, Dad. Gotta go. Thanks for the advice."

"I'm always here for you," he replied with a strange chuckle.

****

Now that's pretty cool. I didn't know I was going to get a speaking part in this story. Given that my brain has been downloaded, maybe I should give you a 'heads-up' (pardon the pun) about this whole 'Braintrust' thing. Once they discovered how to do 'cranial downloads' it made sense to link the data from a whole bunch of the smartest people around to form a kind of 'database of wisdom.' You see, the COI folks figured out how to take all of the information that comes out of the COH meetings and put it all together. That is done in their division called Circles of Consensus, or COC. They call it that because they can ask the seven billion people in their groups what they think or feel about something and put all of the answers together. They can determine what percentage of the population likes applesauce and how strongly they feel about it. That kind of information can be handy for people who grow fruit so they know if they should plant more apple trees or something else. COC data is now available to every government and corporation in the world, which allows them to know what the people like and want.

Where Braintrust comes in is that once COC defines the wants and needs of the people, Braintrust develops strategies that helps governments and corporations fulfill the mandate of the people. It's actually pretty simple. Even I understand the concept despite the fact that my cranial download wasn't Braintrust worthy. Oh well, not everyone can be a genius.

I think it's time for us to see how Hai is making out after his first shift of intense labor.

Chapter 19
November 14, 2058. Southern China.

Even though it was the middle of the night, the bright lights simulated daylight, but that didn't make Hai any less exhausted. He had begun the shift with a shovel in his hands and was instructed to act as a swamper for the front-end loader that was filling trucks with overburden that was to be removed from the open pit mine. He hadn't figured out where they were taking the rock, but clearly any valuable minerals had already been separated away and this debris was of no value. He couldn't help but wonder if the rock was at all radioactive. Halfway through the shift the operator of the loader spiked a fever and had to be hauled away with about as much ceremony as the deposits he was digging through. One advantage of growing up on a farm was that Hai had been around equipment all of his life and there was not much that he couldn't operate or repair. Even though this loader was approximately twice the size of anything that he had ever seen, it appeared that the basic operational concepts were the same. Eager to stop the initial onset of blisters on his hands, he volunteered to take over the machine. Since no one else seemed to care one way or the other, before he knew it he was sitting in the cab of the monstrosity, overlooking the massive bucket. It was at that moment that he realized how much larger it was than anything that he had ever operated. Within an hour, he had captured the basics of how to get the work done without killing himself in the process. Hai was fully aware of the fact that in virtually all sanctioned mines in the world, the heavy equipment being used was designed to be autonomous and controlled robotically. As he operated the outdated loader, his body became increasingly happy about the fact that the mine had been forced to utilize outdated equipment from the days when the mine was operating legally. It had been a long time since he had done manual labour. Finally, the shift ended and he was torn between finding a bed and passing out for as long as he was allowed or heading to the dining hall and getting to know some of the workers who would be getting off shift. As much as he needed the sleep, he dragged himself off in search of information and food.

Silently he followed some of the other men, expecting they would know where they were going. When they reached the central building the smell of strong tea drew him forward. In the middle of the room a row of battered and filthy trays and a row of covered dishes had become the primary focus of the workers who swatted away the flies in an attempt to consume the bare essentials of sustenance. There was no banter or laughter to be heard. With barely a word spoken, the men shuffled past the table, filled their bowls with rice and some unidentifiable stew or soup. Then, each of them robotically found an isolated position at one of the many long tables to consume their revolting rations in peace and quiet. 'This could be a challenge,' Hai thought to himself. As he approached the food table he was instantly relieved to know that he would survive nicely on the provisions he had brought with him, but he took some of the gruel so as not to stand out. He saw the other loader operator sitting alone and headed to a nearby position that would allow access while maintaining a respectful distance.

"Any tips for the new operator? Looks like you have been running that thing for quite a while," Hai initiated what he hoped would become a conversation with a compliment.

"Eight years," came the brief reply followed by nothing. Apparently he wasn't interested in sharing his craft.

"That makes sense," Hai tried again after a few long seconds of silence. "You must know this place pretty good."

"Yes," came the monosyllabic reply.

Hai decided that the end of a long shift was not the time to push ahead. They would be back here in about ten hours before their next shift. Maybe some sleep would make him a bit more conversant. At least he had identified a possible target.

"Good night," Hai said as he rose to leave and received a grunt in response.

Chapter 20
*November 20, 2058.
New York City, USA.*

"Good evening everyone. My name is Jason Wolfe, welcome to the Wolfe Pack. When we decided to focus on the population strategy this year, we had no idea it would become this fascinating so quickly. This past week there was a Circles of Humanity event that focused on the information, statistics and psychology behind the topic of population. We will take you inside COI and let their people tell you what they think and feel about the results of those meetings. Also, the recent public unrest in protest of perceived Global Council policies seems to have found itself a face. We will tell you who has stepped forward to lead the revolution and what may be motivating him to do so."

Claire watched as her new boss turned about two hundred and fifty man-hours of research and scripting into less than an hour of conversational news. Jason had once told her that he was now able to insert almost twice as much relevant information into a show than he had been able to twenty or thirty years ago, but it seemed to her like they were just scratching the surface of what was available to say. That was what Jason called the 'comprehension gap'. It wasn't that the audience wasn't capable of understanding the issues, but most people weren't trained to deal with the complexity that exists in life. That detail was what their website was for. It provided background for interested viewers to research and agonize over if they chose to dig deeper. The one-hour show was basically an advertisement for the website, designed to entertain and entice the audience while fairly representing the facts of the story.

"Let's assume that each of you watching this show were in attendance at your COH event last week with your own individual group. I know I was. We all listened to Doctor Julie Peters as she discussed the social attitudes and values as they pertain to giving birth and dying. She talked about aging and approaching death, and how some of those perceptions have been changing for those who have the resources to get cranial downloads. I know how I felt during that part of the session, but we would like you to go on our website and quantify how you felt. We believe that it is important to verify the validity of the feelings we are receiving through the Circles of Consensus feedback loops by receiving independent feedback from our viewers. This will ensure that the information we receive from COI is real and not manufactured, which is part of what they are being accused."

"Then, the COH session delved into a statistical analysis of the global population's perceptions and what they will mean to the Global Council. I recently spoke with Doctor Peters and she admitted she was concerned about the optics of that information session. She was concerned they would be perceived as betraying the trust of their users by selling a message from the Global Council rather than just dealing with absolute truths as they always have. We had a frank and open discussion about it, and the one thing I can assure you is that she is sincere in her desire to provide open support."

"The portion of the COH session I want to dig into is how they dealt with the situation regarding the violent demonstrations that have been occurring around the world. They exposed us to the concerns of the demonstrators, allowed us to consider and discuss the merits of those issues and then measured our level of concern before, during and after we had become informed. We have reviewed all of the data that came out of that segment and it is clear that statistically speaking there is no issue here. Only seven hundred and forty-seven groups showed any real concern at all after being exposed to the concerns of the demonstrators, which is less than twenty-thousand people out of seven billion. There were more than twenty-thousand people at each of the demonstrations that were chanting and wreaking havoc. What I would like to understand is, what happened to those people? Why didn't they show up in the numbers? If so few of us really are concerned about this issue, then why am I wasting my time talking to you about it and why are you listening to something you don't care about? These are the questions that we will attempt to answer in the coming weeks because in my experience, when things don't make sense, something is wrong."

"That leads us to the second major event of the week. Less than an hour after the COH session ended, an independent video feed hit the air. If you are more than about forty years old you would have instantly recognized the face on the screen as belonging to Spencer Watt. From the years 2007 until 2021 he was the top grossing Hollywood movie star each and every year. He became one of the most recognizable faces on the planet, and throughout his career he became increasingly outspoken with respect to political and social issues. If you remember, Circles of Influence, and the effects it was having on society, was one of the items on his social agenda back in the twenties. He was very outspoken about the potential dangers of that organization. Well, we all know who won that one. COI has gone on to transform our global society and Spencer and so many others like him have drifted off into obscurity."

"To his credit, Mr. Watt gave his time and his voice to a number of issues of that past era that needed attention. He became very popular for his actions as well as his talents. So the question is, why now? What has prompted him to become the face of this current revolution and more importantly, did he join it or did he create it? Spencer Watt has agreed to come on to my show in two weeks time and talk to us all about what is motivating his current actions, so that is something we can all look forward to."

"I will leave you with this one thought and a plea." Jason began his summation. "We live in an interconnected world where the actions of a few impact the reality of us all. If you, individually, have personal concerns about the motivations and actions of the Global Council or with the mandate of Circles of Influence, then by all means follow your inclinations and let your voices and concerns be heard. In doing so however, please be mindful that damaging and destroying lives in an effort to preserve life is not only hypocritical, but just plain wrong. Be heard, but be safe. Thank you and good night."

Chapter 21
November 25th, 2058. Trenton, USA.

"Claire! Jermaine! God it is so good to see you both. Let me hug you."

Cayley ran toward her children who had finally arrived for Thanksgiving.

"Can we just stay like this for the next two days?" she pleaded, not wanting to let go of them. "As wonderful as technology is, there is no replacement for physical human contact."

"This is nice mom but my back is cramping up," Jermaine laughed as he began to pull away.

"We can keep going for another minute or two," Claire suggested to the amusement of her now disconnected brother.

"So insecure. You always needed to be the favourite child," he teased.

"I already am. That's why Mom is still hugging me."

"Okay you two, start talking. I have't seen either of you since the summer. I want details of everything you have been up to."

"Can we go for a walk while we catch up?" Jermaine asked. "We've been sitting all afternoon and it's really nice out."

"Great idea, I'll grab my sweater. Put your bags in the bedrooms and we can go. Does anyone need a snack to take along."

"Let's just pick something up on the way if we get hungry," Claire suggested.

"Perfect, lets go." Cayley was so exited to have her children around, she could hardly contain herself. They crossed the street to the park that spread out ahead of them.

"How is your new work assignment, Claire?"

"Pretty cool so far. I am working for this old guy who knew Grandpa."

"Really, what's his name? Maybe I know him."

"I don't think so, Mom. His name is Jason Wolfe. I didn't mean that they were friends or anything. It's just that he knew about Grandpa's work and everything. He's really more like your age."

"Wow, so he really is an old guy."

"Well, not that old really, I guess," Claire tried to backtrack.

"So what are you doing there?"

"We are reporting on the Global Council population story. I'm doing background and monitoring events."

"Wow, that's a big story," Cayley observed, "they must really like you to have you working on that."

"Right? That's what I thought."

"So what have you found out so far?"

"Probably things that you already know, Mom. Like that old movie star dude who is leading the protests against the GC. People really seem to like him. And he might be right. It seems like in a few years there isn't going to be enough food to feed everybody, so they are going to have to do something, don't you think?"

"There's going to be enough food," Jermaine threw in his opinion. "In fact there's going to be more than enough. The new urban farms have been a big success and outside of the big cities there is still plenty of arable land to sustain the local populations."

"But aren't a lot of the areas becoming too polluted?" Claire asked. "Especially in Asia where there are so many people and they are producing less and less? That's why they are going to have to eliminate some of those people somehow. Otherwise, they will starve to death which would be even worse."

"Where are you getting your information from?" Jermaine asked before Cayley had a chance to.

"Recent crop statistics from Southeast Asia. Aren't you supposed to know about that sort of thing? You are a biological engineer aren't you?" Claire teased.

"I design urban farms, I don't count grains of rice."

"Well, if you did, you might realize that I am right. Over the last ten years, crop yields in those areas have decreased by about twenty-five percent. Soon there won't be enough food to go around."

"Does anyone know what is causing it?" Cayley asked. "And if they do, is it reversible?"

"I don't think anyone knows for sure," Claire responded.

"I did some work on the urban farm in Shanghai and at first the crops were below expectations but after a few growing seasons things started to improve," Jermaine provided his insights to the discussion.

"Where did they source the plants from that didn't do well at the beginning? Maybe they were taken from areas that were already diseased or something and then they recovered in a controlled environment," Cayley postulated.

"Yeah, maybe. But if the crops in those areas have been affected by something then we just need to figure out what it is and eliminate the problem."

"Good idea, Jermaine, maybe we can do that after supper so we have enough food for Thanksgiving dinner tomorrow."

"I'm just saying that if there is a problem, then you figure out what it is and do something about it. You don't just assume nothing can be done and that the crop yields will decrease forever."

"I hope you're right because people are going hungry over there and it isn't their fault," Claire stated defiantly.

"How many urban farms have you worked on so far, Jermaine?" Cayley asked, making a mental note to find her friend Hai so that he could explain the ramifications of what they had been talking about. If anyone knew how serious the problem was and what could be done, it would be Hai Nguyen, wherever he is.

"Seven so far. Johannesburg, Buenos Aires, Shanghai, Mumbai, Jakarta, Beijing and Mexico City."

"That's amazing. It must be so interesting designing them and working out the logistics."

"It would be if I was responsible for more than just nozzle distribution efficiencies. Hopefully in time, I will get exposure to more of the tens of thousands of technical specialties that go into the overall design and I will get to be the project manager on one of them."

"I'm sure that one day you will," Cayley supported in true maternal style. "But your current specialty is very important. You are figuring out how to grow the most food with the least amount of water. That's critical!"

"I think you're spraying it on a bit thick Mother," Claire laughed "and maybe adding a bit of fertilizer in the process."

"Maybe you're not the favourite after all," Jermaine taunted her with a laugh.

"I'm not worried about that but it's nice that she sees the good in you too."

"Can't you two even fight and tease each other properly?" Cayley interjected. "As an only child, I would have given anything to have a sibling to torment and make fun of and you two are just wasting the opportunity."

"Why would we focus on doing that? She's the only sister I have. We're on the same team," Jermaine responded, confused by his mother's apparent disappointment in them.

"Against who?" Cayley enquired.

"What do you mean?"

"If you are on a team, then you are competing against someone, so who is it? Is it me?"

"What? Of course not. Why do we have to be against anyone?" Claire wanted to know.

"That's what teasing is. I can't believe you two."

"Maybe you shouldn't have enrolled us in all of those Pre-Adolescent COI Human Understanding Programs if you wanted us to be able to fit in and cope with your world of negativity and bullying," Claire suggested with a straight enough face that Cayley couldn't figure out if she was serious or not.

"Teasing isn't bullying. You only tease the people you love."

"That's a funny way of showing love. There must have been a lot of love flying around when you were growing up."

Cayley tried to respond but couldn't think of what to say. There was no doubt that over the last thirty years, including all of her children's lives, young people had received the benefit of being taught the basic principles of humanity at an early age. Prior to that, everyone seemingly knew how hard it was to transition from childhood to adulthood with your self-esteem and basic moral fabric intact. The problem was that no one seemed to want to do anything to help young people understand the world they lived in and teach them how to treat other people. It had always been considered a parent's job, but who had taught them? As societies changed and pressures and situations seemed to become progressively more difficult for each generation, the mental health of our population as a whole grew worse and worse. The first mandate for Adam Stapleton, when he developed Circles of Influence, was to provide education and peer support for young people. Like a triage doctor assessing where to spend his time, it was clear to Adam and Julie that it was best to try to reach the young and to help them while they still had the ability to develop positive traits. Now that the first wave of those young people have become parents and influential members of our society, the positive results of those early educational programs have become obvious. The generations that have followed since, and who are currently enjoying their formative years, will enhance society with their self-actualized approach to life.

"Mom, are you still with us?" Jermaine inquired as his mother was walking between them but staring ahead absently.

"No. I mean yes, I was just thinking about how much I love you both."

"Of course you do."

****

"They slowly walked and caught up with each others lives. The sky gradually began to shift from blue to red as dusk revealed the passing of time and made them aware of becoming hungry."

"I am planning to cook a Thanksgiving Dinner for us tomorrow, but tonight I thought that we would eat out."

"That's great, Mom," Claire agreed enthusiastically, "it will be nice to go to one of your regular restaurants and meet some of your friends and neighbours."

"Should we go home and change first?" Cayley wondered aloud.

"I don't think we need to," Jermaine stated definitively. "I'm starving, lead the way."

They rustled through the leaves to the west entrance to the park and crossed the street where they entered a restaurant simply called 'The Plate'. The place was warm and bustling with what appeared to be a full contingent of congenial patrons. A family who were located just inside the door turned and greeted Cayley.

"I would like you to meet my son, Jermaine, and my daughter, Claire. This is Ahmed Abbasi and his wife Sanji and I am afraid I have forgotten your children's names. They have grown so much since I last saw them."

Ahmed shook hands with Jermaine and Claire and introduced his three teenage children. Cayley had a brief casual conversation with Sanji while unconsciously scanning the large room where her neighbours typically came to share a meal. For the sake of efficiency, food conservation and socialization it had become commonplace for people to eat communally in local neighbourhood restaurants. Nuclear families, especially with young children, would often still eat together at home, but otherwise the trend was toward eating out in public. In most cultures around the world, this was a routine that had survived the centuries but Western society had become increasingly isolationist. People living alone, eating alone, and feeling alone was a common element that, despite its unnatural human tendency, had become far too prevalent in the western world. Drive-through fast food chains and expensive fancy restaurants were the two most common culinary end points, depending on how much disposable income you had. It had taken quite a while for Cayley to become comfortable with these casual come-togethers but after her husband died and her children moved away it had become her norm. In time, she had developed a local group of friends and acquaintances with whom she was quite comfortable sharing her meals. For the most part, people didn't really care who you were for the rest of the day, but when it came to spending a couple of hours eating and socializing, all that mattered was that you were hungry and friendly. The trend away from sitting alone, or with your family, in front of a television eating a quickly prepared meal had proven to be beneficial on many levels. Getting fresh air and exercise as you walked to your favourite establishment to eat and socialize amounted to what came to feel like a two hour vacation each day. It provided a break from your reality and a chance to grow your world. The food was good and affordable, and after the meal many people would stick around and talk or play games.

Today, on the Thanksgiving weekend, more families than usual were present and the mood was proving to be very boisterous. Cayley had moved to this neighbourhood after the children left for university, so they didn't know any one in the room, but they were adults and capable of being social, Cayley noticed proudly.

"Cayley, it's good to see you." She turned to see the smiling face of Patricia Wilkins. She and her husband lived in her apartment building with their seventeen-year-old daughter, Whitney. "Why don't you and your family come sit with us? We have our son home from college as well. I'm sure they would appreciate sitting with other people their own age."

"Sounds good. Patricia, this is my daughter, Claire and my son, Jermaine," who both turned to greet their mother's friend.

With the introductions made, the two families sat down and began to visit.

"What are you taking at college, Chad?" Jermaine enquired.

"Geology, with a mining specialty and a minor in chemistry."

"That sounds interesting. Have you had some good work terms?"

"The one I'm into now involves the mining of rare earth elements."

"That's pretty topical these days, not to mention controversial."

"Yeah, it is but it really doesn't need to be. Now that the demand has stabilized there is no reason we can't produce all we need in a responsible manner. It's not a question of supply; we just need to protect the local environments. I really don't know what all of the fuss is about."

"Probably just left over sentiment from decades ago when it wasn't handled very well. For a long time the only places they were mined was in the remote regions of China where it was totally unregulated. Because of that it got labeled as being toxic and dangerous and most countries didn't seem to want anything to do with mining them," Jermaine contributed from his limited knowledge of the subject.

"That was until it got so expensive that companies and countries decided it was worthwhile controlling their supplies. During the tech boom, before sustainable product development methods became enforced, REEs became the new oil of the past century. Cell phones, televisions, computers, and electric cars, all of which were designed to be obsolete in one to five years, demanded an abundance of raw materials making REEs the new hot commodity."

"Yeah, no kidding. If society hadn't begun changing during the boom in demand, we would have definitely be fighting wars over this stuff."

"It sounds like you're a history buff," Chad observed. "War is a pretty antiquated term."

"No, not at all, I'm an Agricultural Engineer, but my grandfather used to tell me lots of stories about how things worked in his day."

"From what I hear, they didn't work very well at all."

"That seems to be the consensus. I think we're pretty lucky to have been born when we were."

"I couldn't agree more. How about you, Claire?" Chad asked, making an effort to bring her into the conversation.

Claire hadn't really been listening to the conversation around her but caught the gist of the question. She had absently been observing her mother interacting with the friends and neighbours surrounding her. She was so happy that her mom had made friends in her community that would help fill the void of becoming a widow. She had a remarkable mother who deserved to be happy. Jermaine may be right about being lucky because of when we were born, but the more important factors seem to be where and to whom we were born. Being born to Cayley Wilson in the United States in the middle of the twenty-first century represented the best of all worlds. It was time to straighten these guys out.

****

Cayley was at ease as the conversation around her flowed effortlessly. She looked over at her daughter, who was almost the same age as she had been when she was released from prison and spent time on an island under the clinical supervision of Adam Stapleton. She still remembered being so socially inadequate that having to socialize at a meal like this would have sent her into a sense of panic. In stark contrast to that, Claire and Jermaine had easily accepted a room full of strangers and were participating in conversations they seemed to be thoroughly enjoying. After her Mother's death, Cayley had spent a decade of her life blaming the world for her own failures because she felt sorry for herself. She had spiralled downward into a self-destructive pit of despair and anger. It took a month of intense support and education from Adam, and the benefit of a new friend in Julie, to allow her to even recognize that she had an alternative life course available to her. Between that experience and the continued benefit of the resources of COI, she was able to make something of herself. She had finally learned to like who she was and be able to give something positive back to other people and to the world around her. But here her children were, also losing a parent at an impressionable age, yet seemingly fine with their lives. They could have made the same excuses and mistakes she had made at their ages but they didn't. They accepted support, dealt with the pain and loss in a healthy manner and gradually moved on. Cayley sometimes wondered what would have happened to her if she had been exposed to the youth education program before her mother died. Would she have demonstrated the same strength of character that her children have shown? Would she have been better prepared to deal with the inevitable adversities that exist in life? Maybe in retrospect it was good that everything unfolded as it had. A few years ago, Adam had told her that she had been a significant part of the inspiration behind the change in focus of his life's work. Prior to their first encounter, he had been working solely on research relating to the understanding and manipulation of human behaviour. He knew his objectives were not aligned with those of his financial backers in the government, but he wanted to get results and he had his tenure and reputation to consider. He told her that it was her transformation that lit a fire under him. Her success had reminded him of the impact that education and support could have on individuals and he became driven to move that process forward on a larger scale. At that point he changed the focus of his COI website and began to develop education modules for young people. He became convinced that proactively providing social psychology education would help young people avoid emotional turmoil by supporting them during their formative years. Witnessing the young people around her in this restaurant, who had become the beneficiaries of his programs, it was clear that Adam's change in focus had become an influential change for mankind. The idea of her being his muse made her smile, which broadened as she continued to observe her children.

****

The moonlight softly illuminated the path ahead of them as they enjoyed the cool dampness of the evening air. The cushion of leaves on the ground being disturbed was the only sound that competed with their conversation.

"Let's play that game we used to play when you were young," Cayley suggested, too enthusiastically to be ignored. "Tell me the best and worst things about your careers." Beginning when they were about ten years old, each day at supper, Claire and Jermaine were encouraged to tell their parents the best and the worst things that had happened to them that day.

Jermaine remembered that he wasn't always enthused about having to share his feelings with his parents. At his most unwilling moments he would rely on reporting that 'The best thing was that there was no bad thing that happened and the worst thing was that there had been nothing good.' He remembered getting away with that answer a few times, perhaps for no other reason than the sheer inventiveness of having thought it up, but long term he was obliged to play along. Then one day in one of the COE talks he was watching, they introduced a method of actively searching for the moments of each day that are amazing. They were encouraged to search for and recognize positives as a means of maintaining and re-enforcing a favourable attitude. They were to see the good in people and in situations that otherwise would go unnoticed. It was explained that we get to decide how we feel by what we observe and think. When he brought this pearl of wisdom back to his family and associated it with their game, his parents applauded his ability to make the connection. He could tell by their reactions that they already knew exactly what he was talking about. Jermaine remembered asking why they didn't just tell each other the good things each day so that everything was always positive and he had never forgotten the answer he was given.

'Bad things can always happen and we need to be able to talk about them and learn how to help each other deal with them. Life is meant to share the good times and help each other through the bad times.'

"I'll go first," Jermaine proclaimed trying to match his mother's enthusiasm. "The best thing about my career is that I get to learn a lot of things from all of the people I meet and work with from all around the world. On any given project we can have hundreds of people focusing on a single farm in a city that will feed millions of people. We are all motivated to solve a common problem and feel good about our successes."

"That's really exciting Jermaine," Cayley beamed. "Do you realize that what you are doing would have been impossible thirty years ago?"

"Yeah, some of the technology is pretty new."

"It's way more than that. For example, people from different regions didn't communicate and interact the way they do now, not because the translation software wasn't available but because there were too many cultural, social and political barriers. International funding wasn't nearly as prevalent as it is now because of protectionist and competitive political and business interests. It would have been unfathomable to get a global initiative to be able to devote the funding and manpower necessary to go into a single location to solve a local problem," Cayley explained how things worked in her day.

"But a global problem is just a whole bunch of local problems put together. Hunger isn't an isolated issue and it can't be eliminated by dealing with one person, city or country at a time," Claire professed.

"You are right, of course. I completely agree," Cayley responded, "but what I am telling you is that even though people may have understood then what you do now, the way the world worked didn't allow for the same solutions as we have now. People were conditioned to think more about themselves as individuals than as part of a society. I can remember when I was in university, a group of experts from the United States in a variety of fields like health care, finance, taxation, education and law were tasked with working together and determining the ideal way of setting up the systems that dealt with each field. They spent a long time and finally came up with a collective plan that would deliver the best results for Americans as a whole. Then they presented the plans to focus groups that made up the equivalent of the cross-section of the American population and overall the ideas were widely rejected."

"Why would that be?"

"That's what they wondered and so they proceeded to try to answer that question."

"And?" Jermaine prompted, clearly engaged in the discussion.

"They came up with a couple of reasons for the failure to persuade people to accept the proposed changes. Change needs to evolve from within the understanding and acceptance of the people who the change will affect. People can only comprehend things that make sense to them from within their own frame of reference. Imagine if a new law was passed that forced everyone to give half of their money and belongings away to strangers. In a world dominated by capitalism, wealth and possessions, which defines the world I grew up in, the people would not comply willingly. They would resist because that law would make no sense to them and would threaten their core survival. You cannot work for forty years for the primary purpose of gaining financial security and then just give it all away. It would have threatened the way we were raised and our basic survival instincts would have violently rejected the idea. If that law had been passed forty years ago, there would have been widespread anarchy throughout the developed world. If the same law were passed today, I wouldn't want to lose half of what I own, but I would likely see the merits in doing so. The two of you, on the other hand, would think nothing of it. Money has never been a motivator for you. You do your jobs for pride, satisfaction and for the betterment of the world you live in. Any money you have has been given to you as a convenience, not a reward."

"That's interesting," Claire surmised. "So you are saying that the people rejected the good ideas just because they were different from what they knew. That seems pretty closed-minded."

"Maybe," Cayley admitted, "but the other reason for the rejection was that as individuals we had been influenced to be isolated from others and focused on our own individual interests rather than those that would serve the common good. We had been divided and conquered and unable to see beyond our own noses. What we were doing locally on an individual level, our governments and corporations were also doing globally. Your grandfather blamed the media for that and, to a large degree, I expect he was right because it was controlled by the elite few who determined everything."

"But what I like best about my job in the media is that we get to share information with all of the people," Claire refuted her grandfather's criticism of the media. "We get to find cool and inspiring stories and discover truths that let people see things clearly. Could it have really been so different when you were young?"

"I think we're going to have to accept Grandpa's opinion on that. He was the expert."

They exited the park and walked across the street returning home chilled but with an internal warmth that had developed throughout their evening together.

"Do you really credit your friends with changing everything about how our world works?" Jermaine enquired.

Cayley thought for a moment as she remotely opened the front door for them, providing access to the small vestibule that had just become automatically illuminated. The obvious analogy struck her and she answered her son's question.

"Adam and Julie just opened the door and shone a light on things. The billions of people who have been alive since then have done all of the heavy lifting."

****

The moment they returned to Cayley's apartment it became clear that something was happening. She had purposely ensured that all three of them had left their electronic devices at home while they went for dinner to enjoy a couple of hours of quality time without distractions. That time had just ended. Every abandoned device was making noise, vibrating or flashing in an attempt to gain their attention. 'There is something you all need to know' was the collective message. Cayley went to her console and activated the screens, which became populated by a deluge of messages and videos. The dominant one, based on her activity history, was loaded and ready to go.

"Good evening my fellow citizens of the world. My name is Spencer Watt and I would like to speak with all of you this evening so that you can understand the importance of the next two weeks to the future of mankind. This is the time for us to stand up and be heard. We need to let the heads of COI, Braintrust and the Global Council know that we will no longer be lied to and manipulated. We have to remind them that every life is important and that we will not let innocent people be killed in an attempt to control population growth. We have been lied to and misled. We are being told that there is plenty of food to go around and that there is no need to control our global population, but we know that is a lie. Throughout Southeast Asia, China and India, where almost forty percent of the world's population lives, the local crop yields have decreased by almost thirty percent over the last couple of decades and the situation is getting worse every year. But they want us to believe that everything is fine. Well, it's not fine and we aren't going to accept the lies anymore. The Global Council knows that it has a major catastrophe on their hands and is throwing money and resources at the area, but despite their efforts the situation is getting progressively worse. My friends, there is no way it is a coincidence that this year, when the Asian crisis is at its worst, population control happens to rise to the top of the agenda at the annual GC meeting next month. They are creating schemes to do some terrible things and we are the only ones who can stop it. The one thing we have in our favour is that all laws and mandates require the support of us, the people. Through your COH group, you have the ability to stop them from killing us. We can tell them that murder is not acceptable. Healthy, caring human beings do not commit murder. We all know that to be a certainty. If it is not the collective message of the people that COI reports back to the Global Council, then we will know that the people of Circles of Influence are working with them to promote their lies and deception. Over these next few weeks it is imperative, my friends, that we turn up the heat on those who would deceive us with their propaganda."

"Next week there will be meetings at every office of the COI group. I implore you to take to the streets and make them see us. Make them hear us. Thou shall not kill. The week following, the Global Council will be holding their policy meetings. We need to keep the heat on them to do the right thing. Thou shall not kill! On

December 15th, when we are to be told how our leaders will implement plans to carry out our wishes, we need them to know that thou shall not kill! Don't forget, my friends, we have the power, and together we will force them to do the right thing. I am only here to help you get what you know is right. I am here to help you be heard. I am here for all of us and we will be heard! Thank you and good night."

"Oh my God!" Claire gasped. "I have to get to work. I am glad we had a few hours together because I don't think I will see the light of day until Christmas. This can't be for real, is it? I mean he's basically accusing you and the Global Council of premeditated murder. Everyone knows that is insane. You wouldn't manipulate the data and the GC wouldn't do it anyway. Who would believe this?"

"I expect we are about to find out," Cayley surmised glumly.

"He's not totally wrong about the situation in Asia. Something has been damaging the crops and people are starving, just like I told you earlier," Claire reminded them.

"But he has to know that we're not going to go around killing people so they don't starve," Jermaine stated the obvious.

"I'm sure he does," Cayley sighed, "but he wouldn't be the first person who became famous for stopping a threat that never existed in the first place."

"That's what you think this is?" Jermaine asked incredulously. "You think he is just creating fear out of nothing to get attention and play the hero? That makes no sense at all."

"Maybe not, but it seems to be working for him so far. Two weeks ago I had never even heard of him and today he's heading a revolution," Claire observed. "Crazy!"

Chapter 22
November 26, 2058. Southern China.

Hai had to concentrate on his work to ensure he would safely end the twelve-hour shift he was in the middle of. It had been over a week since he arrived and while he was getting better at operating the loader, they were being forced to work at the limits of the equipment in order to move the necessary amount of rock. Each bucket load he picked up was precariously close to toppling his machine as he moved across the uneven terrain toward the waiting trucks. The good thing was that he had finally managed to have two informative discussions with one of his colleagues. It had taken far longer than he had expected, as he had planned to be home in Vietnam by now. Finally, a worker named Laing Ji had unknowingly provided him with valuable information about the mine, specifically as it pertained to water handling and releases into the nearby stream. He had managed to discretely get some soil and water samples from within the operation that could be compared to the downstream samples he had taken during his approach to the mine. Those were well hidden back at his hillside terrace.

He had just filled the bucket to almost overflowing and was turning to inch toward the empty truck when he felt a gun barrel being pressed against the back of his head, courtesy of a guard who had climbed up onto his machine without being noticed. The assailant shifted to his right side where he shouted for Hai to lower the bucket.

Without understanding how he had been found out, Hai quickly assessed his limited options. He nodded his head in understanding and activated the bucket. Instead of lowering it, and stabilizing the massive machine, he quickly raised it as high as it would go. Hai then turned the behemoth sharply to the right causing the world to turn upside down as the guard, along with the machine unexpectedly toppled over sideways in slow motion and eventually trapped the man, literally between rock and a hard place. Hai meanwhile used his dexterity and anticipation to scale down the left side of the machine as it became the top and he quickly worked his way to the ground like a lumberjack on a giant rolling log. Seeing that the driver of the truck had run to the assistance of the trapped guard, Hai scampered into the driver's seat of the unattended and massive getaway vehicle. A few seconds later he was heading toward the mine entrance, hoping the gate the trucks entered and left through would be unmanned and open. Even if it wasn't, there was no way he would be stopping for directions or for permission to leave.

Chapter 23
*November 27, 2058.
New York, USA.*

"Welcome to the Wolfe Pack. I'm Jason Wolfe. I hope all of you Americans had a wonderful Thanksgiving and the rest of the world is equally as thankful for the blessings they enjoy," Jason spoke, opening the show.

"Because tonight falls at the end of the Thanksgiving weekend, and because it had been a quiet week, we planned for a nice relaxing nostalgic show. We planned to take you back through history and reflect on the positive aspects of the past. For those of you who don't know, the first American Thanksgiving was in 1863, as declared by Abraham Lincoln. The first Thanksgiving in North America was held in Newfoundland, Canada in 1578. It was organized by Martin Frobisher, who was an explorer. Similar harvest-related holidays exist in parts of Asia, South America and Europe. Obviously, this concept is nothing new and it points out the fact that for centuries, people have had reasons to be thankful. It recent years, some of us have developed a bad habit of looking at the past and merely giving thanks that it is over with. We sometimes feel so privileged to live in our current society that we fail to appreciate the positives that have persisted throughout our recent history. In an attempt to do something about that, we thought it would be a good idea to scan back over the past one hundred years and review some of the significant positive events that have taken place."

"We will start with the 1960s. Besides the music and a generation of young people promoting love and peace, the first successful human heart transplant occurred, a man walked on the moon, and Mao Zedong launched the Cultural Revolution in China," Jason began the segment by listing the positive events to a backdrop of relevant music and video. "The Peace Corps was founded and Japan built the first bullet train. Martin Luther King inspired millions and the first Kwanzaa was celebrated. Not bad for the first decade. Now let's look at the 1970s. It was then that the United States pulled out of Vietnam and that country became united as one. The Skylab space station was built and the Apple Computer Company was formed. The Aswan Dam was completed in China and Mother Theresa was given the Nobel Peace Prize."

"There is no doubt that there were terrible things occurring around the world during the same time frames, but by focusing on the positive achievements, you allow yourself to create a picture of success." What he hadn't told the audience was that, in the process of researching the positive achievements of the past, more than ninety percent of the events he had come across as being significant were negative. The process of harvesting the gems of positivity was not as easy as he had expected. He wondered if that truly was reflective of human nature or merely a comment on the media that created the lists of newsworthy achievements.

Jason continued on through the following decades. The fall of the Berlin Wall and the creation of the internet occurred in the 1980s. The release and rise to power of Nelson Mandela and the end of Apartheid in South Africa happened in the nineties, along with the end of the Cold War, the initial uniting of the European Union and the launch of the Hubble Telescope. He continued to provide examples right up to the positives taken from the 2040s to provide memorable achievements that his younger audience could relate to. All in, his viewers were treated to thirty minutes of positivity that was meant to create human pride and positive reinforcement.

Claire watched the segment and had to wipe the occasional tear from her eyes. The combination of visuals, music, and positivity created a powerful message that she was pleased she was not immune to, no matter how many times she watched it.

"We at the Wolfe Pack hope that you enjoyed that presentation of past positivity. We certainly enjoyed putting it together for you. I would dearly love to end the show on that upbeat note, but we had one more piece of nostalgia that occurred this past week. On Thursday evening, we had a dramatic return of the Thanksgiving turkey, but this one was not called Tom and did not receive a Presidential Pardon. This year's turkey was in the form of Mr. Spencer Watt, who took another opportunity to spread negativity during a time of thanks. I can assure you that if we discover someday that his warnings are rooted in truth, then I will thank him, personally, to his face. On the other hand, I don't appreciate having my precious family time being interrupted by these continued messages of fear and accusation. I, for one, am confident that the truth will be revealed and that we, as a society, will continue to move forward, progressively, together. Good night, everyone."

****

That was a nice touch, tying Thanksgiving into a segment on positivity. I lived through all of the events that were just reviewed in that video and as a journalist I reported on many of them. The trouble in those days was the focus in the media toward the negative events that existed. Go ahead, turn on your computer and search the news events of any decade in the past and you will see that there are at least ten negative stories to every one that is even remotely positive. That didn't happen accidentally and it wasn't representative of the daily lives of average people. Those who controlled the media, and me for that matter, dictated an environment of fear and negativity. Day by day, year by year, each of us just gradually became conditioned to it. Thanksgiving, as Jason just reminded us, is a day, once a year, where we are encouraged to be thankful. What did we do on that day? Turn on the TV and watch football or plan our shopping trip to the mall. When I grew up there was a pervasive reference to 'the good old days.' Now, it seems, the people in this book keep referring to 'the bad old days.' It makes my downloaded brain wonder if there is a trend or is it just a question of personal perception. Was life good in the 1950s, bad around the year 2000 and good again now? Based on historical information, it has always been bad, with a few positive things sprinkled in for good measure.

If you spend your entire life looking through a single window, your world view will be limited to what is available to you. You will be biased toward your specific and limited observations and be unaware of other possibilities. Your life will be perceived as good or bad depending on your personal choice between optimism and pessimism. If you allow your window to expand, then so will your viewpoint. Typically, the reality of experience will re-

define our views but it opens us up to external biases. In the negative environment of perceived limitations that the media used to present, we were likely to become pessimistic and narrow. The current world does not have to deal with the backdrop of pervasive negativity. As a result there is no anchor holding everyone back. It has been my experience that individuals have been as likely to have a good life at any period of time over the past century, but today, the majority of people have learned to be happy. This came as a result of the current environment of positivity.

Chapter 24

November 28, 2058. Seattle, USA.

Joshua Li sat at his workstation and tried to focus on the growing amount of work that needed to get done before the upcoming COI meeting. Try as he may, his attention kept being side-swiped by thoughts of his Yeye, which was one of the few words of Mandarin that he knew. He had no idea if his Grandfather was alive or dead and the lack of knowing haunted his every waking moment. Even knowing the truth, as horrific as the news may be, would be better than worrying about what might be. What if he is being held captive somewhere against his will, needing help, and no one is looking for him? Josh shook his head as if he were trying to shake the negativity out of his ears. Trying to refocus, he scanned the screens in front of him which displayed the latest data output report. He had been hoping to recognize some clue as to why their COH data didn't seem to be meshing with the Braintrust recommendations. He really needed Cayley to get him access to the combined data set to understand how the integrity of their internal data may have been affected or compromised in the merging process. As he scanned the screens, a notice appeared from an unknown caller who wished to speak with him. Usually he would have ignored unsolicited interruptions, but his thoughts flashed back to his Yeye and, just in case, he activated the accept response and addressed the mystery caller.

"Joshua Li, how can I help you?"

"Mr. Li. Thank you for accepting my call. My name is Spencer Watt and I am afraid I have some bad news for you."

Josh sat speechless for a moment not knowing what to say. He didn't want to mention his grandfather, but what else could this possibly be about.

"Yes?" was all that he could muster.

"Mr. Li, I realize that we don't know each other and I am sorry to be the one who has to tell you this, but if you are not already aware, your grandfather in China has been taken from his family and has been killed. Our investigators in China have made it very clear to me that this has been a government-sanctioned action. Once again, you have my profound condolences."

"Do you know where he is? His body, I mean. I need to have some proof of this!" Josh responded sharply.

"I understand completely, but unfortunately this is all of the information I have. We have a list of eighteen people from that region who have suffered the same fate. We are still investigating for more details."

"Why are you calling me to tell me this?" Josh asked, his head spinning.

"I just thought that if you didn't already know that you had a right to. Since the government isn't admitting it, then how else are the grieving families going to find out what has happened?"

"And you are absolutely positive that what you are telling me is true?"

"As positive as it is possible to be without standing over the lifeless body."

"I did already know that he was missing. Even though they were warned not to, my family informed me of that fact. I hoped that…" and then his words just dropped away as a wave of grief passed through him and anger began to rise from within.

"How can they do this? They're not going to get away with it!" Josh snapped despite himself.

"You are right. We won't let them. We are working with as many people as we can attract to expose what is happening. I am spending my own money on this and hoping to gather as much information as possible so that we can definitively prove what is happening," Spencer stated, hoping that Joshua's anger would last long enough for him to be manipulated further. When he had first entertained the plan to create this mirage of global social concern, he looked for a point of weakness within the COI group that would allow him access inside the juggernaut that they represent. It was clear that the principle founders and most senior staff were not likely targets but the head of their IT group seemed like a possibility. Researching his family allowed Spencer to find out that Josh's parents and grandparents lived in northwestern China near Chengdu, and it was a simple matter to hire a couple of men to put on fake uniforms, abduct his grandfather from his home and keep him hostage. Depending on how this all turned out, the old man may have to be eliminated, but that would be a small price to pay for all that would be achieved. Realistically speaking, the old man was already on borrowed time given his age and the hard life he had lived.

"What can I do to help you?" Joshua asked, caught up in his emotions and looking for a way to avenge the his grandfather's death.

Spencer smiled with the satisfaction of a sport fisherman who had just felt a tug on the line, indicating that his prey had just been hooked.

"I'm not exactly sure right now. That certainly wasn't my reason for speaking with you today," Spencer lied. "One thing just occurred to me, though. I wouldn't want you to get into any trouble, but if there was any way to learn about discrepancies between the Global Council's actions and the will of the people as revealed by our COH groups, that would be very useful. We need to demonstrate that the GC is acting irresponsibly and lying to us about it. We need to catch them at their game if we have any chance of forcing them to stop doing these terrible things to people like your grandfather," Spencer replied, hoping that poking at the man's open wound once again would serve as a strong motivator.

"I will see what I can do. How can I communicate with you?" Josh enquired.

"I will leave you my private contact info. We also have our website available. I will look forward to hearing back from you."

"I will see what I can do and let you know," Joshua concluded. "Thanks for contacting me."

"I just hope that in some way we can help you by preventing others from having to experience the pain that you are going through," Spencer responded with as much fake sincerity as he could generate.

****

I've been following along with the storyline and I can't help but think that this Spencer Watt character is a pretty lame villain. When I was young, the books and movies had mass murderers and psychopaths who left a trail of devastation in their wake. This guy is nothing more than a washed up actor that nobody cares about anymore. There have been a few people killed and injured in the demonstrations, but Watt didn't even get his hands dirty. Is this the most tension and horror we can expect from a story based in some future nirvana? It may make for a wonderful society but it doesn't provide much suspense. Hell, there hasn't even been a good car chase yet, which makes sense since there doesn't seem to be many cars around. Maybe the author is appealing to our intellects rather than stimulating our visceral emotions. Perhaps the intent is to enlighten rather than scare the hell out of us. Hmm, positivity over fear. That's starting to sound familiar. Maybe I should just let you get back to the story.

Chapter 25
November 29, 2058. New York, USA.

The sun shone brightly, creating swaths of diamonds on the surface of the Raritan River that her train was crossing. A firestorm of coloured leaves stubbornly clung to the branches that bowed down towards the water's edge along both shores of the river. It had been a beautiful summer and fall. Winter still seemed a long way off. Cayley reflected back on the days when the world was fixated on looking for the doom and gloom inherent with almost every aspect of society including the seasonal forecasts and the occasional drastic climactic event. Perfect days like this would be ignored as being insignificant. Global warming, is now merely one of the world's manageable issues, despite being the mantra of a generation that sought change. It ranked right up there with other issues such as segregation, the Vietnam war and sexual orientation. Like trying to change a light bulb in the dark, any task can be next to impossible given unfavourable work conditions. As ineffective and disruptive as the environmental movement may have been, the need for change was necessary. Using an adversarial approach to the real and serious problems of overconsumption and unsustainable processes did little more than polarize stakeholders and alienate efforts toward positive goals.

Fortunately, the primary contributors to the earths greenhouse effect have been negated as a result of societal changes in other areas. The move toward pervasive vegetarianism, which came as a result of the Global Famine, and eliminating nearly seventy-eight percent of all travel and transportation related energy consumption through technological advances have controlled global emissions. Another primary advancement was the promotion of long-life product design that precluded having to buy new electronic devices every year or two. It was something that would never have occurred had the corporate model not have completely changed as a result of the global financial revolution. Once business and political leaders from around the world began working toward the best interests of society as a whole, the problems began to fade away.

Collective and inclusive thoughts and actions were the tonic required to heal the plague of individualism and negativity that had gradually and invisibly taken hold of society. And yet, Spencer Watt had somehow created a virus of fear that had unexpectedly arisen in small pockets of society and threatened to spread. After decades of relief from fear-based societal conditioning, renewed anxieties had resurfaced as senseless and powerful as ever. Fortunately, the tools now existed to combat the spread of fear and Cayley was confident that reason and calm would prevail.

The train began to slow as it approached its destination at Grand Central Station in New York. Cayley suddenly realized that it had been thirty minutes since they had crossed the Raritan River, which had swept away her previously constructive work thoughts. She should have been mentally preparing for the COI quarterly meeting she was heading to and reviewing the notes she had made for the presentation she was about to deliver. Instead, she had let her mind wander like a time-traveller going back and forth between thoughts and opinions spanning decades of historical recollections and future possibilities. Cayley had to refocus on the tasks that lie ahead. She knew there was absolutely no validity to the recent concerns claiming that the Global Council would invoke drastic measures to control population, but it wasn't good enough to merely convince the public of that reality. They needed to expose the scheme that Watt had developed and reveal to the public the fatal and destructive methods that he had used for no other purpose than feeding his own ego. She gathered her things when the train stopped and rose to meet the challenge of the next three days of meetings and discussions that were deemed too important to be facilitated by remote attendance. This was why their computers were still housed in buildings with offices and meeting rooms. Once in a while, people still needed to sit together and be present with their colleagues to deal with the major issues. They would still be interacting online with other groups of employees who would gather at their local headquarters around the globe, but no longer would a hundred or more people fly around the world to meet in a single location. Even the United Nations and the Global Council did that just once a year.

****

As Cayley approached their office building, it became clear that this wasn't going to be a quiet morning. She could hear the protesters before she turned the corner and saw the demonstration that had engulfed the entrance to the COI headquarters. It took her back to some of the events from thirty years ago when the Establishment waged an all-out war on them through the media and branded them as anti-American traitors and worse. It lasted for nearly a decade as the people of the world became enlightened and the governments and corporations became threatened. Here we go again, she thought, as she approached the crowd and braced herself for the verbal onslaught that would be coming her way once the crowd realized she was attempting to enter the building. She hoped the assaults would only be verbal. Cayley tried to understand what was motivating these people to stage a demonstration. The crowd was dominated by people who appeared to be over forty years old. Maybe they were just having a bit of nostalgic fun for old times sake. They didn't look like they were having fun. They seemed intense and engaged.

'What a waste of energy,' Cayley thought to herself as she tried to blend in with the group. As she got close to the front door, she noticed the security personnel posted by the entrance. The plan she developed, just at that moment, was to approach in a serpentine manner, suggesting she was just an onlooker and not the enemy. She wished she was carrying a placard instead of a brief case. There were seven or eight hundred people holding signs and chanting 'Thou shall not kill'. 'Well, at least they shouldn't kill me,' she surmised nervously. Cayley got close to the front entrance and made a dash for it. Some of the people noticed her at the last second and made remarks and shoved her as she swept past them, but soon enough she was inside the building, shaken but safe. 'How could people still be driven to act like this?' she wondered. It seemed impossible to believe, but it was real and somehow they needed to put it to rest.

"Good morning, Cayley. Are you okay?" Aziza Korir inquired as he approached her. Aziza was the office manager who would be facilitating the meetings for the next three days. The New York office was conveniently located close to the United Nations Headquarters and less than three hours by train to Washington DC. The employees who worked there were responsible for dealing with business development, corporate communication and government liaison. Cayley was considered to be the top-ranking member of the local staff of about three hundred people. Given that she had chosen to live in Trenton, she rarely came into this office which was why the meetings were organized and run by Aziza and his staff. The COI Psychology Centre was located in Seattle and it also housed a strong computer technology staff. The primary computing hardware and data centre was located in Phnom Penh, Cambodia, and smaller satellite offices existed in Brussels, Brasilia, Nairobi and Jakarta. In total, a staff of about six thousand people worldwide provided a service tasked with the objectives of educating and binding together seven billion people and, in the process, providing emotional support to all.

"We are set to begin in about fifteen minutes," Aziza informed her. "We have Doctor Stapleton cued up online for the opening comments and then Doctor Peters will follow him. Your address will be third on the agenda, probably in about one hour from now. Is that okay?"

"Perfect, Aziza. I will be ready, thanks."

Cayley walked into the boardroom that was set up auditorium style with three large screens at the front and a podium where she would deliver her report. Fifty or sixty people were already seated at a series of tables that filled the rest of the room. She saw a place card with her name on it reserving her spot at one of the front tables. She smiled as her mind flashed back to the San Juan Islands and her first exposure to COI. Just the sight of her name on a place card invariably took her back to that low point in her life that was the beginning of everything. A time when something as trivial as whose name was printed next to hers was cause for extreme anxiety. That is where she first learned about synapses and that correlation had obviously been reinforced and cemented in stone.

As Cayley made her way forward she stopped a number of times to have brief conversations with colleagues whom she didn't get to see very often. Finally the lights began to dim and the COI logo appeared on the two end screens and a view of a vacant podium was visible on the centre screen. Taking his cue, Aziza took his position in the spotlight.

"Welcome everyone. This meeting will be streamed live to and from all of our offices in Europe, Africa and the Americas, as well as to the remote computers of all of our employees and associates. As usual, the reports from Asia have been prerecorded given the hour. To begin today's agenda it is my honour to introduce our founder and the Chairman of the Board, Doctor Adam Stapleton."

Instantaneously, everyone in the room rose and applauded the image of the man who had made all of this possible. As he stood at his podium in Brussels, he graciously accepted the love and respect that was being bestowed upon him before encouraging silence.

"Good day to each and every one of you present and to those of you from our corporate family who will view the meeting offline in the coming days. Thank you all for your remarkable work that continues to exceed my expectations on a daily basis. I am sure the reports we will review and discuss over the next three days will demonstrate the objective we all strive for which is continued excellence. As proud as I am of your continued achievements, as we gather to review our progress it is clear that as an organization and as a society we are under attack. Our integrity has been questioned and nothing is more important than that. A seed of fear has been planted into the collective mind of our global society and fear is a very strong emotion to combat, but together we will do just that. Because of the unusual circumstances that have prompted this social unrest, we will respond in a manner that is fitting with the moral code of our organization. All of my words this morning and everything that we discuss over the next three days will be streamed live to the media outlets and private monitors worldwide."

A murmur of surprise spread through the COI meeting rooms.

"I have made this decision unilaterally just this morning. No one else knew I was considering this action, which means that every report being presented was prepared with the expectation that it would be part of a private internal process. We have nothing to hide and at all times our objective is to promote openness and clarity. We represent nothing more than the seven billion people around the globe who we serve and we welcome their scrutiny. I encourage each of you at these meetings to share your information and thoughts openly as you would have at any of the previous quarterly reviews. The fact that our end users may be watching should only make us more eager to solve our problems and celebrate our successes. Thank you all and I look forward to a productive three days."

Cayley had to admit that she was shocked at the announcement of holding an open meeting. Adam was right about the fact that they had nothing to hide, but there was a lot of complexity to what they did and she was worried that it may be too much for many people to take in. There always seemed to be some technical issues that needed to be worked through and psychology isn't what you would call an exact science. Oh well, Adam is the boss and after nearly four decades of knowing him, she trusted his judgment completely.

"Thank you, Doctor Stapleton," Aziza responded as he regained his role as the facilitator of the meetings. "I must say, I have never addressed such a large audience before. I wish I had chosen a more impressive suit to wear today."

His comment created a chorus of laughter in the room.

"The first report will be delivered by our CEO, Doctor Julie Peters."

Cayley watched as Julie's image appeared on the screen, seeming calm and relaxed with the trademark sparkle in her eyes that betrayed her ascending years. If she was concerned about Adam's decision to open up the meetings, she didn't show it.

"Hello everyone and welcome to the year-end review for 2058. For those of you who will be sitting in for the first time I hope you end up feeling that it was time well spent. We will be reviewing some very detailed and technical reports. If you find some of it difficult to follow, don't feel bad. My eyes gloss over during the complex portions of some of the presentations as well. Remember, this is a work process not entertainment."

"Because this is our final meeting of the year, I will begin by providing an overview of the past twelve months at Circles of Influence. You can be assured that everything I touch on in this presentation will be dealt with in much greater detail in the coming days."

"Of primary importance is the fact that our user base increased by more than one hundred and eighty-million people last year. Circles of Humanity membership and the participation in our education modules once again led the way in growth. We lost nearly seventy-five million people to death and poor health, welcomed one hundred and ninety-three million eight year olds who enrolled in our youth education program and have included one hundred and sixty-five million new, young members of Circles of Education into Circles of Humanity. We are now providing services to seventy-nine percent of the population of the world and we look forward to surpassing eighty percent early in the coming year."

"Given that my talk will potentially be watched by billions of people who may not be completely clear about us as a corporation, maybe this would be a good opportunity to provide some background as to who we are as an organization. Circles of Influence is a not-for-profit charitable organization that was initiated in 2018 by Dr. Adam Stapleton. At that time he was inspired to create a website designed to help educate and support people, especially young people, who otherwise would fall between the cracks in society. He became convinced that the youth in our mainstream society were lacking the necessary mentorship, education and support that is required for them to survive puberty and reach adulthood as well adjusted and confident human beings. Issues such as bullying, substance abuse and suicide were all increasing in Western societies and he became inspired to do something about the problems that existed. I was fortunate to be one of his graduate students at that time. His COI website became incredibly popular as a place where individuals could log in anonymously and gain knowledge and support from both peers and professionals. Within five years the website was being used by people from around the world in seven languages. During that time, Adam began creating self-development courses designed for the youth in an attempt to teach them life skills and basic psychology. By 2026, portions of these courses had been adopted into the curriculum of formal education programs in more than seventy-five countries around the globe. At that point we formalized Circles of

Education, or COE, which now provides on-line education around the world for eight to twenty-five year olds from primary school through to undergraduate university programs. Circles of Education continues to be the world leader in child- and adolescent-focused supplemental learning programs. This year, in the entire world, ninety-four percent of children aged eight to eighteen are enrolled in our program. These courses have merged with formal brick and mortar schools at all levels to ensure that our youth have the tools necessary to understand themselves as clearly as they do the world around them. In the coming year we will also be celebrating our fifteenth year of providing post-secondary education to capable and motivated young adults through a combination of online and co-op work programs. This year we had the opportunity to hire more than five hundred students to work within our organization and in total there are over one hundred million students in the program and half a billion graduates who are now working for governments and corporations, contributing to the betterment of our global society."

"Also during the early 2020s, Circles of Humanity was beta-tested and then rolled out to deliver a methodology of building understanding and trust on a group level. I think we all know where that has led. Circles of Humanity continues to grow in participation and the threshold age has been lowered to sixteen, with the permission of a parent. The early goal of this program was to develop emotional support while building acceptance and understanding within diverse groups of twenty-five strangers. Over time, the vast majority of those involved discovered that they, as individuals, are each a unique member of the one true collective, which is humankind. This global realization finally eliminated centuries of fear-based divisiveness that encouraged people to create groups of alienated stereotypes who often utilized aggressive and extreme methods to gain recognition. As transformative and purposeful as COH has become, I believe that just as beneficial to society, on both the individual and collective levels, are the recent technical advances that allow us to use feedback loops of the combined thoughts and feelings of our entire society. With this recent tool, we can do everything from directing the Global Council to providing emotional connective support to every individual from the rest of society. In doing so we are fulfilling a core human need which is to feel that we are loved and accepted."

"You will have to forgive me for letting my inner psychologist out," Julie apologized, "but I really love this stuff."

Cayley laughed out loud despite herself. Her best friend in the world had just demonstrated her own special brand of humanity with intelligence, wit and intensity. In a few short minutes, she had painted an image of their vision. Julie was going to be a tough act to follow, she realized.

"The fastest growing segment of our programs is Circles of Consensus which was spearheaded in the year 2036. As you may know, it is our only commercial enterprise and although it is a not-for-profit organization, during the past year it generated almost seven billion dollars in revenue. It has paid for each of our programs and contributed nearly a billion dollars worth of charitable donations to the United Nations. COC is the application of utilizing our Circles of Humanity database to provide detailed and trending information to the Global Council, national and regional governments at all levels and corporations from around the globe. This accumulated data helps its user understand the will of the people and their associated needs, which helps them facilitate the design of programs, products and work flow to best achieve the most effective and desirable results. Having data that is linked to the minds of over seven billion people is an amazing tool to have at your disposal and it is being utilized more and more each year."

"We are now in the third year of our joint venture with Braintrust which, as everyone knows, is a collective database of the cranial downloads of prominent intellectual and accomplished people. The organization that has perfected this process was asked by the Global Council to merge their database with ours. The result has been a remarkable marriage that defines what humanity wants and needs with the collective wisdom and experience to act on those wishes in the most effective manner. During the past couple of months there have been suggestions that there may be issues with some of the output data and that is something we will be discussing in detail later today."

"If you will bear with me for one more minute, I will just finish up talking about Circles of Influence, which interestingly is the only segment of our business that seems to be failing. There are significantly less people signing on to this part of the website than ever before. Despite efforts by our staff to keep it current and relevant I guess we have to recognize the fact that it has served its purpose. For that reason alone, I congratulate every person who has contributed to COI over the past thirty-nine years. The website was designed to support healing and to let those in need have a place to seek answers and support. The fact that this website is being utilized less and less is a testament to the fact that it has done its job. People have healed. Society has healed. We will never be finished feeling better about ourselves and helping others do the same, but we have made tremendous progress. We have come to realize that, as individuals, we may be many things, but above all else we are human and we are one. Thank you for your time," Julie ended, as she looked into the camera and smiled one of her infectious smiles. She had just done what all leaders are meant to do, inspire.

"Well done, my friend," Cayley spoke softly. "Now it's time to get down to business."

****

Following her introduction, Cayley stood at the podium with her keyboard and display monitor in front of her. She wasn't there to give a speech but rather to be productive. She scanned her prioritized list of objectives, which were also on the large screen on the wall for all to see. She had been a bit shaken when Adam announced his decision to make the meetings public, but she wasn't about to compromise this opportunity to deal with her departments internal issues for the sake of privacy. As Adam had said, 'We have nothing to hide.'

"Hello, everyone, my name is Cayley Wilson. Now that our leaders have inspired us, I will initiate the first of the departmental reviews that are designed to review the status, issues and workflows that exist within each of our departments. As the head of Government Liaison and Communication, it is my responsibility to ensure that all internal and external dialogues are clear and efficient and that any existing issues are brought to light in order to assure that they are dealt with appropriately. In addition to the Global Council, our client base includes twenty-six hundred and fifteen government departments from federal, state and municipal levels as well as eight hundred and twenty-three corporations that we do business with through Circles of Consensus. That is an increase this past year of fourteen percent in the number of clients and seventeen percent in revenue growth. We are very proud of that, but what we are more concerned with is that we continue to receive positive feedback regarding our working relationships and our effectiveness in providing relevant information."

"There are two areas of concern that need to be addressed during the next three days as we work though the details of each segment of our organization. Firstly, there have been some internal concerns about the consistency of the COC / Braintrust interface and, personally, I cannot imagine anything more important to investigate than that. Each of our projects need to be reviewed meticulously to ensure that, if there are issues, we can identify and resolve them. Secondly, I want each of us, over the next three days, to keep foremost in our minds that there have been recent allegations made about the integrity of Circles of Influence as a whole. If anyone in this company sees any areas of concern that could negatively affect our workflow and our effectiveness, then it is your responsibility to make those concerns known. We cannot maintain our high standards if we are not on the lookout for weaknesses and problems."

Cayley continued with an overview of her department and then went into specific detail regarding their customer survey results where every negative comment was discussed at length with the representatives from the relevant internal groups. About three hours later they were done and it was time for a meal and a mental break.

****

"How do you think the first session went, Cayley?" Julie asked.

Julie, Cayley and Adam had each grabbed some food and gone to their offices where the three of them could connect online in privacy and discuss the progress of meetings.

"Good, I think, although I must admit, Adam, you threw me for a bit of a loop when you decided to open up the meetings to the public," Cayley responded.

"Maybe I should have given you both a heads-up, but I was concerned that it might have detracted from our productivity and restricted the open discussions about our internal problem areas if you had the time to rethink your approaches. So far I think that it has gone well and I really believe it is something we needed to do."

"Are you thinking this will happen at all of the future meetings as well?" Julie asked.

"It's probably too early to tell. Let's see how this one goes and what the external mood is next time we meet," Adam suggested

"I think we may be in for some trouble in the next session when Josh Li gives his presentation and we review the information technology aspect of COC," Julie mentioned. "There has been something off with him lately. He seems to have it in for Braintrust and he has seemed really preoccupied any time I've seen him."

"We can't very well muzzle him. Besides, if he's right, then we need to know about it and try to figure out what issues we might have," Cayley weighed in with her thoughts.

"Of course, but we also have to keep an eye on him given his state of mind and the fact that the world is watching."

"You're right, Julie, so let's stay on our toes," Adam instructed. "Between the three of us we should be able to handle anything that arises. By the way, Cayley, I really liked the way you followed up two and a half hours of focus on negative reviews by reminding everyone that ninety-three percent of our reviews have been positive. Then you complimented everyone for a job well done. For that, I am complimenting you."

"Thanks, Adam. I must have had some good mentors somewhere along the line."

****

"Welcome everyone to the next session where we will talk about two of the most important parts of Circles of Influence. Computers and data," Joshua Li opened his remarks after being introduced by Aziza. "This past year our system has dealt with just over seventeen zettabytes of data, which is about six thousand times as much as the entire world produced fifty years ago. Needless to say, my department is kept busy. Accessing and keeping track of that amount of data is a remarkable task and the people working in our group have done a great job. Our growth has been steady at about fifteen percent per year in terms of staff, computing power and data. I am happy to report that, internally, we have no outstanding issues that are currently causing any problems. However, I believe that we have two problems that are affecting us from the outside. I have personally reviewed the COH data that we are merging with Braintrust and I looked at the combined output that goes to our end users such as the Global Council. The Braintrust data must be sporadically corrupting our data because the integrity of the message is not always being represented in the output data."

"Do you have any examples of this that we can look at, Josh?" Julie asked.

"It's kind of tricky because it can be subtle and interpretive. We wrote a program that was designed to identify context and directive variables that would be able to do a statistical analysis on the output data streams."

"And in words that the rest of us can understand, what does that mean exactly?"

Josh thought for a minute and then replied, "We compare what the data says should be done with what the people said that they want."

"That sounds good," Julie commented. "Does the program work?"

"Of course it works, but it can only point out and calibrate discrepancies. Then we have to figure out why they happened."

"Can you give us an example, Josh?"

"Sure, Julie. By definition, Braintrust is not allowed to recommend any individual action that does not have at least a sixty percent COH approval rating by the people and any comprehensive strategy needs to have a seventy-five percent combined approvals rating."

"And does your software show occurrences where these conditions are not being met?" Cayley joined in to the conversation, intrigued by the discussion.

"There have been a few that are clear departures. It's interesting that some of the major problems involve issues dealing with the elderly. For example the 'End of Life Protocols Bill' that was tabled last year was one of the most obvious ones. Our program indicates that the combined COH support for the forty-nine individual variables involved in the Bill is only sixty-three point four percent, well short of the seventy-five percent that is mandated. Despite that fact, it was recommended by Braintrust and was easily passed by the Global Council with limited discussion."

"I remember that one," Cayley recalled. "We had a meeting about it and we finally concluded that because of the delicate and emotionally complex subject matter, it was too difficult to quantify some of the issues. Since both Braintrust and the Global Council were very supportive of the overall strategy then it was approved."

"We showed clearly that we could accurately measure the approval rating of forty-one of the forty-nine variables and that statistically the Bill was illegal but they wouldn't listen," Josh insisted. "The deeper I dig, the more examples I find of the Global Council doing things that the people do not uniformly support. They were all reviewed at the time they were presented but each one was approved despite the disapproval numbers."

"If they won't pay attention to single examples, can we put together a report that shows all of the examples of divergence between our data and their recommendations?" Cayley asked.

"I already have a list made. We can go through it together if you want," Josh replied. He had created the list after his conversation with Spencer Watt. He had yet to send it 'out of house' because he wanted to deal with it first in these meetings. He hoped that they could get the results that were required within COI so that he didn't have to breach corporate confidentiality by sending the data to Watt.

"Good," Cayley responded. "Why don't you continue on with your review for the rest of the day and then we can all go through your list first thing in the morning when we are all fresh? This is important and we need everyone's eyes on it before we create an issue."

"Sounds good," Josh agreed as he continued on.

****

"Can the three of us wrap up the day with our thoughts on how it went?" Adam requested as he contacted Julie and Cayley privately after the meetings had ended.

"I admit that I don't know a zettabyte from a zebra but I thought Josh's review was excellent. They do a lot of work making statistical sense out of thoughts and feelings. It's impressive," Julie commented.

"It is if it's representative of societies thoughts and feelings," Adam confessed. "I'm always leery of measuring and quantifying human emotions to the decimal point

"Spoken like an old school psychologist," Julie teased.

"I know, I know. I'm a dinosaur and I readily admit it."

"Josh is certainly emotionally engaged in this thing with Braintrust and he seems to have a mad on for the Global Council as well. Have you talked with him about any of this, Julie?" Adam enquired.

"We don't see each other a lot, but lately he has seemed to be more stressed than usual. I just assumed he was pre-occupied with getting ready for these meetings."

"That would make sense. I know I do," Cayley admitted. "He seems pretty sure about the Braintrust issues and the possibility that most of the focus is on issues dealing with the elderly. That could tie in with the population strategy discussion. Do you have any thoughts on that, Adam? After all, you are a member of both components of that discussion."

"Ouch! Just when I was enjoying the feeling of being downloaded into Braintrust because I'm considered smart, you bring up the possibility that I am there because I am old."

"Don't be so sensitive. I assumed you had your ego under control."

"You would think so wouldn't you? Admittedly, most of us who are in there are older, and there are mounting numbers that have passed on. I can tell you that, since my downloads, my dreams have become different somehow. It seems that when I am asleep, and my conscious brain is at rest, my subconscious seems to be dealing with something. I've been unable to define what it is but I have certainly been very aware of it. In the mornings I will sometimes have a feeling of uneasiness but I won't remember anything specific. I was telling Julie the other day about some rumours that spirits are somehow communicating with their downloaded brains."

"With what, a Ouija board?" Cayley asked laughing.

"Look, all I am saying is that there are some interesting things happening and I for one don't believe

I know enough to discount any theories when it comes to downloaded brains, active ones or spirits. The energy of life is beyond me."

"I guess you're right, Adam. Who am I to say anything? I talk to my deceased father for life advice."

"Hopefully not your love life?" Julie couldn't resist.

"At the moment, that seems to be as dead as my dear father."

"I think that's too much information for me ladies," Adam stated. "You can talk about that stuff later."

"Fair enough, back to boring stuff like ghosts infecting Braintrust. Is that something you want to talk about tomorrow? If their system is somehow not working the way it should then it impacts us a great deal. Our reputation is on the line here."

"That's true, Cayley, but our part is to make sure our data is accurate and to point out the discrepancies that occur when it is merged with Braintrust. It's not our job to figure out what their problems are or to manage their business. We need to keep the two things very separate. We can always go back to just providing the COC data to our customers without Braintrust and let them figure out how to honour the wishes of the people," Adam clarified his thoughts on the issue.

"I agree with all of that," Julie said. "So what about our session with Josh tomorrow morning? He has really dug his teeth into this and seems to be taking it personally."

"I think that's good. We need to demonstrate to Braintrust that we have some issues with our combined data. If we don't take it seriously, then they won't either. Let's just make sure that he is focused on what we are trying to achieve and make sure there isn't some other agenda he has going on. Julie, can you talk with him and get that message across. Maybe you can also see if you can pick up on anything else that may be bothering him."

"Yeah, I'll do that right away. I'll see you two tomorrow."

****

Julie left her office and took the elevator down to the IT department where she knew Josh would still be. It had been a busy day for everyone and even though it was still mid-afternoon on the West Coast, many of the employees were already heading for the exits after an early morning and a productive day of meetings. Passing through the bullpen full of cubicles, desks and tables littered with computer hardware she could see Josh ahead in his office making data fly around his smart-screen like a man possessed.

"Someday I am going to have you teach me how to do that," she said as a means of introducing her presence.

"Then what would I do around here? I definitely don't want your job," Josh said as he turned toward her. As usual, Julie couldn't tell if he was joking or taking her literally.

"That's good, because you are already doing a great job of yours. I was just talking with Adam and Cayley and they wanted me to pass along how happy they were with the afternoon session."

"And?"

"And what?"

"What else did they ask you to do that brings you down here?" Josh wanted to know, feeling very defensive.

"Nothing," Julie replied, not sure how to proceed. "I just thought I would come down and see if there was anything you need from me to prepare for tomorrow morning," Julie attempted, hoping he would fall for that and get the conversation started.

"You still can't work a smart board, right?"

"Nope, not like you."

"Then I'm good. Thanks"

"Listen, Josh," she began slowly not wanting to overreact. "Is everything okay? It seems like you have been distracted or something lately. Is there something you'd like to talk about?" Julie asked, immediately regretting the stereotypical psychological question.

"I thought that you said I was doing a great job. The only distraction is you coming in and disrupting my focus."

"If there is nothing wrong, then why are you reacting to me the way you are right now?" That's better, she thought. Engage with his intellect and conscience rather than patronize his feelings. "The last time I looked, we were friends first and colleagues second."

"We are friends and I don't know why I am reacting like this. I have a few family things going on. Maybe that's it. This whole Braintrust and GC thing is making me crazy. They are doing it on purpose and we have to stop it." Josh stated defiantly,

"They who, and stop what exactly?"

"The Global Council. They are already killing people and we have to stop them or they will take us down with them."

"You're starting to sound like Spencer Watt." Julie observed.

"He's not wrong about this."

"What, about? Saying that we are manipulating data and lying to the people?"

"That's what I mean. We are being lumped in with them and we shouldn't be. We aren't doing anything wrong. They are killing people and we are being blamed for it. It's all going wrong and we need to stop it."

"Isn't that what we are planning to do in the morning? We're going to create a report for Braintrust and the Global Council to help them sort out the problems they're having." Julie spoke slowly and purposely, trying to appeal to his reason.

"They don't care. They're getting exactly what they want so that they can continue on with their plan."

Julie watched her friend and observed how shaken he was by their discussion. "Why are you so convinced that the Global Council has a negative agenda? They haven't demonstrated that before. Why now?"

"I don't know? Maybe Braintrust is pulling the strings somehow but it's going to affect the population strategy and it's not going to be good."

"Okay, look, Josh. I can see how important this is to you and I will try to help. Let's go through your report in the morning and then Cayley will take it directly to Manuel Rosales. She will find out what's going on and we will keep you involved throughout the process. If they are doing the types of things you say they are, then we will find out and stop them. Are you okay with that?"

"What about Cayley? Is she on our side or theirs?"

"I have known her for forty years. Trust me, she is on our side all of the way, but we don't want there to be sides. We just want to find the truth and make sure that the will of the people is protected. Agreed?"

"All right. Now leave me alone so I can get back to work. Okay?"

"Consider me out of your hair. See you in the morning."

Julie left his office more concerned than when she had entered. Something significant had set him off and he was on the verge of losing his way on this. If he blows up in the morning in front of the entire world, it will be bad for everyone, except maybe Mr. Watt. She was going to have to warn Adam and Cayley to be ready for damage control.

Chapter 26
December 4, 2058.
New York City, USA.

"Are you ready for tonight's show, Jason?" Claire asked as they sat down to review the last minute changes to the notes.

"I'm always ready to be in front of the people," he answered without it sounding at all arrogant. "What about you? This week must have been hard for you given that the entire focus is on the organization your mother has worked at for the past three decades."

"Yeah, those people are like my family, which is why I know they haven't done anything wrong."

"What about media objectivity?" he smiled.

"I have put in over eighty hours this past week going through every soundbite and verifying every statement to make sure that we only present the truth. Knowing I did that confirms to me that COI has nothing to worry about. They are part of a complicated system that needs to be monitored and I am glad that we are the ones doing it."

"Fair enough. Are you going to give me the hook if I go off script?"

"Why would you do that? We have laboured over getting the facts perfect."

"Yeah, but sometimes perfect isn't very entertaining."

"Really, after all the lectures you have given me about integrity and how bad things used to be and you want to do a 2020 flashback."

"I didn't know you were listening to my lectures." He enjoyed it when she didn't realize that he was teasing her.

"Everyone listens to you. You are Jason Wolfe and you have to live up to that."

"Thanks for the pep talk, Claire. I think someday I am going to be working for you. Sometimes it seems like I already do," Jason added after taking a moment to think about it.

"Sorry for coming on so strong," Claire backed off, realizing how emotional she had gotten. She really was worried about this show and how it might affect her mother

Jason took his seat on camera and got his 'game face' on.

"Good evening, I'm Jason Wolfe. Welcome to the Wolfe Pack. We have a lot to cover tonight and it all seems to involve our friends at Circles of Influence," Jason began while sneaking a quick look over at Claire who was following along with the script. "For those of you who just came out of hibernation let me review the details of what's happening. This was week one of the political events that occur in December of each year. The week when the people of Circles of Influence hold their meetings where twelve months worth of data encapsulating the will of the seven billion people who belong to Circles of Humanity is assessed. Each of their departments discusses their goals, achievements and issues. They do a complete internal review of the organization to ensure that the data that is presented to their external partners is valid and accurate. So far, so boring, right? Well, not so much this year. It all started a few months ago when the Global Council announced the major initiatives to be determined for next year and one of the items was a new global population strategy. Then out of the blue, about a month ago, a series of worldwide public demonstrations began to occur. It was kind of like pulling your grandfather's old 2010 Corvette out of the garage. We were transported back to a time where public unrest and violence was a part of who we were as a collection of insular societies. Keep in mind there are two generations of young people alive today who had never seen such a thing. Naturally it attracted a lot of attention and unfortunately the direct death toll is now up to seven with many hundreds of others seriously injured. What we don't know for sure is whether the demonstrations developed organically or if they were part of an orchestrated predetermined plan. Is someone or some organization really willing to see people be killed to advance the cause of raising awareness that people may die? I hope I am not the only one who sees the tragic irony of that scenario. We at the Wolfe Pack have worked tirelessly in an attempt to find out how and why these demonstrations happened and what has caused the senseless deaths. So far we don't have anything concrete to share with our viewers but we will not stop looking into this."

"The next development that happened a couple of weeks ago brings us to Circles of Humanity which held one of their regularly scheduled group hugs, but that one was a bit different. They actually had an agenda. This was a focused approach to communicating with the masses about topics relevant to the global population. They were very open about what they were doing. They wanted the senseless violence to stop and hoped that if everyone could openly look at the topics involved, then the fear and anger would be identified and either authenticated or else go away. It kind of reminded me of Mom and Dad sitting down the fighting children and forcing them to talk out the problem."

Claire sat and observed her boss as he delivered his monologue, so far sticking pretty much to the script. She still wasn't sure if she liked the approach that he took toward delivering the stories. To her, he came across with a smug attitude that suggested he knew something, or was in on a joke, that he was still deciding if he would share. Jason had a sort of cavalier arrogance that, in her growing opinion, was detrimental to the concept of having a sincere and open friend telling you the truth. Maybe her sheltered youth, growing up in a benevolent society, had ruined her for the harsher realities of life, but if she were running the show it would be done differently.

"Immediately after those meetings," Jason continued, "a hero was born. Ex-movie star and activist Spencer Watt told the world that he would become the face of the revolution. We will have Mr. Watt on the show tonight so that you can decide for yourself what his motivations may be."

"This past week has been about Circles of Influence. They held their most important meetings of the year, given that they provide the first step toward developing the Global Council annual agenda. There was an interesting twist that was announced at the beginning of the meetings by the founder, Dr. Adam Stapleton. It seems that he unilaterally decided to open up the entire three day meeting to the public in a move that was designed to once again demonstrate their willingness to provide openness in the face of public criticism by Spencer Watt. We will also have Dr. Stapleton on the show tonight. Now keep in mind, neither of our guests are actually here in New York, so we can't put them in a room and let them duke it out, but perhaps we will be able to create a dialogue that will be both entertaining and illuminating."

"As I said, the COI meetings were available online for each and every one of us to witness the details of what they do. Now, I don't expect that many of you were inclined to sit through twenty-four hours of meetings that you weren't obligated to attend, so we have taken it as our job to do that for you. We have watched, analyzed and summarized the entirety of the sessions into a twenty-minute segment that we hope you will find interesting. I hope you enjoy the summary and I will be back with you soon."

Claire sat and watched her monitor where the video she had laboured over came to life. She had tried to ensure that the content was assembled in such a way that it honestly reflected the mandate and spirit of COI and its varied departments. She had been surprised how much she learned about the organization and the amount of work that goes into achieving their results. Editing the hours of available video into a short review was challenging. She wanted to emphasize the human component of the organization while clearly demonstrating their methods, achievements and willingness to tackle their internal issues publicly. Hopefully, the presentation would be useful and well received.

"Thanks for sticking around," Jason welcomed the audience back to his part of the show, once the video had ended. "I hope that what you have been presented with has given you a sufficient understanding of the current state of COI and how they achieve their mandates. As a reward for sticking around, we are now ready for the main attraction.The final segment of the Wolfe Pack for this week will be a discussion with our two headliners. Dr. Stapleton. Mr. Watt. Thank you both for joining us."

The images of the two men occupied the screens on either side of Jason Wolfe. The three of them exchanged pleasantries and prepared for whatever was to come next.

"Let me start with you, Dr. Stapleton."

"Please, call me Adam."

"Okay, Adam. I understand that for the past forty years, your sole focus has been the Circles of Influence Organization. Is that an accurate statement?"

"I do have family and friends, but yes it has been the focus of my career."

"Is it fair to say that you almost single-handedly took the beleaguered old world we had in the 20's and turned it into the semi-utopia that we enjoy today?"

"My colleagues and I developed and applied the concepts that have helped mankind to more closely reach its potential if that's what you mean."

"Right, and for doing so, I expect you believe you deserve some respect."

"Every human being needs and deserves respect, Jason. Fortunately, in recent years as a collective, we are getting much better at understanding how to earn respect, which is often tied to giving it," Adam explained. "The goal is to learn to respect yourself and, through that, become impervious to negative feedback from others and learn not to require their approval. At the same time it is critical to recognize the qualities of others and give them the respect they deserve and need. Hopefully, at my age, I have learned to do exactly that."

"I think I saw that information somewhere on your website," Jason commented, with just a hint of sarcasm.

"I am happy to hear it's being used. Hopefully you found it enlightening."

Jason smiled his famous condescending smile. "Most definitely, thank you. When you hear the sort of things Mr. Watt has been saying about your organization, how does that make you feel? Gee, look at me. I sound just like a psychologist."

"Maybe you should send us your resume, Jason. We are always looking for good people," Adam played along, trying to keep things light. "When I hear the things Mr. Watt has been saying, it makes me feel like we need to sit down and promote understanding, so I thank you for facilitating this meeting tonight."

"But it must be painful to hear accusations about an organization you have poured your heart and soul into for the past four decades."

"It is disturbing to realize that, after all of this time, it is still possible for people to fail to understand what we stand for. And to see anyone fall back to the old methods of negativity and divisiveness is disappointing. Especially when there are far more productive ways of solving problems."

"Did you watch the overview of your recent meetings that we just finished presenting?"

"Yes, I did. I'd say you did a pretty good job of diluting three days of meetings and twelve months of work by thousands of people into a twenty-minute piece."

"Thank you. We try. So why do it? Why open up your meetings to the public? Weren't you afraid of what we might see?"

"Whether as an individual or an organization, any time you expose yourself to others you run the risk of them seeing all of your warts and blemishes, but it also demonstrates your inner being. We made ourselves vulnerable to anyone that wanted to know more and each person watching would have seen something different based on what they were looking for. The important thing is that we are okay with that because we want everyone to know who we are and what we do. We interact directly with seven billion people every month. We have no secrets. Problems will come up and we will deal with them as best we can."

"One problem that came up at your meetings last week was that Joshua Li, your head of Information Technology, accused the Global Council and Braintrust of not honouring the will of he people. That can't be good for your working relationship with them."

"Josh identified an issue that has been concerning him. We encourage him to discover issues that may arise. That is part of his mandate. He generated a report quantifying a problem that may exist. That means he is doing his job. We will take that information to the end users and determine if the problem is real. If so, I am sure that they will take the necessary steps to remedy the problem."

"Mr. Li also inferred rather strongly that the Global Council is already acting on strategies which do not align with your data. I got the impression that his views and those of our next guest, Mr. Watt, may be closely aligned."

"That may be true but the difference is that Joshua, with the full support of COI, is identifying a potential issue and acting to resolve it. Mr. Watt, as I understand him, is merely throwing around accusations and promoting civil unrest."

"Then perhaps we should include him in this conversation and see what he wants to throw around tonight. Good evening, Mr. Watt."

"Spencer, please."

"Okay, Spencer. So far you have remained quiet. Has that been difficult for you?"

"Not at all. I have a lot of respect for you and for Dr. Stapleton. I am happy to listen and learn."

"But now it is your turn. What would you like to add to the conversation?"

"I would like to begin by congratulating Dr. Stapleton and his associates for making such a dramatic contribution to our global society. I believe it has been the most transformative process in the history of mankind. Running an organization that utilizes the skills of thousands of people to shape and measure the thoughts and feelings of most of the people on the planet must be as rewarding as it is difficult."

"Unlike many of our viewers," Jason refuted, "I am old enough to remember some very different comments that you made about Adam Stapleton and Circles of Influence in years past. You were openly very critical of their agenda and methods when they were first establishing themselves a few decades ago."

"That is true, Jason, and in the context of that era, I can still stand by my comments. A lot has changed since those days but the need for critical oversight still exists. My current concern is that an undertaking as broad reaching as Circles of Influence carries with it a great responsibility. It has been my experience that organizations that grow to attain as much significance as COI enjoys can eventually become hindered by their own scope, growth and success. The control and power that he and his friends wield is almost beyond comprehension. That can, and does, change people. If you compare our situation today to how it was forty years ago, all that you will see is that presently there is just a different small elite group of people running the world than there was back then. Today's elite is going about it differently and have wrapped themselves in a different identity but can they really be trusted any more than the people they threw aside in their rise to power? COI claims that they represent the people of the world, but so do I and my message is a warning. You have to be careful when you blindly put your trust in anyone. People with the age and experience levels of the three of us will understand that, but the younger generations who have been influenced by Dr. Stapleton's approach since they were born do not have the luxury of perspective. I don't want to replace Circles of Influence to become a supreme ruler who indoctrinates people into a new system of government and society. I just want to support those who are willing to stand up to the Establishment and make sure that the system is really doing what they say it is doing. If the existing power structure proves to us that they will enact the laws and strategies that the people want, then I can go back to my private life knowing that I helped make that happen. But, if the Global Council continues to promote sanctioned murder for the sake of a flawed population strategy, then I will stay and fight."

"You have repeatedly suggested the existence of a strategy that they are planning which has already been determined and that there have already been deaths occurring as a part of its implementation. Do you have any proof of any of this?" Jason probed.

"Only what I have been told by the people who initiated this effort. I am merely giving them a voice."

"And what about you, Adam? Do you have any knowledge of such a plan already existing or being implemented?"

"Not at all, Jason. I do know for a fact that such a thing would not align with the wishes of the broader population, so the Global Council would not be authorized to do such a thing. My concern is that this entire situation has been created by some old-fashioned misinformation that has been designed to create fear. The thing I can't figure out is who would do such a thing and for what purpose."

"Are you suspicious of Spencer Watt being the 'who' that is behind the whole thing?" Jason pushed in an attempt to inflame the discussion.

"I have no reason to believe that," Adam answered diplomatically, even though he wouldn't be that surprised if it were true.

"And Spencer, do you have any reason to believe that Adam is deceiving us all and is purposely acting against the wishes of his seven billion followers?"

"Jason, if I may," Adam interrupted, "I would like to point out that in no way do I have seven billion followers. The reality of the situation is that our organization is the single follower of seven billion people who are leading us toward what they want."

"Fair enough. I stand corrected. Your response to the question, Spencer."

"No, I do not believe that Adam, or COI for that matter, is purposefully deceiving the population and going against our wishes. What I do fear is that they have created a system that is beginning to veer out of control and they are all too close to it to recognize the dangers of where we are headed. That is why I am here. There are people in the world who are already being negatively affected and they need to be listened to. I have listened and now I am attempting to allow them to be heard."

Jason tried to figure out what else he could ask either of these men that would create conflict of some sort. They were both far too skilled to have been tricked into saying something stupid and creating something of interest for his viewers to remember. "Well, I must say in conclusion that this has to rank right up there as one of the most anticlimactic debates of all time. Based on what I have heard tonight from the two of you is that neither of you want the Global Council to invoke a strategy that kills people and both of you want the voice of the people to be heard and followed. If I didn't know any better I would think that the two of you orchestrated this meeting so you could promote your common agenda of making me look silly trying to initiate conflict between the two of you."

Claire studied the faces of their two guests as they tried to figure out how to respond to the impromptu end to the show. Neither of them did.

"Thank you to my esteemed guests for appearing tonight and I invite all of our viewers back next Sunday to the Wolfe Pack. Goodnight."

Chapter 27
December 4, 2058.
New York/Trenton, USA.

"Hi Mom, do you have a moment?" Claire's recognized and approved voice passed through Cayley's inbox.

"Hi hon. Of course. How are you doing?"

"I just wanted to make sure you're still talking to me after tonight's show."

"Of course. You are going to have to introduce me to Jason some time. The first time I met Adam, I spent a month trying to get the best of him in verbal warfare. I have never seen him speechless before. Well done."

"The part at the end of the show was totally off-script. It just sort of happened. I thought you would be mad."

"Why would I be mad? The program was a fair and open dialogue. Besides, Adam can handle himself. When he was first asked to appear he was going to nominate me to take his place. I'm glad he didn't."

"Yeah, me too."

"I just wish you guys could figure out what Watt is up to and expose him. Someone needs to prove to the world that he is just stirring up trouble to feed his own ego."

"We've been looking but there is no evidence of that so far," Claire confided. "I'm sure Jason would love it if we could."

"We'll keep our fingers crossed, I guess. I miss talking with you, Claire. We have both been so busy lately there just hasn't been the time."

"I know, me too Mom. I'm really looking forward to Christmas. By then this whole Global Council stuff will be over until next year. We can actually relax and just hang out."

"I'm really looking forward to that."

"Me too, Mom, gotta go. Love you."

"Love you too, Claire."

Watching her daughter's image disappear, Cayley realized how fortunate she was to have two remarkable children who filled in all of the gaps in her life. It was far more than she had ever anticipated. Christmas couldn't come soon enough, but first things first. She had a week of integrated meetings with Braintrust and each of the UN agencies beginning in ten hours followed by their joint presentation to the Global Council the following Monday. Ho, ho, ho!

Chapter 28
December 6, 2058.
New York, USA.

Once a year, Cayley went to New York in early December for the UN meetings and, despite the demands of the job at hand, she always looked forward to it. Unlike the COI meetings a week ago, she was far more relaxed during these meetings given that she was in no way the focus of any attention. Walking past the Christmas tree in Rockefeller Center, going for a walk in Central Park and feeling the energy that exuded from the masses of people in the streets was all good. It was a world removed from her sleepy little Trenton that she would be eager to return to in four days time. She had been fifty-one years old the first time she had encountered Manhattan in person. The experience was like meeting your best friend for the first time after years of intimacy. She had lived there in the movies and on television. There were iconic buildings and districts that seem to represent the story of America as it had been revealed to us through the generations. Triumphs and tragedies alike were woven into the fabric and history of its people and landmarks. New York City was akin to a barometer with which to measure the state of the developed world. This once-a-year exposure was like a real life time-lapse video of the evolution of Western urban society. It was like drawing a stick man on the bottom of each page of a notebook, as her father had shown her when she was young, so she could watch the funny little man dance along the pages as they were flipped through. So too, with her annual glimpse of New York. Over the past fifteen years, she had seen recognizable changes from a time-lapse perspective. The obvious things were the lack of private cars and taxis and an abundance of people friendly pedestrian streets that encouraged an outdoor social life that existed even in the frigid December climate. The less obvious but more significant change she had begun to pick up on over the past few years was that increasing numbers of friendly people were populating the streets. There were more children and more smiles. The ever-present energy was still there but it had softened. The previously prevalent horn honking and engine roaring had been replaced by laughter and music. Perhaps Manhattan was still not in contention for the 'Happiest Place on Earth' moniker that Disneyland maintains, but it had become a very livable and workable oasis at the self-proclaimed centre of the universe.

    It was a pleasant morning for early December and Cayley decided to walk from her hotel room to the United Nations Headquarters. She preferred to stay in the heart of the city just south of Central Park. Somehow it seemed more like a holiday that way. Strolling along East 44th Street, the UN building complex gradually came into sight. It was one thing that had not changed appreciably since she began coming to New York. The buildings lacked the grandeur of the national monuments in Washington, DC but at one time, they would have been considered ultra-modern. Now they were little more than an aging understated afterthought of anyone passing by, unaware of the significance of what was transpiring inside its walls. That is where the true transformation had occurred. The UN of the past had been a sort of idealistic attempt at global synchronicity and diplomacy, which unfortunately lacked the required authority. Their agencies had produced significant achievements in a number of isolated fields but had lacked the support or ability to dictate actions that had been necessary to invoke long-lasting change. Then, a growing global epidemic of starvation and death finally forced the alienated world governments to form a co-operative alliance. The UN was provided the funds and support to create a necessary change in how food was grown and distributed. A five-year-long collaborative assault on hunger prevention and food production created dramatically positive effects. That success provided proof that a collective global approach to problem solving and project implementation was far superior to isolated and often conflicting national and corporate agendas. The overwhelming success of that approach, headed by the United Nations Food and Agriculture Agency, led directly to a heightened human awareness. The people of the world realized that what they desired was a global approach to all of the complex issues that exist beyond national borders. The message of that new common realization was captured in Circles of Consensus data and led to the permanent creation of the Global Council under the newly mandated United Nations. In most of the nations around the world, the citizens demanded that their governments relinquish their authority over global issues to the new and empowered United Nations. Born out of a crisis of starvation came a tipping point that created positive change that has grown over the past decade and a half. As she walked through the front doors of the headquarters she was met by a courtesan who was waiting to escort her to the meeting hall. Cayley knew that, even before she entered the building, unseen scanners and cameras had identified her and confirmed her expected arrival. She was aware that highly trained security personnel did exist and would appear in a split second should the need arise, but she appreciated the subtle approach to security that existed in today's world. One that reflected the people and the attitudes that prevailed, rather than the small fraction of one percent who represent potential dangers.

"Cayley, welcome. It is good to see you in person," Manuel Rosales greeted her as she was escorted into the meeting hall. "I always enjoy spending time with my valued friends and colleagues at these annual meetings."

"Me too. You are looking well, Manuel. If you have some time, I was hoping we could carve out a bit of time to have a short discussion about some issues that have arisen."

"I will have my assistant speak with you about my schedule. I am sure that we can work something out."

"Great, thank you. Oh, by the way, have you seen Hai Nguyen? We have been out of touch for quite a while and I have been worried about him."

"Indeed I have. We had a meeting earlier this morning. He has some interesting details to share with us all. He is tied up right now, but we are scheduled to meet again after today's sessions. Perhaps the three of us can get together then and we can discuss your issues as well."

"I would love that," Cayley responded as she glanced around the hall. "It looks like we are about to start. I better get to my seat. I'll see you later then."

She headed off to her seat in the semi-circular room that she had seen in movies when she was young. In those fictional representations there would be delegates from each country sitting behind their national plaque and flag, demonstrating a division based on Dominion. Today, the heads of each of the UN agencies who would each be giving a detailed presentation populated the curved rows of tables. In addition, there were members of the Global Council, representatives from Braintrust and her, the lone COI representative. This group of about fifty people would carve out the basics of the international agenda for the next year and plant the seeds for the constantly evolving five- and ten-year plans. The thousands of expert contributors to the work that would be discussed over the next four days would be watching from their homes or various satellite agency offices located throughout the world. In addition, it had become common to have approximately two to three billion viewers watching at least portions of the talks in order to stay educated on the various topics of interest to them. In what had become a hybrid of news, entertainment and politics, the completely transparent access to the process of running the world's affairs was available for all to witness. It allows the billions of people, who enjoy the reality of having ownership of the process because of their involvement in Circles of Humanity, see the results as they develop.

"Hello Cayley," came the greeting as she approached her seat. For the fifth year in a row, it became obvious that she would be sitting beside a brilliant woman whom she was about to speak with for the fifth time. Once each year, they had sat beside each other for four days of meetings and on each occurrence, as their familiarity grew, so did their conversation. Lillian Yao was the head of the UN Natural Resources Agency. Cayley was convinced that her surname consisted of only three letters to make room for all of the other three-letter acronyms that described the extent of her varied and extensive educational achievements. The thing she appreciated most about Lillian was that her humanity outshone her academic conditioning.

"Hi, Lillian. I have really been looking forward to catching up with you" Cayley beamed as she greeted her friend. "How has your year been?"

"It has been a very busy year, but definitely satisfying. Sarah got married this year and our son gave us our first grandchild. A girl. It has been so exciting."

"That's wonderful. Congratulations."

"What about you, Cayley?"

"The kids are doing great. Jermaine is really enjoying his work with developing urban farms and Claire is thriving with her work-terms that are associated with her college degree in Communications. I am so proud of them both and what wonderful people they have become."

"It is very rewarding, isn't it? Especially now that the world has straightened itself out. They don't see it, of course, because all that they know is what they have experienced. For those of us who are old enough to have seen the way the world used to be, the change has been rather remarkable. I had an older brother who refused to have children because he didn't want them to have to grow up facing all of the problems that existed and were perceived to be worsening."

"I knew people like that as well, but thanks to you, and your colleagues at the UN, it is different now."

"I believe there are a few other people to thank," Lillian commented.

"When is your presentation?" Cayley asked.

"Tomorrow morning."

"Are you nervous?"

"No," she answered, looking perplexed as to why she would be nervous. "There have been some interesting recent developments with rare earth element production and I am excited to discuss a solution."

Cayley loved being around brilliant people who are able to set aside irrational human frailties as they attack problem solving with an enthusiastic and intellectual vigour. Of course Lillian wasn't nervous. She was too excited to even consider the possibility. Cayley couldn't help but wonder how she ever ended up in this room full of over-achievers.

✶✶✶✶✶✶✶

As Cayley entered the restaurant, she spotted Hai and Manuel already seated and deep in conversation which allowed her to approach without being noticed.

"Is there room for one more at that table?" she asked as she reached the table.

Instantly Hai jumped up and gave her a huge hug, which betrayed his reserved cultural upbringing.

"I have been so worried about you, my friend," Cayley scolded him. "Where have you been for the past month?"

"I am sorry to have worried you but it was a necessary action that I was required to take."

"I'm just glad you're okay. Where were you and why didn't you even tell your son where you went?"

"Because I didn't want him to worry and because he would have insisted on going with me and that wasn't possible."

"This is all way too cryptic for me. What have you been up to?"

Hai looked across at Manuel who nodded, as if giving his approval for Hai to fill her in on the details. Cayley's concern was morphing into confusion.

"Okay. Well, as you know, for the past number of years our crop yields throughout large parts of China, Southeast Asia and India have been dropping. Our group has been investigating and trying to understand the causes. All of the primary river systems in the entire affected area have their headwaters in the Himalayan

Mountains. Recent water studies indicate increasing levels of toxins being carried into the river basins that contain the arable lands that produce our crops. At last year's meetings I recalled Lillian Yao mentioning an anomaly in the data regarding the production and utilization of rare earth elements. It seemed that industry was using more Rare Earth Elements than were being produced, which of course is impossible. It concerned me that there may be a link between the two issues. I did some research and found that back at the turn of the century there were some REE mining sites in the Southwestern China that had been shut down due to environmental concerns. These are in remote areas adjacent to the headlands of some of our major river systems. Documents from the Natural Resources Agency show that these mines have been shut down for the past forty years, but I got ahold of some satellite images that show sources of light and heat from nine of the old sites that are supposed to be in mothballs."

"So you called up Lillian and asked her to look into those mines and find out if they are active." Cayley prompted.

"That was the first step, yes," Hai acknowledged. "We picked one of the sites and a team was sent out to investigate. When they arrived, there was no one around and the place was locked up. They looked around the perimeter and were not convinced it had been abandoned for four decades, but nothing conclusive came from it."

"Which meant that if it was recently being mined, then whoever was controlling the mining had been tipped off that they would be receiving company," Cayley concluded.

"Exactly," Hai continued, "so we wanted them to believe that the Agency's concern was officially over and laid to rest and that a report had been filed to confirm as much."

"And then you gave them some time to resume production and privately hired inspectors to investigate further," Cayley prompted.

"That might have been the rational next step, but I couldn't put people in harm's way based only on my hunches or paranoia. I needed to check it out myself."

"What are you, a Vietnamese James Bond?"

"Who?" Hai asked, having no idea who or what Cayley was referring to.

"Never mind. It just sounds really dangerous and unnecessary."

"Well, I am here safe and sound and it was very necessary. I confirmed that the illegal mining was happening and found out who was purchasing the black market REE's. Then we traced the money back to the people who were behind it all. We even discovered the person who tipped them off to the inspection. He had also been falsifying production reports. All and all, our efforts were successful."

"How long was the illegal mining taking place?" Cayley wanted to know.

"It looks like about twelve years."

"Wow. It's amazing to me that they would get away with it for so long. I don't even understand why they would do it at all."

"It's hard to know what motivates people sometimes," Manuel spoke up. "There is still a use for extra money in this world and it may be as simple as that. Maybe just left over bad habits from the past when that sort of corruption was commonplace."

"Yeah, maybe. So what will the fallout be from all of this?" Cayley inquired.

"Well the principals that ran the mining operation will be fined and imprisoned as will the person who worked with them to falsify the documents."

"Are there still prisons around to send them to?" Cayley asked. It struck her that there are so many things, like her father's cherished CD collection that she had to purge when he died, that just lose relevance due to technological and societal change. Recalling her time in a correctional facility made Cayley rejoice in the reality that the need for such institutions had almost been eliminated. Privatized prisons, which for years had been a growth industry in the United States, had now become the modern equivalent of a Blockbuster video store, a butcher shop or a car wash.

"What will happen to the companies who knowingly purchased the illegal raw materials?" Cayley asked.

"They will also be fined. The money will go to reclaiming the mine sites and cleaning up the residual environmental damages. The good news is that we have begun to calculate revised future crop yields as the groundwater becomes cleaner again. We can already see that it will create higher sustainable population levels throughout the region which positively effects the global population strategy results," Manuel concluded.

"That's great. So I suppose you are a big hero, Hai. Will they be throwing you a parade for making us all worry to death about you?"

"It doesn't serve any purpose to reveal the details about how the overproduction was discovered. We have only told you because you are a concerned friend. Dwelling on the negatives that still remain in our society is an unproductive exercise that we don't wish to support. A report will be filed but the details of the clandestine actions of your good friend sneaking around remote areas of China will remain between the few people who need to know," Manuel dictated.

"Fine by me." Cayley responded. "Does Lillian know? We sit together at these meetings. I don't want to spill the beans accidentally."

"Yes, Lillian knows all about it," Hai responded, with a strange look on his face. "What way would you spill beans, other than as an accident, and what does that have to do with anything?"

****

"Good morning Lillian," Cayley announced herself as she approached her seat. Lillian was already seated and concentrating on the papers arranged neatly on the desk in front of her. She was probably just reviewing her documents in preparation for her presentation, scheduled in two hours.

"Hello Cayley. How was your evening?"

"Very nice thank you. I had dinner with Hai and Manuel last night. Your name came up in the conversation."

"In a good way, I hope."

"I can't imagine how it couldn't be good. You are one of the most impressive people I have ever had the privilege of knowing and working with."

"What a nice compliment. Thank you, Cayley. I suppose part of your discussion last night was about the REE overproduction that Hai uncovered. He took quite a risk going out there on his own without even telling anyone."

"Right? That's what I told him. Fortunately it ended up well. How could something like that have been happening for so long?"

"I'm sure your friends at COI could explain the human failings that would allow people to act illegally, to the detriment of society, better than I can. From a technical point of view, the rare earth elements, especially strontium and yttrium, are in strong demand given the dependency we have on electronic devices and technology. Just like gold, diamonds and oil in the past, they are increasingly valuable due to basic supply and demand principles. Even though the wealth that can occur by selling these elements is no longer tied to power, money is still a favourable commodity in our global society and apparently motivating enough to take risks for."

"I am afraid I do understand the human frailties that promote those types of behaviours but it is hard to understand how they got away with it for so long," Cayley shook her head.

"You have probably never been to the wilderness areas of south and west China but when you are hundreds of kilometres away from the closest living soul it is amazing what is possible. That is how the mines started in the first place nearly seventy years ago. During the early technology booms, it became obvious that these elements would increasingly be in demand. A century ago all of the production of these elements occurred in Brazil, India and South Africa. Then in the 1960s the United States became the dominant supplier for about thirty years. After that, my country began massive production about the same time as the US gradually reduced its production due to environmental concerns. By 2010, China produced ninety-five percent of all REE's worldwide and began to use this monopoly as a geopolitical tool. Recognizing the increasing value and demand for the elements, they halted all export of the raw materials so that other countries would be dependent on Chinese manufacturing to provide the world's goods. The demand for the elements was so great that many illegal mining sites in remote areas were developed. Many of them paid no attention to the significant environmental damages that were occurring. At the time, China was willing to ignore the problems in the quest to control REE production. To their credit, however, they did shut down many of the worst offenders, which were the unregulated illegal mines. The group that Hai discovered had secretly begun mining operations at nine of those remote sites about fifteen years ago and of course environmental damage was of no concern to those people."

"When I went to university in the late teens and early 2020s, there was some talk about rare earth elements but it didn't seem to be a big deal," Cayley recalled.

"It was talked about more in China, where I went to University, but for some reason the environmentalists in the West seemed to be single focused on fossil fuels."

"Yeah, the whole global warming thing just seemed to take off and gained political and social traction."

"It did seem to be well done overall. Adding an element of fear to the constant reality of climate change and preying on the existing disdain for large corporations effectively captured the attention of a whole generation who accepted the flawed logic and created positive change for all of the wrong reasons," Lillian summarized a lengthy and complex historical process. "Thankfully, the focus eventually turned to producing all raw materials in a sustainable manner rather than just shutting down broad segments of our resource streams. Today more than forty percent of our energy is still sourced by non-renewable resources because they are the most efficient and cost-effective energy sources in certain situations. Step changes in making the production processes environmentally acceptable allowed for a reasoned approach to developing a global energy strategy."

"I think the other positive contribution that occurred in synch with the global warming scare was the recognition of the need for conservation, recycling and the development of sustainable practices," Cayley added her thoughts to the discussion. "Unfortunately it took the use of fear to get society's attention. They used fear a lot in those days it seems."

"True, but it did get results. Once manufacturing practices changed toward creating long-life products and consumerism began to decline, the overall demand for natural resources began to drop," Lillian commented.

"Fortunately so. If the demand for disposable and unnecessary leisure products in the developed world had spread to the densely populated developing nations, we may no longer be around to talk about this. Fortunately, the more equitable levels of consumerism that exist throughout the globe today have been stabilized far below the ludicrous levels of my father's generation. Now we can all have what we want, and need, without destroying the world in the process," Cayley concluded, recognizing how simple things seem in hindsight.

"Yes," Lillian added, "as of this year we are using thirty-seven percent less energy to provide products and services to three hundred and twenty-three percent more people than we did twenty years ago."

"It sounds like you've begun your presentation," Cayley teased as she smiled at her friend. "Given the phenomenal impact of those statistics, it's no wonder humanity had become a united entity.

Chapter 29
December 9, 2058. New York, USA.

"Good morning, Jason. Are you ready to begin?" Claire asked as she knocked on the already open office door.

"Yeah, come on in. Time's a wasting." They both sat in front of the large smart screen in his office ready to prepare for the Sunday show which was only sixty hours away.

"What did you think of the UN meetings?" Jason inquired of his young protege.

"Really interesting. I've watched them before, in the past years, but I have never paid as much attention as I did this time."

"I'm glad to hear that. What did you learn?"

"Mostly that there is an incredible amount of information available to us if we want to take the time to understand it. And I guess I gained an appreciation of the interconnectivity of so many things."

As Jason listened, he was impressed by how well his young assistant was taking to her assignment. "Like what?" he prodded.

"Well, as we know, the dominant topic this year is to develop a population strategy. To do that you need to understand so many things like health and welfare, which leads to how many people are born and die each year. Then you need to factor in agriculture, natural resources and environmental data to understand how many people the world will support. There are moral and religious implications, manufacturing processes and technological factors that all relate to sustainability. Then you can throw in extra-terrestrial and marine habitat innovations for alternative population groups. It's all so complicated."

"It sounds like you listened to all of the talks."

"Every minute of every day," Claire reported with an exhaustion of pride. "My brain hurts."

"I'm not surprised," Jason commented, "which is why we want to distill it all down to another one of your twenty-minute summaries for our audience. How do you think we should do that? What were the highlights of the four days?"

"I think the biggest thing was about the Agriculture Agency discovering the reason for failing crop trends in Asia and sourcing it back to some illegal mining of rare earth elements in southwest China."

"That was interesting," Jason agreed. "Now they are projecting a twenty-four percent increase in crop yields over the next ten years, which completely changes the population sustainability numbers."

"Yeah and the World Health Organization is predicting a one point seven percent increase in life spans for people living in the affected areas downstream from the mines."

"And what about the manufacturing fallout?" Jason wondered aloud.

"That's what I mean about everything being so inter-related. With less strontium and yttrium being produced in China, it alters the supply chain management details, affects quotas and impacts pricing. The numbers have already been reworked with minimal impacts but still, it really gets complicated."

"That it does. It's a good thing we have the best minds in the world working on the solutions," Jason Wolfe remarked, using his on-camera voice to put her at ease. "Did you glean any other interesting tidbits out of the meetings that might be useful. Was there anything you noticed that most viewers would have missed?"

"Not anything concrete with respect to what was presented but more with the way it was done. The mood of the meetings struck me as being very relaxed and matter of fact. In the face of the current civil unrest and allegations being aimed at the Global Council, it surprised me that the agency heads appeared to be calm and confident. The optimism was universal throughout the talks and the discussions. It's like they know something we don't. That's what I noticed the most."

"Okay, good. If they do know something we don't know, how do we find out what that might be?"

"I don't know. Can we ask them? We could interview one of the Agency heads on the show and ask them directly," Claire suggested, not the least bit confidently.

"And how exactly would you word that question?" Jason probed, seeming to enjoy pulling her thoughts apart.

"I'll have to think about that," was all that she could offer after a few moments of thought.

"No problem, let's go down another avenue of thought. What is the purpose of this week's show?"

"Um, to help the people understand what was covered in the UN talks and to prepare them for productive COH meetings next week where the will of the people will be determined."

"So we're interpreters then? We take the details and technical information that was presented and dumb it down so everyone can understand the important aspects of what was said?"

"Well, I suppose," Claire responded. "But that doesn't give much credit to the intelligence of our viewers."

"That may be true but I think you have to ask yourself why we have viewers at all. If they were interested or capable enough to watch the meetings themselves, then they wouldn't watch our show, unless they want to get a second opinion or merely wish to be entertained. And if they aren't interested or capable, then they need us to tell them what they need to know."

"Yeah, I guess that's right. So why are we looking for angles or insights that regular people didn't notice? That sounds a bit like the negative part of the news shows of the past that you criticized when I first met you. Why don't we just list the important information from each Agency talk and discussion?"

"Because they have already done that. By this afternoon the UN summary will be online for everyone to read."

"Really? Do they do that every year?" Claire asked, surprised at the information.

"It looks like someone hasn't been paying attention after all," Jason teased.

"There's no need to, is there? I trust the process and I get to voice my opinions in my Circles of Humanity group, so it's all good."

"But where do your opinions come from?"

Claire thought for a few seconds before responding. "From my observations of society and from discussions with friends and family."

"Not from watching the Wolfe Pack?" Jason led her on.

"Not before I started working here," she confessed.

"Ouch! And why was that?"

"I don't know. I guess that I didn't think it would add anything to what I needed to know. The world seems to be revolving quite well without me being involved. I preferred to spend my time having fun with my friends."

"So that explains why we struggle with our ratings. Then how do we change things around here so more people would want to watch us?"

"We could let me host the show instead of you," Claire suggested sweetly.

"That would probably get us more male viewers in the sixteen to forty demographic, but that wouldn't necessarily make it a better show. What makes us relevant?"

"We are convenient, useful and reliable," Cayley stated proudly.

"That sounds like an advertisement for my toaster. Hopefully we can do better than that."

"Why? You use your toaster every day don't you?"

"Touché, but I guess I would like to think of us as more than an appliance."

"That sounds like your ego talking. Is that why you try to make the show entertaining and a bit controversial? You want it to be special so that people will notice us."

"I want the show to be the best and most watched news show available because it is what we do and I want to do it to the best of our abilities."

"You're absolutely right. Pride, satisfaction and self-respect. They are the ultimate motivators," Claire confirmed. "Is it true that money used to be the primary motivator back in the olden days? I saw something about that in one of my psych classes."

"It definitely was one of them. It was far more of a motivator than it is now. Before everyone were provided with the Base Living Allotment, most people needed money just to survive. That's a pretty strong motivation. Due to the dominant focus on money in our society back then, there were a lot of people who were completely driven by it."

"Wow, that's hard to believe. How sad." Claire shook her head trying to imagine what that would be like.

"There was a pretty interesting debate when it was decided to initiate the universal allotments. There was a strong sentiment in society that compared it to welfare, which many people thought was highly demotivating. It was actually humorous that the acronym BLA was pronounced 'blah' by those against the program. They said that getting everything given to you would give you the 'blahs' and your motivation to achieve anything would disappear."

"What's welfare?" Claire asked.

"How young are you?" Jason responded, realizing how much had changed in his lifetime. "It was a program in the Western Industrialized Nations where people who couldn't support themselves would get money from the government."

"That makes sense. Why didn't all of the countries do that?"

"Mostly because they didn't have enough money. In many of those cultures it was the responsibility of the family and the community to care for each other."

"The people who were against the BLA were obviously wrong," Claire surmised. "I don't know anyone who isn't motivated to work hard and do their best to make our society better. It makes them feel good about themselves and their achievements."

"You are absolutely correct based on your personal context, but that's only because you and your peers were raised to feel that way," Jason responded. "Your education and development from the age of eight included socialization studies which helped you all understand the science and practicality behind happiness, self-esteem, motivation and self-actualization. You were raised in sync with how society was adapting and with programs like BLA being phased in on a generational basis for those who were psychologically and socially prepared to handle it. There had been trial programs in the past where a group of people were given a base monetary allowance. They were unsuccessful because the people who received it were raised in a society where they were conditioned to having money as a primary driver. If you took away that incentive, they lacked motivation. In your case, your Circles of Education background made you compatible with the existing premise of a universal allowance. Things need to evolve to be successful. You can't just flip a switch and expect people to change on a dime. There used to be a thing called lotteries where people would buy tickets, one of which was picked randomly. The holder of the winning ticket would get a large amount of money, sometimes millions of dollars. Over time, studies showed that the winners would often become more screwed up and worse off than they were before because they had never been conditioned to deal with large amounts of money. Their lives would invariably change for the worse."

"Then why would people buy the tickets?"

"Because of the motivation of money in the society of the day. Everyone wanted to be rich, but unless it came slowly and you were conditioned to it, the rapid transition was like a minefield."

"Wow!" was all Claire could think to say.

"When it came time for you to move away from your mother and become independent, your portion of the family BLA was transferred to you to cover your needs. It seemed like a natural thing for you as nothing really changed and you still lived your life guided by your natural human motivations. When I reached the age of eighteen, a few years back," Jason continued, "I left home and went to college. Fortunately, I had some help from my parents, who had saved up a small education fund, but I still had to take out student loans and get part-time jobs to pay for my school and living expenses. By the time I graduated college, I was about fifty thousand dollars in debt. I needed to work to cover my living expenses and pay back the loans. I wanted to get a good job and be successful like most people, but the short-term focus of my attention was being able to pay off my loans. Money was my prime motivator and that made sense to me because it conformed to the societal view that attaining money defined success and freedom. It messes with your priorities and your decision-making. It's like a disease and it can infect anyone, rich or poor. I am what used to be called a Millennial, which is someone who was born around 1982 and who graduated high school around the beginning of the 21st century. It was the general belief of Millennials that when we grew up we wanted to be rich. The focus wasn't on what we would do, but rather on the end result and that was simply to be wealthy."

"No offence, but that sounds pretty shallow," Claire commented cautiously.

"Perhaps it was, but the important thing to understand is that you are what your environment teaches you to be. Because the world revolved around money, so did the people. It was all we knew. Even many of the people who became wealthy and self-sufficient couldn't stop letting it dominate them. Some would become hoarders and others would just keep fighting for more money and the power which was often associated with wealth. It could be like an addiction."

"It may have been shallow, as you suggested, but look how well I turned out," Jason laughed. "And I think your mother is almost as old as me, so be careful where you tread. Speaking of your mother, she was at the meetings this past week. Have you talked with her about them?" Jason asked, realizing that they had a lot of preparation for the next show to cover and their trip down memory lane wasn't about to get the work done.

"We chatted last night for a few minutes, but she was pretty exhausted so we really didn't talk about much. Besides, it really doesn't feel right using her position and inside knowledge for my gain."

"Our gain," Jason reminded her as a partial joke, but then let it go.

Chapter 30
December 10, 2058. Spencer Watt's Global Broadcast.

"My dear friends. My name is Spencer Watt and I come before you today to keep you all informed about a new development that has occurred which I believe should be considered critical to us all. We now have specific knowledge of an elderly man who has been taken from his family and killed by the authorities. This action came with a warning by the uniformed government agents to tell no one of the incident for fear of additional consequences. This speaks to the reality that the agency sanctioning this heinous act is aware of the fact that the action would be severely disapproved of throughout society. To give further credence to this account, given that some of you viewers may still doubt my sincerity, the direct source of this information is the grandson of this recent victim and he is a high-ranking employee within the Circles of Influence management team. My thoughts go out to this individual who has asked not to be identified. He and his family are in shock and despair over their loss at the hands of a government that has sanctioned actions they refuse to admit to and are not authorized to undertake. We are only ten days away from the Global Council making their proclamations for the strategies and work-plans for the upcoming year and we need to collectively ensure that they hear us and guarantee that no more lives will be lost to this unsanctioned and illegal process."

"I am here tonight to demand on your behalf that the Global Council pass a law that prohibits them from sacrificing even a single life for the sake of population control."

"I am also asking each and every one of you to communicate with us about any knowledge you may have of people who are being taken from their loved ones. These occurrences need to be documented and stopped. Contact our website and we will keep a data base of all suspicious disappearances. They have to know that we are watching and that we aren't going to let another person die in vain. Thank you for your time. I am here for you."

"How did that sound?" Spencer asked the producer. "Did I come across as being sincere?"

"Absolutely. That was perfect," he responded, happy to be able to film the brief message in a single session without significant editing. 'This guy really is a pro,' he thought to himself.

"Glad to hear it. Thanks for your help with this," Spencer added. He headed for the door and felt good about this most recent appearance. 'I guess I'm still a good actor,' he acknowledged to himself, as he chuckled and left the building.

Chapter 31
December 10, 2058. Trenton/Seattle, USA.

"Did you see the latest Watt performance?" Julie asked Cayley whom she had called the moment it had ended.

"Yeah, I did. For the sake of curiosity I have flagged any of his blogs or videos to try and keep current with what he's up to. Do you think he's talking about Josh?"

"It seems likely given the way he's been acting. I still don't know what is going on with him but I am concerned," Julie admitted.

"So what are we going to do?" Cayley wondered aloud.

"Somebody needs to talk with Josh and get to the bottom of this. If he is communicating with the man who is publicly trashing our reputation, then we need to do something about that. I have already tried and struck out with him."

"Do you want me to try?" Cayley offered.

"I was thinking either you or Adam, although I hate to get him involved."

"Why don't I try and talk with Josh? Maybe my connection with the Global Council will give him a reason to open up since it seems to be them he has an issue with."

"That could go either way," Julie observed. "It's not like we need to worry about anything that Josh could expose, assuming it is him who Watt was referring to."

"No, but our data is like our life blood. If it makes its way out of our control, there is no saying what could be done to it. Besides, Josh clearly is having issues and that needs to be looked into and rectified. We need to get to the bottom of this, not only for his sake, but also to protect everything we do here."

"You're right, Cayley. We definitely need to deal with this issue. Are you sure you want to be the one to talk with him?"

"Why not. We don't work together in any direct manner so maybe that separation will make it easier for him to confide in me."

"Okay. Let me know how it goes."

"Will do. Later, Jules."

Cayley took a few minutes to collect her thoughts. As she considered her approach, all of Joshua's personal information and work history showed up on the screen in front of her. He was an only child, the son of a couple from Western China. His only other immediate family were his grandparents who were also still in China. Josh's education records painted a picture of achievement and he had been recruited out of university by COI where he had steadily outperformed his peers and taken on a stream of roles that had lead to his current position. He was thirty-two years old and single. Maybe they needed to give him a little time off to build a life, Cayley considered as she wondered if she had learned anything that would be of use when speaking with him. You could never tell what trigger would provide the best results. 'I might as well just get to it,' she decided and proceeded with the call. Since they were colleagues, she had direct access that would pass her personal request directly to him.

"Hi Josh," she spoke, knowing that he would hear her voice as long as he was in the office. "It's Cayley Wilson. Do you have a moment?"

Josh had just finished listening to the speech by Watt and knew that someone would soon be in touch. He was afraid that it would be Dr. Stapleton. Cayley wasn't nearly so intimidating.

"Hello Cayley. Yes, I can spare a few minutes. What can I do for you?" he asked innocently, already knowing the answer to that question.

"I was wondering if you watched the recent Spencer Watt speech."

"Yes, I did. I guess you must have seen it as well."

"I did indeed. That was terrible news that he related. Do you think it's true?"

"Which part? That someone has died or that there is a connection back to us?"

"Well, both I guess. Was he talking about your grandfather, Josh? I'm so very sorry if that's the case."

"Yes. He called me a while back and told me he had direct knowledge of the death of my grandfather at the hands of the government. Before that my father had called me to let me know about the abduction."

"Oh my God, Josh. That's terrible! What can we do? Do you have proof that he really is dead?"

"Not absolute, but it sounds pretty certain."

"Oh Josh, I am so sorry. You must be devastated."

"Mostly, I'm angry."

"I don't blame you. I would be too if I were in your situation. How are your parents and grandmother holding up?"

"Hard to say. I have only spoken with my father once. I wanted to find out what was going on before I contacted them again but I don't know what to tell them now. I don't think they could have heard this Watt thing. I need to tell them but I just don't know how. I need some answers first."

"What can I do to help?"

"I need to know who did this and to believe that they won't get away with it. The trouble is, if it was the Global Council that mandated it, then nothing will ever be done."

"I'm going to look into this, Josh. If it really came from Braintrust or the Global Council then I will find out, but I really think there must be some other explanation. One way or another we will get to the bottom of this. I can promise you that, Josh," Cayley proclaimed defiantly.

"I hope you are right."

"Are you still in contact with Mr. Watt?"

"Just the once so far, but I will get my answers from wherever they can come, including him if necessary."

"Have you sent him any of our proprietary data?"

"No. Not yet," he added. "But I will if I think that it will help."

"Fair enough. I can understand that. Please, just give me a few days to see what I can find out. Can you do that, Josh?" Cayley pleaded.

Joshua considered her request for a moment and then agreed that for now he would not send any information to Spencer Watt.

"Thank you, Josh. I will get back to you as soon as possible. Is it okay if I speak to Julie about our conversation?"

"For what purpose? I am still doing my job. Nothing has changed with that."

"I'm sure that's true, but she is worried about you and would want to be there to support you as a friend."

"I guess it's okay, but I don't want people feeling sorry for me. I just want to find out what happened."

"And that's what we'll do. I promise."

Chapter 32
December 11, 2058. New York, USA.

"Okay, listen people. We are running out of time on this," Jason Wolfe addressed the small group of people who were all meeting remotely. "By this time next week we need to have definitive answers when it comes to Spencer Watt and his possible connections with the public demonstrations and anything else he might be linked to. I want all of his communications and movements tracked over the past two months. He's the wildcard in all of this. We also need to find out whom he was referring to at COI and follow up on that person. There's a lot of work to be done in a short time. Is everyone clear on their responsibilities?"

All he could see were nodding heads without any comments to the contrary.

"Okay then. I know you have all been working hard on this but it's crunch time. Let's bring this home."

Jason ended his meeting and headed across the hallway to Claire's office.

"Walk with me to the studio," he ordered his young assistant. "Any last-minute advice or ideas?"

Claire rose to her feet, grabbed her tablet and considered his question as she moved past him into the hallway.

"I don't think this will be your best show by any means. Other than the Watt announcement, it was a pretty slow week. It's hard to make the UN meetings exciting. The best you can probably do is just get them geared up for next week for the big finale."

"You might be right but let's not write off this show just yet. Maybe I will surprise you."

"That's what I am afraid of. Just don't mention my mother. Please!"

They reached the studio and took their respective positions, Jason in front of the cameras and Claire seated facing him. She didn't know if their positioning was so she could watch him or visa-versa. She had to admit that, even after a month into her work term, she had neither figured him out nor had she begun to understand her compatibility to the career path she had chosen. She had decided to take Communication in college because she believed that the name itself was the single most critical aspect of society on both the individual and the global levels. For her minor she chose Psychology. When she had to choose the topic of her primary thesis, which would define where her career path would go, it was not an easy decision. Maybe it was her mother's unspoken influence. Claire had grown up observing her mother contribute to issues on a global scale. Maybe it was the need to keep up with her older brother as he sought to feed millions of people by contributing to urban farms. Some people are meant to improve the world one person at a time while others seek to cast a wider net. She knew that one was not better than the other and that both were necessary for the well being of society as a whole. Finally, she decided to emulate her mother and brother. The title of her thesis was to be 'The Psychology of Mass Media'. It was a strange topic for her because she had never really paid attention to the media. She rarely watched any kind of news program. It seemed so unnecessary to her as she was growing up. Anything external to her family, friends and the city she lived in remained in the background and was of little significance to her. Her modern history class in high school brought with it an awareness that prior to her short span of time on earth, the world seemed to be a far different place than the one she was a part of. Much of what had happened in the past seemed to have been either incredibly conflict oriented or else unbelievably superficial. She hadn't understood, until going to college, how being born in the year 2037 would impact her and her entire generation. The entire social and power structure of the world was changing well beyond the understanding of a newborn infant. By the time she had begun to receive societal education at the age of eight, courtesy of Circles of Education, the world order had shifted. The World Famine Initiative (WFI) was demonstrating a better way to deal with global issues through unprecedented cooperative methods. A blueprint for a cohesive global society was being created and generations of young people, like her, were being raised educationally and morally in the spirit of positivity and co-operation. What was a new and exciting transformation for society was her norm. By the time she became a teenager, the WFI had been successful, the Global Council had been formed and was facilitating the world's affairs in a manner that correlated to the wishes of billions of Circles of Humanity members. There was no drama or sensational storylines to pique the interest of a sixteen-year-old who was just happy to hang out with her friends. The news media was as insignificant to her as she could possibly imagine. Her mother kept track of what was being broadcast but that seemed to be a requirement of being able to do her job. In college, Claire began to gain a better understanding of the comparisons and contrasts of her world to the one that had come before and how corporate and social media had both contributed to and hindered the societal evolution. It seemed so incomprehensible to her how divided and adversarial the world, and individuals alike, had been a mere thirty years earlier. Fairness and equitability seemed nowhere to be seen. Fear and negativity were used as tools for the sake of power and control and much of that was done through the media. It was that seeming abuse of power that piqued her interest and helped her realize how influential the entire media had been and it made her wonder if that was still the case. A book she read in a second year philosophy course, called 'Sapiens: A Brief History of Humankind', changed how she saw pretty much everything. The author, Yuval Noah Harari, laid out the premise that a human is only capable of knowing about one hundred and fifty people well enough to have complete trust and faith in them. Beyond that general number, we have to rely on other people's opinions and judgments and use them as our own, which can become problematic. Because of this social limitation, it was impossible to form large unified groups of people. The desire to create larger groups, as was inevitably the motivation of those who wished to lead or dominate others, generated the need to create 'myths' that could form the basis of a constructed commonality. The book explained that there were three such myths that dominated and took root in our evolving societies throughout the world. They were Dominions, the Corporate Economy and Religion. Collectively they have survived the centuries and become the primary pillars upon which the society of mankind is supported.

The concept of 'Dominions' illustrates how millions of people can rally together under the concept of a distinct flag representing the citizens of a specific geographic area. They will feel a part of a commonality relating to formerly agreed upon yet arbitrary lines of latitude and longitude that define a country's borders. Millions of lives have been lost in wars designed to protect these imaginary lines across the earth's surface. Similarly, a gold coin or a dollar bill is only valuable because it has become accepted by large numbers of people who control the global economy and who agree that it has a specific value relative to other things.

The book goes on to note that patriotism, wealth and religion have created the best and the worst of mankind. At the heart of each of them was the desire to hold power by bringing together and controlling large numbers of people. None of them are concretely real but are merely visions of what is agreed to by large groups. The book provided an interesting concept that Claire had never considered. She remembered an evening a year ago when her mother had invited Dr. Stapleton over for dinner and the three of them sat and visited for a couple of hours. She had mentioned reading the book Sapiens and talked about the premise of the three myths and how hard it was to grasp the concept based on her experiences. None of those three pillars were remotely negative aspects of the current society she had grown up in and it was hard to think that they ever could have been. Claire remembered Dr. Stapleton listening intently to her with a bemused smile on his face. When she was done relating her story, he congratulated her on reading the book and for grasping the concepts that it contained.

Then he told her that it had been a combination of that very same book and her mother's inner strength that had become his inspiration to create Circles of Influence forty years earlier. At that time, he explained, those three pillars were dominant aspects of the world structure, as they had been for centuries. He told her about a letter he had seen in a museum at a fort that guarded the city of Barcelona. The General of the army that had just conquered the city sent that letter to his Monarch. He outlined his views on how to continue to suppress the defeated people of the region so that they could control the wealth that would be created by the local resources. His recommendation was either to leave behind a large army, which would enforce the Dominion of the Monarchy or to build a church and use religion to keep the local population under his control. In that era, it seemed, church and state were not distinct entities. The story explained how intertwined the three pillars were even in the fifteenth century and Adam related that nothing had changed much since then until Circles of Humanity was developed. He had recognized that the one true pillar or commonality which exists within mankind is its 'humanity'. Every living person on the earth has the same basic needs, which are to give and receive love, to touch and be touched and to care and be cared for. Independent of race, gender, age, wealth, nationality or religion, we are all fundamentally the same with respect to our needs and motivations. After centuries of being divided up into adversarial groups based on our superficial and mythical differences, he took it upon himself to bring us together in an effort to concentrate and build a society based on our one true commonality.

He developed Circles of Influence to support the well-being of each individual, Circles of Education to enlighten the youth as to their emotional potential and Circles of Humanity to bring previously diverse groups of individuals together in an environment of trust and understanding. Today, less than half a century later, Religions are jointly providing a spiritual base of support, Corporations have evolved to become efficient tools that create products and solutions for the betterment of mankind and Dominions had become unified and cooperative entities which provide collective services to those who share the commonality of geography. The positive aspects of each of these pre-existing pillars have flourished in response to the human transformation from divisiveness to cooperation. The transition from fear-based negativity to positivity occurred because seven billion people had become united and would accept nothing less.

Claire remembered thinking later that night how future history lessons may include talking about Adam Stapleton along with other influential people such as the Dali Lama, Alexander the Great, Julius Caesar,

Beethoven, Adolf Hitler, Mother Theresa and Bill Gates. They were all leaders and influencers who had left their marks on society. If Adam hadn't been a close friend and mentor of her mother, Claire may never have seen his face or heard his name mentioned because of his desire to stay in the background. He could have gained unbelievable power as a result of the social transformation he initiated, but that seemed to be the last thing on his mind. Adam's sole motivation was to help fix the world one person and one COH group at a time. It was that evening when the field of psychology grabbed her and gave her a direction. Combining it with the media, which had been in her blood forever thanks to the stories her grandfather had told, seemed to create a perfect pairing. And now, here she was, an associate helping produce a top-ranked news show which she just realized was already underway. Seemingly it had been for some time based on where Jason was in the script.

'I hope Jason didn't notice me being off in some other dimension instead of hanging on each of his well-delivered words,' Claire thought to herself as she brought her attention back to the task at hand.

"Fundamentally, the discovery of the illegal REE mining has created a ripple effect throughout numerous disciplines," Jason was orating, "and will undoubtedly create a very different outcome for the population strategy which will be presented eight days from now. If you factor in the manufacturing, economic, agricultural and environmental effects of this discovery, it will be interesting to see if the sentiment of the COH groups will be altered in any way as the people digest and develop current attitudes around this recent development."

"To wrap up tonight's show, we will review the latest events relating to the social unrest which seem to have been adopted by Spencer Watt as his own personal agenda. We are happy to report that there have been no public demonstrations for the past week, which we applaud. The senseless violence and loss of life was completely unnecessary and hopefully a thing of the past. In their place have been targeted but controlled demonstrations outside of the United Nations Building in New York and in regional headquarters around the world. Even though this may be viewed as an ineffective tool representing nothing more than a waste of human capital, we can't help but applaud the recent trend away from violence and toward a peaceful show of consolidation. This is a throwback to a time almost a hundred years ago in the 1960s when the youth of the day in western cultures chose to drop out of society in protest of wars and social injustice. The interesting contrast is that our recent demonstrations have been largely devoid of young people, who seemingly have not been attracted to the current message. We are going to show you a compilation video created from our historical archives to give you a sense of what it was like to be a flower child in search of the Age of Aquarius. We hope you enjoy the videos which is set to the still popular music of that decade."

The segment began and Jason took the opportunity to get up and head over to Claire's desk. "Good idea suggesting this segment," he commended. "I watched it this morning and still can't get the music out of my brain. The audience is going to love it. There is something about the time and place that just seemed so right. I often wished I had grown up in San Francisco in the sixties instead of Milwaukee in the early part of the twenty-first century. Even the descriptor is lame. Who says I grew up in the tens?" He shook his head in dismay.

"You looked like you were having some issues with the early part of the show, Claire," Jason continued. "I noticed some strange expressions on your face. Did I miss something? I didn't mention your mother did I?"

"No. Not at all, it was all good," Claire responded, hoping he wouldn't press it any further.

"Great, well I guess I better get ready for the big finale," Jason said as he bolted off, grabbed some water and settled back in to his place on camera.

"Welcome back everyone. I hope you enjoyed the video as much as I did. It's really hard to believe that those pictures and songs are almost one hundred years old. Getting back to the present, I want to re-emphasize that since Spencer Watt has become the self-appointed face of the revolution there has been a switch away from violence and toward more orderly demonstrations. If this is anything other than a coincidence, then we thank you, Mr. Watt. What hasn't diminished are the verbal assaults he has been throwing around in his personal attacks on the Global Council, Braintrust and COI. He is pulling no punches when it comes to allocating blame and making demands. In his latest speech, which aired last night, he revealed the fact that they have firsthand knowledge of a recent killing in China attributed to a government sanctioned population control strategy. Watt is demanding a new law which would put an end to any such deaths. We have approached Mr. Watt to request proof of his allegations but, to date, we have not received a response. In a strange twist, a senior employee at COI was, in fact, revealed to be the grandson of the latest known victim of this alleged program. It looks like it is shaping up to be an exciting night a week from tomorrow when we kick off the year-end political extravaganza. We will have interviews with all of the major players and details of each of the new global strategies, live as they are released. We will encourage each of our viewers to submit, in real time, their independent approval ratings of each of the approved projects and compare our results with the existing Circles of Consensus numbers. In doing so, perhaps we can judge for ourselves the effectiveness of the Global Council and its collaborative system. It's the night we all look forward to each year and we will provide you with our best Wolfe Pack coverage. Have a great week and we will see you in eight days."

Chapter 33
December 12, 2058. Jermaine's COH Group Meeting.

Jermaine settled into his work station to prepare for his Circles of Humanity session scheduled to begin in ten minutes. He did the math in his head and realized he'd been attending these meetings for eight years. He had been integrated into a group initially formed in 2029. He had a couple of friends who had been assigned to a new group with twenty-four other people who had never met and had nothing in common other than being human. He and his two friends were in total disagreement as to which type of entry into COH was the best. It was interesting to find that each of the three of them felt their experience had been the most favourable. Jermaine found that joining in with an existing and cohesive group as the twenty-fifth member was highly beneficial because the other people were interested and motivated to include and accept him into the group. The dynamics were already set and the hard work involved with building trust and acceptance was but a distant memory. Both of his friends on the other hand felt it was advantageous to have been a part of the group bonding process. They felt that experiencing conflict, misunderstandings and closed-mindedness was a unique experience they would otherwise have never witnessed. Somehow, experiencing the dark side of humanity gave them a new found respect for their current reality. One which they had previously taken for granted. They believed the act of group-building was a challenging experience which had enhanced their appreciation of what had been achieved due to their newfound understanding of how much work it took to get there. Outside of their families, most of their previous relationships had been with peers who were all raised and educated in a relatively uniform manner, which meant there was little to discuss and learn from each other. His mother had once divulged to him that there was a lot of effort and planning that went into assembling individual COH groups. There had to be a specific amount of diversity while ensuring that complete alienation would be avoided. It certainly wasn't an exact science but after more than thirty years of experience, utilizing specific profile data, they had gotten pretty good at matching group members who could achieve success together.

    According to Jermaine's timer, the session would begin in two and a half minutes. Fourteen of his group members had already logged in to the meeting. Jermaine ran to the kitchen to fill up his coffee cup and grabbed some water and a muffin for later, in case the meeting went on longer than he expected. He reached his seat when they were about to begin. He logged in, attached his cranial cap, and looked around the circle of friends. Truth be told, there were still a couple of members he was somewhat ambivalent about but he could honestly say there was no one involved who he hadn't come to trust and respect. He hoped they all felt the same way about him.

"Hello everyone. This is Julie Peters and we are about to begin the most important meeting of the year. As you all probably know, Circles of Humanity was developed for the purpose of connecting people from around the world to promote understanding, acceptance and support. It has only been during the past decade that your unified voice has defined the mandates of the Global Council, your local, regional, and national governments and numerous global corporations. Today is the present-day representation of what used to be called an election. The difference is, instead of voting for people, you will be voting for actions. For those of you who are experiencing their first COH year-end meeting, we hope you enjoy the process. Today you will be discussing the various options recommended by the United Nations agencies based on the input from COC and Braintrust. You are being asked to review, discuss and choose between the various options developed by the experts in each UN agency. Each COH group will rank the various aspects of the options outlined for you. The data will be tabulated and combined with the rankings from the other two hundred and eighty-million groups in order to determine which actions are supported by the majority of the seven billion people involved. In addition, your feelings and thoughts, as they pertain to each of the options, are also being calibrated. This provides us with two separate measurements of how well the proposed plans fit with the desires of each and every one of you. The results of this entire process will be revealed next Monday at the Global Council year-end review when they provide the details of their plans for the upcoming year along with the calibrated support for each one."

"Obviously, this meeting represents democracy in action. Each and every person represented in the world gets an equal voice and the opportunity to influence others with their ideas. We at COI hope you treat this process with the respect and importance it deserves. Your individual group facilitator will guide you through the process at whatever pace you require to complete the required inputs. Take your time and be thoughtful and decisive as you make your feelings and opinions known. Thank you for your participation in this proud and productive event," Julie concluded.

Jermaine looked over at Jawad Ghadazi who had been their group facilitator for the entire eight years he had been included. Jermaine had always been impressed with Jawad's organizational abilities and respectfulness, which were combined with his efficient mannerisms. Their meetings had run well in the past with everyone receiving an opportunity to speak their minds but kept from dominating the conversation.

"Welcome everyone," Jawad began. "Before we get into the tasks at hand today, does anyone have any personal comments, concerns or greetings they would care to share with the group?" He stopped and looked around to provide ample opportunity for someone to speak up.

"I would like to congratulate Farah Nariji on participating in her first COH year end meeting," Aiko Furuta commented. "This is meant to be an exciting time for a sixteen-year-old to be able to give his or her voice to the process of how the affairs of the world are determined and managed. I remember my first one. I was nervous but excited to participate. If everyone is okay with my idea, and if you wish, Farah, I would like to suggest that you present your thoughts first on each of the topics we review and discuss. It would give the rest of us the benefit of a fresh viewpoint without overloading you with our thoughts. Does it sound like something you would like to do?"

"Your suggestion would be very nice if it is okay with everyone," Farah responded quietly. "Thank you, Aiko, for considering me."

"Does anyone have a concern with Farah going first?" Jawad asked the group, who voiced no objections. "Okay, does anyone else have anything they would like to say before we begin the exercises?"

"I was wondering if it would be a good idea to talk about our thoughts of this whole Spencer Watt thing and the allegations he has been throwing around. Since we are approving plans for the Global Council to authorize, it seems relevant to talk about how much we trust them," Frederik Hultzinger suggested.

"It seems like a reasonable thing to do," Maria Fuentes agreed. "The topic is bound to come up at some point in the discussions, so why not get it out of the way first."

"Does anyone object to discussing this first?" Jawad enquired, and no one did. "All right Farah, it looks like you are on the spot. Would you like to tell us what you think about Spencer Watt and the things he has been doing and saying?"

"I have to admit, before the last month, I had never heard of this man and I have never seen the kind of violence and anger he seems to be representing. He hasn't shown any evidence to prove what he has been saying about COI, Braintrust or the GC. I think we should ignore him until he is able to confirm the allegations he's making. The GC has never lied to us before, so why should we think they are now?" Farah concluded, sounding tentative and somewhat nervous.

"Those were good observations, Farah. Thank you. Does anyone else have any thoughts on this?"

"I agree with Farah," Jermaine spoke up. "I don't understand where all of this negativity and distrust is coming from. None of the groups he is attacking deserve our distrust because they have never done anything to warrant it. Just because some guy who used to be famous starts trash talking, people are all going crazy. I don't get it."

"I understand what you are saying Jermaine but you may want to consider that you and Farah may be coming from a limited and somewhat naive position. You were both raised with COE as a base foundation from the age of eight. Neither of you have seen the types of things some people are capable of," Fredrick offered. "You haven't had to experience the realities that can exist where people still lie and cheat. This lack of exposure can make you prone to being taken advantage of because you don't recognize the signs of the negativity."

"But why would you want to look for something bad that isn't there?" Farah asked.

"Because it might be there and if it is then you better be able to recognize it," Frederick explained his thoughts.

"I have an idea," Jawad interjected. "I would like everyone to think about how much they believe the things Spencer Watts has been saying and how possible it is that the Global Council has already authorized the killing of people as a part of their population strategy. Write down a number between zero and ten where zero would mean that you don't believe any of it and ten being you believe that it is all true. When everyone is done we will reveal our numbers."

Jermaine grabbed a pad of paper and wrote down a zero. Maybe it was because of his mother's influence and his connection to COI, but he just didn't believe any of it.

"Okay everyone. Now, before we show the results, I would like you to write your age below the number you wrote."

Everyone completed the task and then they held up their numbers for everyone else to see. It took a few seconds to scan the other twenty-four sets of numbers but it took no time at all to distinguish the relationship that existed. The numbers people wrote ranged from zero to six, but the interesting thing is the almost a perfect relationship between increasing numbers of believing the negativity with the advanced age of the person. The range of ages in their group was from sixteen to eighty-nine years. By design, it is common to have participants about three years of age apart throughout the spectrum as one aspect of group diversity.

"I wondered if this would happen," Jawad commented. "Does everyone understand what is being demonstrated?"

"This might help," Jermaine commented. "I just plotted the belief in Watt and his distrust of the system from zero to six on the x-axis and our ages on the y-axis and have just posted it for everyone to see. The resulting plot is almost a perfect straight line except there is an inflection point at age thirty-five, which is about the age you would have to be less than to have entered Circles of Education at age eight. All of us who are thirty-five years old or less entered zero to two for our belief in the negativity. Those of us who are between thirty-seven and eighty-nine registered numbers which gradually grew from two to six as our ages became higher."

"So I guess it shows that we all see what we are conditioned to see," said Michelle Dufour, a woman in her sixties. "If we were raised and grew up in a society containing deceit and negativity, we are more likely to anticipate its existence. It seems that since the highest score in terms of accepting Mr. Watt and his view of the world is only six out of ten, it means we have all been somewhat affected by our exposure to the positivity and connectedness of COI and the world has evolved under its guidance for the past forty years."

"Well, I was almost sixty years old when I first heard about Circles of Influence and seventy-one when I joined this group, so you might say my ideas were pretty well formed before this whole thing got started," Richard

Tompkins spoke up as the elder statesman of the group. "I voted six out of ten not because I think Mr. Watt is right about what he is saying, or because I like his ideas, but it wouldn't surprise me at all if he is right. I have met a lot of people and seen a lot of things in my eighty-nine years and it is hard to surprise me. People of my generation were raised to be skeptical, to distrust and to keep an eye open for what could go wrong. I admire and envy you youngsters who have been taught to be different and who see the good in everyone and everything, but those still aren't necessarily the people who run this world. The power still rests with those who are dominantly fifty to seventy years old and some of them are likely to be more like me than like Farah. They once had the taste of power or were at least raised in an era of things like bullying, confrontation and the concept of me first. That tends to rub off on a person and, as much as we all seem to have changed for the better, you can't escape your past."

"That's true Richard, but shouldn't we be aiming higher?" Aiko found her voice. "What we think controls how we feel and the more we reinforce the old way of thinking, the more slowly the positive evolution will take."

"Idealistically I agree with you, Aiko, but aiming high shouldn't get in the way of seeing things clearly. There is still going to be some carry over in our society from the past that we are trying to leave behind and the carry over is most likely to be in circles of power with those of us who are older. It defines most of the members of the Global Council. It doesn't mean they are corrupt and can't be trusted, but the possibility exists and shouldn't be dismissed," Fredrick tried to make his point.

"They should be considered innocent until proven guilty though, don't you think?" Jermaine asked.

"In theory, yes," Richard responded, still leaving it open. "In my experience, which you all must agree is extensive, there are very few absolutes in life and to make things so, at either end of the spectrum, can be an unwise approach."

With that warning, the conversation died. It had been initiated with the blind clarity of youth and concluded by the wisdom of age. The process, seemingly, gave everyone pause for thought.

"Okay, I think we should begin with the task at hand," Jawad prompted. He introduced the first of the six decision topics they were charged with working through. While previewing the process earlier, he had noticed they had left the population strategy to the end of the process. They were being asked to begin with the less complex topics, some of which were building blocks to the later issues.

"I have now put on your screens the background data for our first item which deals with the strategy toward allocation of resources for energy development. Please take a few minutes to familiarize yourselves with the data and then we will begin the process."

Jermaine looked at the preamble. There were statistics of current and projected worldwide energy demand and supply which were broken down by region and by energy source. He had taken a course in college that dealt with this exact topic which perhaps was the reason it seemed so clear cut and simplistic to him. The course had talked about the history of geopolitical events, peak oil and the OPEC oil cartel. The fear of nuclear energy due to potential terrorism and natural disasters and the failed experiment with biofuels making corn too expensive to eat were all discussed. The whole fossil fuels versus the environment debate was covered in the course. All-in-all, looking back on it now, from the present frame of reference, it seemed rather ridiculous. Jermaine wondered if there was a past tense of 'science fiction'. Disruptive and adversarial approaches to decision-making was wasteful and non-productive. Energy from all sources is a precious commodity that requires efficient production methods, conservation practices and environmental scrutiny. Like water and food, energy is a necessity requiring co-operative management rather than political manipulation.

The proposed plans for 2058 were to build infrastructure to allow for the transport of more oil and natural gas from Iran and Oman to supplement geothermal energy in northern India. Other infrastructure projects were planned for pipelines in central and east Africa and additional wind farms in South Africa. In South America there were continued efforts to bring energy to Argentina in order to support the increasing population in the region. With abundant energy resources in Venezuela and Brazil, the entire continent was in good shape. The overall plan was to use local resources for local solutions just as was done when overhauling the agriculture system. In the past, Japan had to buy expensive energy from half way around the world because of their poor relationship with China which was resource rich. The societal disease of isolationist politics and power blocked simple solutions that could have resolved many of the past global issues.

Jermaine decided to stay quiet on this one and see how the rest of the group made out. It was really a pretty simple exercise. He couldn't understand how, in the past, wars had been fought and lives lost over a commodity. So much of the past was hard for him to understand.

December 12, 2058. Cayley's COH Meeting.

Cayley listened as her group clarified their thoughts and opinions regarding the energy supply strategy options laid out for them. Pretty much it was just a case of understanding the reasons behind something and agreeing to it. There was little reason for disagreement. The UN Energy Agency did a good job of assessing local needs and building the required infrastructure to provide the most appropriate type of energy from the nearest possible source. Environment, economics and conservation were all primary factors when it came to determining the proper mix of projects, and these factors appeared to be well thought out for each of the ones being proposed. As a result it was easy for her group to support each of the proposals.

The next topic to be covered was from the UN Food and Agricultural Agency. Once again a brief overview provided the prioritization of the issues still facing this agency. It had been twenty-seven years since this group was formed and given the authority to revolutionize the manner with which global affairs were dealt. By the year 2030, mounting famine and disease had created a global pandemic due to polluted and depleting ground water, agricultural inefficiencies, regional poverty and substandard living conditions. Food shortages led to fear-based hoarding which made the supply issues even worse. It became clear that the situation could not be remedied without some sort of cooperative worldwide agenda. A collection of humanitarian agencies under the technical guidance of the United Nations called upon the governments of the world to support a unified approach to combating all aspects of the issue. The United Nations Food and Agriculture Agency was strengthened and provided the necessary funds and expertise to build a global system to govern, design and implement a system of providing clean, sustainable water and food to all regions of the globe. New international laws were created and ratified where it came to such things as trade, quotas and funding for the necessary projects. It took ten years for the project to develop and begin to show progress. Five years later, the global agency had demonstrated dramatic successes, which made people realize that a collective global approach was required to deal with most of the worlds other issues. That was twelve years ago, and the almost five billion participants in Circles of Humanity saw the need to form the Global Council. They in turn pressured their national governments to transfer the authority for all of the global affairs over to the newly formed Global Council. The first issue dealt with was the monetary system, including trade, followed by energy, manufacturing, mining and human resources. One by one, the dominos fell as the balance of power shifted from governments and the elite to the people. Globally, the developing world grew sustainably while the excesses existing in the upper middle class of the Western nations, and in select pockets of all nations, were systematically eliminated.

"Do you have any thoughts on this topic Cayley? Your son works on these projects doesn't he?" Birget asked, pulling Cayley away from her thoughts.

She was immediately embarrassed because she had no idea what the group had been talking about.

"I'm really sorry everyone. I got distracted and lost track of the conversation for a bit. Could someone please catch me up."

"We were talking about the three new urban farms being proposed," Busar Korir stated. "In Kenya, where I live, we wish to decentralize the population away from Nairobi and I think that would be the case for many countries. Building these very large urban farms in the big cities attracts more people to the larger centres. I believe it would be best to encourage them to decentralize and support rural life which will likely be more agrarian by nature, thereby producing more food."

"Your logic makes sense, Busar," Cayley agreed, "but one thing I have learned about the farms is that they allow us to grow a larger variety of crops in a controlled environment. This allows people in every part of the world to enjoy the same healthy diet regardless of geography and climate. It is a critical factor when it comes to eliminating the need for transporting food long distances, which adds cost, requires energy and reduces the nutrients of the food. I agree that decentralization is an important process, but there are economies of scale which make larger urban farms more efficient."

"I can guarantee you we are working on taking the technology that goes into the large urban farms and applying it to smaller versions applicable for less populated areas," Hai Nguyen spoke up. He didn't like getting in the way of discussions involving the agency he was responsible for, but there was no reason not to reassure them about the facts.

"There you go," Birget proclaimed. "Direct from the horse's mouth. Are there any other aspects of this we should know about, Hai?"

"I think you all know me well enough to understand that I wouldn't sanction any of these proposals unless I am one hundred percent convinced of the need for and effectiveness of each project. When I first got involved with the Food and Agriculture Agency about five years ago, I was unsure exactly what it would be like. I expected a huge bureaucracy full of inefficiencies. I was surprised to find it was an effective and well-run organization full of motivated and smart people who care passionately about ensuring that every person in the world has access to plentiful and healthy food. I can assure you that any plan developed within our agency is well thought out and necessary, and I am sure the same holds true for the other agencies as well.

The fact is, our plans are tailored to the needs of the people because of the input from all of us through these meetings. This process assures that the projects not only represent the best options available, but tie directly back to what the majority of the people desire. By the time we get to this review process, it should pretty much be a done deal which, based on the discussions up to now, seems to be the case."

"Thanks, Hai for that reassurance," Birget responded, "we really are a lucky group to have both Hai and Cayley with us to provide reassurance that the system works so well. Does anyone have anything else to discuss about the current topic before we move on?"

December 12, 2058. Spencer Watt's COH Meeting.

Spencer Watt sat quietly and endured the discussions that seemed to go on and on as their group worked through each of the agency reports. He had never been particularly engaged in these things, but this time he didn't want to say anything at all to prolong the discussions. He just wanted them to get to the final topic, which would be about the population strategy. He didn't have anything particularly relevant to add on the topic. He had already done so in public. He was curious to see how many of the other twenty-four members of his group had been swayed by his month-long agenda of fear and distrust. He particularly wanted to see what the Human Resources Agency had to say about their recommended strategies. Would they acknowledge him and his requests publicly? That was the success he was hoping for. To be seen as the catalyst for change. He would be seen as the reason the Global Council had listened to the people and acted accordingly. His name would be synonymous with saving lives and changing the course of history.

Finally, they got to the population strategy and the preamble was presented. He scanned the document quickly searching for his name, which wasn't to be found. What the hell? He scrolled back to the top and began to read in more detail. The first part provided statistics regarding population numbers and projections based on trends of births and deaths. Next was a section on sustainability metrics based on available food and water supplies and how recent discoveries in China would improve the ability to sustain larger numbers of people in Asia as a whole. The next section talked about population densities and laid out strategies with respect to migration away from over-crowded areas and toward less inhabited areas. Water supply projects through improved desalination were being designed to increase agriculture and populations in previously avoided arid climatic zones. Finally, near the end of the document was a section on ethics and the respect for human life. Spencer got excited, anticipating that this was in direct response to his efforts. There was a pledge by the Agency to preserve the sanctity of every human life and to ensure that no actions would be taken to threaten anyone in any manner. It then began to talk about birth control education and concepts like planned parenthood, but that wasn't of interest to him. He scanned down toward the bottom of the document in case there was some other mention of the recent public concerns. There was nothing.

He then focused on reading the three strategies which were laid out in detail. The first one dealt with a review of the revised increase in population targets for China, India and Southeast Asia. The targets had been decreasing in recent years due to the mounting crop failures but were now able to begin reversing due to expected increases in crop yields.

The second strategy dealt with the details of increased population targets in the higher latitudes including Australia, Argentina, Canada and the Soviet Union. Spencer thought the third strategy looked more promising as it began with the moral and ethical aspects of conception and end-of-life decisions. He browsed through a detailed report on cultural approaches to both topics. It discussed optimal family size as it related to health, living conditions, ideal mother's age targets, and recommended but non-enforced targets. Blah, blah, blah. When he got to the end-of-life section, he slowed down and concentrated on each word for content and meaning. Self-determination, human rights and personal desires were to all be factored into any actions to be undertaken. Finally, he saw it and his heart fluttered in anticipation. 'No human life will be terminated for any reason by the direct action of any level of government without specific instructions from the individual or their informed family. Recent concerns to the contrary can be put aside as it is the express intent of the Human Resources Agency to preserve all life to the extent that each individual dictates. If this intent is ratified by the Circles Of Humanity collective, then the Global Council will enforce this position by law.' He did it! He could take credit for this inclusion and achieve his intended outcome.

The broad smile exploding onto his face must have given him away.

"Congratulations, Spencer," one of his group members offered. "It looks like your efforts have paid off."

"I hope so," he replied simply, not wanting to sound too consumed by what they were seeing. "As long as they do what they say, I will be happy." His mind began racing as he considered his next steps. Now, while the spotlight was cast squarely back on him, he had to determine exactly what he wanted his new-found status to achieve.

Chapter 34
*December 13, 2058.
Trenton/Seattle, USA.*

Cayley and Julie caught up on each others personal lives as they waited for Adam and Josh to join into the conversation. They typically tried to fit in a half-hour of personal time before scheduled meetings just to keep connected.

"Hello, ladies," Adam announced himself as he requested to be connected.

"I'm here too," Josh chimed in.

"Right on time gentlemen," Julie commented as she initiated the four-way connection. "It looks like we have had another successful COH meeting, based on the average length of the meetings. How long is it going to take to document the feedback and get a report off to the Global Council, Josh?"

"I will have the statistical analysis done by morning and the report ready for your approval by noon Pacific time."

"Sounds good. It will be interesting to see if there are any major concerns with any of the proposed strategies," Julie commented.

"My group seemed to be pretty supportive of everything," Cayley reported. "How did yours go, Josh?"

"There was certainly some discussion about the population thing at the end. I purposely didn't try to inflame anything with my bias."

"Do you feel comfortable talking with the three of us about how you are managing to deal with this Josh?" Adam asked. "As co-workers, we care about you being too close to this thing, but as friends we are concerned about what you and your family are going through. We would really like to be able to help in any we can."

Josh thought about how to reply to Adam's question and offer of help.

"Obviously this has been a difficult ordeal. Especially not knowing if my grandfather is dead. And if he is, to understand what happened to him. I have had a lot of time to consider my emotions surrounding who, or what, has caused this situation and who, if anyone, is to blame. I think I have been able to set aside my feelings of anger enough to approach the situation rationally for now."

Cayley felt so sorry for what her friend and colleague was having to go through. "I spoke directly with Manuel Rosales about this issue, Josh. He assured me he is unaware of anything that could tie back to your Grandfather's disappearance. He told me he would speak to the heads of every related national and local government, as a favour to me, in an attempt to understand what may have happened. He will report back to me with anything he discovers."

"Thank you, Cayley. I really appreciate your help."

"It's what we do for each other. We're going to get to the bottom of this, I promise."

"Have you spoken with your grandmother?" Julie asked. "She must be devastated."

"Unfortunately, we have not communicated directly because it is too difficult for her to get to the community communications centre. I have not seen or spoken with her since I left China. I have kept in contact with my parents and they are caring for her."

"Now that our year-end meetings are over, why don't you take some time off and fly there to be with them. The company will make the arrangements and pay for your flights," Julie suggested.

"I appreciate your very generous offer. I will consider it, but there is still a lot of work to be done."

"Nothing you have to do here would be as important as your family," Cayley added.

"We will see," Josh deferred the decision, unsure if it made sense to travel so far. "Let's get through this weekend before we focus on anything else."

"That's fine, Josh. Just let us know if you decide to go and we will make it happen. Can we reconvene this meeting at two pm Seattle time tomorrow, after we have all had a chance to look at Josh's report?"

"Sounds good. Have a great evening everyone," Adam concluded.

"You too, Adam. Bye, Josh."

The two men signed off leaving Cayley and Julie to themselves.

"Josh seems to be okay, don't you think?" Cayley enquired.

"I think so, but the problem is, he's a very private person and we may never know either way."

Chapter 35
December 14, 2058. Somewhere near Chengdu, China.

The room had gradually grown dark as night closed in. This time of year, just before the winter solstice, there was about fourteen hours of darkness each day. Despite a small electric heater, the cold damp air caused him, at times, to shake uncontrollably. He had lost track of time but believed it had been at least two weeks since he had been taken. He had received food and water but no explanation. Two men in masks had been taking turns tending to him, but for the most part he was left alone to wonder what possible purpose there could be for him to have been kidnapped. They had no money for ransom and no enemies who came to mind. His wife would be beside herself with worry. Thankfully his son and daughter-in-law would be taking care of her until he returned, whenever that might be. All he needed to do was to summon the energy required to wake up each day, a feat which was becoming more and more difficult.

Chapter 36
December 14, 2058. The Home of Jesper Halverson, Oslo, Norway.

Jesper had seen all of the old movies featuring the famous, fictional private investigators. It looked like a lot of fun, following people around, breaking into houses, solving crimes. Sure, there was always the obligatory black eye, but in exchange you also got to sleep with a beautiful woman. Not a bad tradeoff when you think about it. If only this was what being a private investigator was really like. Maybe it was, back then, but now he rarely got to leave the comfort of his home. He was the owner of Superior Surveillance and Security, a private investigative company utilizing high-tech solutions to life's little problems.

Video and data provided every piece of information he required to uncover the details of any situation, assuming it didn't happen in the middle of the Sahara desert. The kidnapping near the small remote village of Lilian, China, could be somewhat problematic. There were only seven public cameras in the entire village from which to gain access points from which to observe. He saw no record of any personal devices being utilized in the dark at that hour, so he would get no help there. He had chosen the feed from a camera positioned on the outside of a government building in the village. It was located adjacent to the main road. He had selected the time frame leading up to and following the abduction, which was reported to have occurred just before midnight.

Assuming the perpetrators would have required transportation, he would watch for any vehicles passing by during the correct time frame. Since personal vehicles were rare, especially in remote areas of China, he didn't expect to see many. He watched as an old, rusted, three-wheeled vehicle passed by heading west along the main road at eleven ten traveling in the direction of the home of the missing man, which was about ten minutes away. Eighteen minutes later a large truck, being followed closely by a motorcycle with one occupant, passed by in the opposite direction. Six minutes later, at eleven thirty-four, what looked like a government-issue jeep was sighted heading east. Less than two minutes later, an enclosed van moved slowly eastward. He continued to log the details of the vehicular traffic up until twelve-twenty. In total there were eleven vehicles observed, only two of which travelled past twice, west initially and later heading back to the east. It seemed likely to him that whoever had undertaken the abduction would have come from the east which was in the direction of Chengdu, which represented the existence of civilization.

If he was correct, then he only had those two possibilities to follow up on. The three-wheeled truck had gone west at eleven ten and then back east at eleven fifty-one. The government jeep had done the same at eleven thirty-four and eleven fifty-eight. Either one of these could be carrying the old man away from the village just before midnight. He followed both vehicles from camera to camera along the road as they passed through each village. By the time the vehicles reached the town of Wenchuan, the government jeep had passed the older truck, but there was no evidence that either of the vehicles had stopped.

Then, somewhere between Shangxia and Ziaoping, the three-wheeled vehicle disappeared. Jesper went through every minute of video for the next ten hours and didn't see the vehicle again. The jeep, on the other hand, had continued on to a military compound just north of Chengdu.

Fortunately, Jesper had been able to get registration numbers off of each of the two vehicles. The government vehicle, of course, was a lost cause, but the old truck was registered to someone named Shuen Yu who lived in Ke Yue Cun, a small village just across the river from where the vehicle had disappeared. Spencer Watt had stated publicly that the government had been behind this abduction and subsequent murder, but he would also look into all of the records he could find on Shuen Yu, just in case something popped up that looked suspicious.

For the past two weeks, since Jason Wolfe had hired them, they had been on Spencer Watt twenty-four seven. Without ever leaving their homes, Jesper and his associates used the Global-com system to be at the side of their person of interest, in real time, without his knowledge. There would have been a time where this type of cyber-stalking would have infringed on a multitude of privacy laws, but somewhere along the line, people had lost interest in such paranoid concerns. Watt was a very visible and active man with many contacts and a busy schedule. They had been with him every moment of the day since being hired. Jason Wolfe was their best client and they didn't want to let him down. They had tracked Watt's communications and financial transactions. They weren't supposed to have those illegal capabilities, but certain specific areas of expertise were the reason they were in such demand. They sometimes infringed on illegal methods, but still had their moral values intact. They would never cross any ethical lines investigating anyone who hadn't previously demonstrated a high level of probable guilt. In this case, Watt was accusing the government of murder, and early on in the investigation they had turned up some suspicious information which didn't bode well for his innocence. Given the high stakes and priority of this situation, hacking into a few data bases seemed a small price to pay to get to the truth. He would be shocked if the government authorities hadn't already figured all of this out. Given the sensitivity towards public opinion however, they probably weren't in a position to be too aggressive against Spencer Watt for fear it would be interpreted as an abuse of power against a vocal opponent. They would have to be careful how they made such a move.

Chapter 37
December 14, 2058. Seattle/Trenton, USA.

"Can you join us, Cayley. It looks like we have a major problem on our hands," Julie's voice interrupted her concentration.

"Yeah, I'm here. What's going on?"

"It's Josh's report. It looks bad."

"I had just started in on it," Cayley reported.

"It seems Spencer Watt has created more of a following than we would have expected. Twenty-two percent of the proposed strategies have not been supported. There don't seem to be any specific trends or departments they are uniformly against but the overall sentiment is negative. Basically, I think we are looking at a protest vote against the system as a whole, which of course includes us. It's not clear to me what this will lead to but the Global Council won't feel very good about these results," Julie concluded.

"Is there any chance these numbers are being affected by something other than the COH results?" Cayley asked.

"I spent all night on this," Josh answered. "There is nothing unusual with the data other than the fact that it is unusually negative. We have run it through all of our algorithms and it all pans out. The people have spoken and some of them aren't happy."

"This is truly disappointing," Adam spoke up. "I really thought we had progressed beyond this. The power of negativity is truly astounding. No wonder it was used to hold humanity ransom for so long. After almost forty years of education and discussion, it appears we can still succumb to it. I can only hope it was primarily old geezers like me who are perpetuating this idiocy. That way, in a couple more decades, we will be out of the way of true progress at the hands of an enlightened society. Too bad we don't know specifically which people are buying into these nefarious lies."

"We specifically wanted to build personal confidentiality into the system. Our groups couldn't have developed the way they have if people were afraid their comments would be made public," Julie commented.

"There might be something we can do to work toward the answer you are looking for Dr. Stapleton," Josh offered. "We can plot average age within each group against the level of dissatisfaction the group voiced against the strategies. It won't be precise but it may give an indication that older groups were more affected by the negativity of Mr. Watt."

"That would be interesting," Adam agreed, "even though it probably won't solve anything, it may make me sleep better at night."

"I should be able to get you the data by tomorrow morning."

"Thanks, Josh. I would appreciate it."

"So are we going to pass this information along to the Global Council as is?" Cayley asked.

"I don't see how we have a choice," Julie responded. "Our job is to provide the data, not make the Global Council happy. If the people are concerned about something, then the information has to be made public."

"I think I'll call Manuel and explain to him personally what the data is showing and assure him that the information is accurate."

"That's a good idea, Cayley."

"It looks like it's going to be an interesting year-end meeting. We are going to have to address this in our upcoming COH meetings. We need to address this reaction to the existing negativity and help people understand how we can better learn to deal with irrational fears," Adam concluded. "It looks like your group has its work cut out for it, Julie."

****

"Hello, Manuel, how has your week been?" Cayley opened the conversation, already knowing what the answer to her rhetorical question would be.

"Five more days until my Christmas break," was his simple reply. "How is your COC report coming along?"

"You will be receiving it within the hour."

"I'm sensing there are some problems, given that you chose to call me directly."

"I don't know if I would call it a problem as much as an unfortunate reality. There has been a distinct increase in negativity toward the recommended strategies and work plans," Cayley began.

"How distinct are we talking about?"

"Twenty-two percent of the proposed projects had negativity levels above the allowable thresholds which give you the mandate to proceed with those specific plans. It seems like Spencer Watt's campaign of fear and negativity has paid off for him. We will be working on developing COH and COE modules to combat any potential future issues, but unfortunately, for now, we are where we are."

"That's fine," Manuel observed. "This development is probably more disconcerting for you at COI than it is for us. This is certainly a setback for the progress of mankind as a whole, but maybe we should have expected a few disappointments along the road to success. Don't forget how far you have progressed the overall state of humanity. I'm sure even your psychological experts must have anticipated some temporary failures."

"Probably so, but they are disappointed in these latest results. What are you going to do for the meetings next week?"

"Whatever the people authorize us to do. We understand our role very well. It is to deliver the will of the people. Our work is not our agenda; it is the agenda of the entire population. As always, we will attempt to provide services to the best of our ability and be prepared to do more when it is requested."

"That's what I like about you, Manuel. You are so calm and practical. I can't imagine many global leaders from any previous era who would have been able to see past their own egos and the potential loss of power which comes with merely giving the people what they want. You have my sincere admiration."

"I thank you for the compliment, Cayley, but you are forgetting something. I am not a leader. I am a facilitator. I only succeed when mankind is happy. Soon enough, you and your colleagues will help them understand how to be happy again and then there will be more progress as a result. From that frame of reference, you at COI are the leaders, and for that I applaud you. However, there is much work to be done so I must go now to serve the people. Adios amiga."

"Adios, Manuel."

Chapter 38
December 18, 2058. Somewhere near Chengdu, China.

The mattress beneath him was hard, damp and smelled of urine. The old man hadn't had a good sleep the entire time he had been held captive. He had not been harmed, but an old deteriorating body could not withstand the abuse of scarcity for long. The food and water had been adequate to keep him alive, but he was still losing ground to the alternative of life. It was impossible to tell how much time was left. The rest his body did receive was more from a state of near unconsciousness rather than what could be considered sleep. Trying to create visions of his wife, son and grandson in his mind, gave him the illusion of doing something productive. He had no idea what time it was, but that piece of information was irrelevant. It seemed to have been dark long enough to be morning, yet the filtered light of dawn had not yet arrived. There was a rustling from beyond the walls of the room. Perhaps it was the arrival of his meagre breakfast. A sliver of light from beyond the door fought its way through the expanding opening. Something was different. The shadow of the expected guard moved too slowly. He curled into a ball on the mattress trying to disappear into the corner behind him. Streams of red light dissected the room as he squinted through the darkness.

Faces existed behind masks but could not be seen. Two massive bodies approached him and lifted his reluctant limp body to an upright position. A finger, placed adjacent to where a mouth should have been, urged him to preserve the silence. It was an unnecessary gesture. He had nothing to say.

Chapter 39
*December 19, 2058.
New York, USA.*

"Welcome to the 2058 year-end presentation of the Global Council Meeting, brought to you by your good friends at the Wolfe Pack. My name is Jason Wolfe, and I can assure you we are in for a fantastic show. I feel like I should be breaking into song for the big opening extravaganza. It still seems strange to me how this critically important meeting, designed to outline the business plan for the world, has morphed into the field of entertainment. There will likely be more than five billion people watching this broadcast which is probably the reason for all of the hype. Maybe we all just want to be assured that our voices are being heard, or perhaps we really care about a wind farm in South Africa. Whatever the case, you are all watching and we will do our best to keep you glued to the screen and to ensure that your time will be well spent."

"Our first guest tonight will be Julie Peters who is the CEO of Circles of Influence. She has a Doctorate Degree in Behavioural Psychology and has been at Dr. Adam Stapleton's right-hand for the past forty years. Welcome, Julie."

"Thank you, Jason. It is my pleasure to be on your show."

"We will soon see if that statement is true," he laughed. "We are going to get right to it. Tell me about fear."

"Well, Jason, there are two basic kinds of fear. One is biochemical, which is universal throughout the human race and also most of the other animals that inhabit this planet. It is a primal, deep-seated response to perceived dangers that is controlled in the subconscious reptilian component of our brains. It controls our basic reactions to stimuli without active logical thought. It is what keeps animals alive when there is a real or perceived threat."

"Like when my producer threatens to fire me when our ratings drop."

"Perhaps, if your producer was a poisonous snake."

"Oh, I didn't know the two of you had met," Jason replied, attempting to add to the entertainment component of the show.

"At this point I am not sure I want to," Julie played along.

"At this point, I'm really not sure I do either. So, if the first kind of fear is biochemical then what is the other kind?"

"It is an emotional response and those tend to be more personalized."

"Such as?"

"Such as being afraid of losing your job or the fear of public speaking. We all have fears that we cannot rationalize and which are specific to our lives. In extreme cases they are referred to as phobias, which isn't a comment on the validity of the fear itself but rather relates to an increased inability to deal with the situation. Some people are afraid of heights, the number thirteen or kittens depending on our conditioning and lack of perspective."

"When Spencer Watt tells us the Global Council wants to go around killing people, which kind of fear does that trigger?"

Julie thought for a second. She really wasn't expecting this line of questioning. "Well, in the broad sense, for the vast majority of people it would be biochemical at its root because the message is that our lives could be in danger. However, given that there is no immediate threat, the situation is more intellectual rather than physical. Because our logical conscious brains are brought into the equation, the key aspect becomes emotional, based on individual experiences and interpretations. For example, if I think they are only going to kill people called Jason, and that is my name, then I would be fearful."

"Hey, that's my name. Do you know something I don't?" Jason exclaimed, thrilled by Julie's ability to play the 'straight man' role to his humour.

"Probably, but I wouldn't lose sleep over it if I were you," Julie teased.

"I'll try not to. Thanks for the advice. Many of our viewers may be wondering why we are talking about fear to start off the show. Julie, would you like to fill them in or should I?"

"Well, you are getting paid to do this and I haven't seen your script, so I expect it would be best for you to let us all know where you are headed with this."

"Fair enough. I have seen a copy of the report sent from Circles of Consensus to the Global Council. It's the report which tells them if the people agree with the strategies and work plans presented to the Circles of Humanity groups. Typically, by this stage of the process, everyone is in complete agreement on the details. It seems that this year the results are a bit different than usual. Is that a fair assessment Julie?"

"Yes, it is, Jason. The overall reaction of the COH groups to the various work plans was more negative than usual."

"And why do you think that has occurred?"

"It seems likely that the recent social unrest that has been occurring over the past couple of months, and the promotion of fear and negativity by Mr. Watt, has influenced more people than we would have expected. The fear didn't exist a few months ago when most of the feedback and policies were being developed."

"And would you categorize this fear as being rational?"

"Fear is a feeling. If you are asking me if I believe that some people's current feelings are justified, then I can't help you. I can tell you, however, that based on my personal information and frame of reference, I have not been affected by the recent fears. However, each individual will attach their own information, experiences and biases toward their decision-making and how they feel about it."

"Fair enough."

"Are you afraid of the scenario Mr. Watt has projected, Jason?"

"I thought I was supposed to be asking the questions."

"Maybe, but don't forget, I am a psychologist. It's what we do."

"Do you want me to lie down on a couch?"

"No, I just want you to answer my question," Julie prompted.

"Okay, I will. No, I am not afraid of what I have been hearing from Spencer Watt."

"And why is that, Jason?"

"How about I tell you later. We just have time for one more question."

"And what would that be?"

"After all the work you and your colleagues have put into the past forty years of education and support for the whole of humanity, does this recent negative reaction feel like a failure?"

"I would be lying if I didn't say it feels like a setback. I am disappointed the negativity was as effective as it appears to have been, but I also see it as a learning experience from which we can all grow stronger. The other reality is that the data shows a relationship between increasing age and the effect the fear and negativity had on people. What this means is that those most vulnerable to Spencer Watt's campaign of fear and negativity are those of us who grew up in that environment and have been conditioned to react to it. I would suggest that almost all of the young people who were born after the year twenty twenty-five would have been virtually immune to Mr. Watt's message. What this information means to me is that mankind is advancing and progressing but it takes time to completely transform."

"Until such a time as all of us hold-overs are dead and gone you mean."

"Or are open enough to be able to learn from our children," Julie provided a more positive option.

"That does sound better," Jason admitted.

"It is important for all of us to understand that what we know, feel and believe is largely determined by the filters of our societal environment," Julie tried to summarize. "As society evolves, so do we. The recent trend toward a society of inclusion and positivity allows us all to exist within our changing reality. This developing societal trend has allowed us to know, feel and believe concepts not widely available to our ancestors. Their perspectives were specific to their immediate lives and localized societies. You can only know what you are a witness to and can only change compatibly while being in step with your culture."

Jason sat and thought about what he had just heard. "I believe it's going to require some time for me to absorb this new knowledge, Julie. Thank you so much for your insights, your time and mostly for your dedicated work with Circles of Influence."

"You are very welcome, Jason, and thank you for having me on your show."

****

"Our next guest is the Head of the UN Human Resources Agency, Mansoor Rasheed. Welcome, Mr. Rasheed," Jason greeted his guest. He was a large imposing man whose sparkling eyes and dark features would have been considered by most observers as being attractive. The more subtle aspect of his appearance was his kind face and the warm smile which seemed to be a permanent fixture.

"Mansoor, please. Formalities are not required."

"Mansoor then. Could I ask you to tell us about yourself? You and I have never met and I am sure our audience would appreciate some background from you."

"Of course, Jason. I am sixty-one years old and I live in Tehran, where I was born. My wonderful family includes my wife, four grown children and three grandchildren. I am hoping for more. I was trained as a medical doctor and have a passionate interest in motivation of all kinds. With my job at the United Nations, I strive to combine my physiological knowledge of people with my desire to help them succeed, both individually and as a whole."

"And your family is well?" Jason enquired. He knew that in many cultures, including that of his guest, you would never initiate a formal conversation prior to asking about their family.

"Very well, thank you for asking. I hope your family is prospering as well," Mansoor responded as he was conditioned to do.

"Unfortunately, I haven't been able to spend much time with my family lately, but my wife assures me everyone is well and looking forward to spending time together during our Christmas break," Jason responded and then got back to the interview.

"How long have you worked for the UN, Mansoor?"

"Two years as the head of the HRA and five years before that as an advisor," he related his personal history.

"This is an important meeting for your agency, given the unveiling of the new population strategy," Jason commented beginning to hone in on the topic of interest now that the pleasantries were out of the way.

"Your statement is true to a point," Mansoor agreed tentatively. "We have been working on this new strategy for the past five years as a part of our long-term planning cycle. That is becoming the standard process within most of the agencies. It allows for a clear direction with constant learnings and improvements. What I am trying to say is that every year is equally important to us, as we try to understand what the people want and how best to deliver positive results."

"And it seems the people may want something different this year. It must be difficult to be able to react appropriately to changing conditions and public sentiments."

"It wouldn't be fun if it wasn't challenging, Jason. Besides, what we will be dealing with this coming year, with the nominal increase in negativity, is a fairly easy issue to handle. You have to remember how strongly aligned our population is compared to the past decades when we were completely fragmented and often enemies. The efforts my predecessors had to expend to get us to where we are today make our current issues seem rather inconsequential. That is not to say we don't need to address them seriously, but we also shouldn't fail to acknowledge how far we have come as a united society."

"That's a point well taken, Mansoor," Jason commented. "Imagine if the first time we met, instead of being today, it had been forty years ago when we were in our early twenties."

"Unfortunately, that doesn't take much of an imagination," Mansoor replied, shaking his head. "Even though we could well have been as similar as brothers, with respect to our personalities and moral values, our differences with respect to nationality, religion and socioeconomic backgrounds would likely have kept us separated. If we had met, we would have been armed with misunderstandings about each other. Potentially we could also have been armed with weapons. The mutual respect and commonalities that exist between us today would not likely have been recognized due to the individual influences within both of our societies in the past. It is a tragedy of our history that we all need to keep in mind as we deal with our present and approach our future. There is no issue we will face together that cannot be resolved co-operatively."

Jason listened to his guest and his elegant and positive responses to the questions thrown his way. 'There must be something I can ask him that will elicit a more controversial reaction from him,' Jason pondered.

"Mansoor, what would you say to the families of the, reportedly, deceased elderly victims of what has been described as a strategy by your agency to facilitate controlled deaths?"

"The first thing of course would be to offer my profound condolences for their loss," Mansoor responded instantaneously and then paused slightly before continuing, "and then I would assure them there is no scenario within our agency, or within the Global Council, that would have dictated such brutal actions. I can think of no social agenda that would require us to do such a thing. I would assure them there have been no actions taken that would have resulted in human deaths at the hands of any of our people."

"So the allegations brought against you are false?"

"Absolutely, Jason. We are as disturbed by the allegations as anyone, but fortunately they are false. If there have been people dying under mysterious circumstances, we are not aware of them and certainly are in no way responsible."

"Then how do we deal with our ever-growing population?" Jason pressed on.

"Our global population is determined by three independent factors. How many babies are born, how long people live and how many people die. We monitor each of these closely for the purpose of supporting situations where infants are born healthy and to mothers who are in a position to provide stable long-term support to the child. The responsibility of all parents is to provide the necessary support to every child born into this world. This understanding is what birth control education is designed around. We do not desire to control how many babies are conceived and delivered in a given year, but rather what percentage of them have the basic conditions provided to them to be healthy, loved and supported. With regard to life expectancy, it is a function of delivering the proper living conditions to encourage nutritional, medical and mental health. Those are three things our various Agencies strive to provide. With regard to deaths, once again we do not concern ourselves with the number but rather with the circumstances. Any individual who has a life they wish to preserve will be provided our support to do so. However, should someone find their life situation to be such that they are not mentally or physically able to maintain the desire to continue on, the support is there to allow them to control their own destiny with dignity."

"That all sounds very nice, but in the meantime our numbers continue to grow. How do we deal with that?"

"You know, Jason, that question would be better answered by my colleagues from some of the other agencies such as the Food and Agriculture Agency. With continued efforts, technology and sustainable practices there is a growing confidence that we can keep pace with our population growth. Then of course there are options such as remote populations in space and in our ocean habitats, but I am afraid those topics are way outside of my field of expertise. The statistical facts, however, indicate that even though our global population is still growing, incremental growth has slowed. When we study the demographic trends, it is clear we will soon see a plateauing of the global population and then a gradual shrinking. Looking long term, if we have a population issue at all, it may be that in time, negative growth will become the real issue. Fortunately, that potential scenario is still a long way off."

"You are a hard man to catch off guard and be made to say the wrong thing, Mansoor," Jason admitted.

"Is that what you are trying to do? Perhaps you just haven't asked me the right questions."

"And what would those be?" Jason sincerely wished he knew.

"Well, you could ask me what I think of my youngest daughter's latest hair style. My answer would definitely get me into trouble," Mansoor laughed through his enduring smile.

"Perhaps I will take that tact the next time we meet. Thank you so much for appearing today. I truly am glad we met tonight for the first time instead of forty years ago under different circumstances."

"I am very happy about that as well and I would like to thank you for having me on your show so that I could speak directly to your many viewers."

"You are welcome, Mansoor. Next we will welcome Manuel Rosales who will provide the details surrounding which of the coming year's work strategies were approved to be implemented and then I will be back on camera with another special guest," Jason reported. Then he and Mansoor rose and moved toward Claire's table as Manuel faced the camera and began his presentation.

"Mansoor Rasheed, I would like to introduce you to Claire, my very capable assistant."

"Pleased to meet you Mr. Rasheed," Claire stammered, surprised that Jason had bothered to bring him over to her during his break. "My mother has told me very positive things about you."

"I am afraid you have me at a disadvantage as I am not sure who your mother is."

"Oh, I'm sorry. Of course not. Cayley Wilson is my mother."

"Well, then that makes you a very fortunate daughter. She is a remarkable woman. I have had the good fortune of meeting her on a few occasions."

"I do feel fortunate. May I ask you a question, sir?"

"Only if you call me Mansoor."

"All right, Mansoor, can you tell me why the HRA continues to view the role of the biological mother as the central cornerstone of the family unit while other parents and potential caregivers are less regarded when it comes to determining the acceptance of an infant's life situation," Claire asked.

The two men exchanged glances.

"Aren't you glad she wasn't conducting the interview?" Jason remarked.

"I believe I am," he responded and then turned to face Claire. "That is a very legitimate and complex question. Biologically the mother can give birth to and initially feed the infant, which of course makes her irreplaceable at the beginning of any life. We have the technology to replace the mother completely, but as a race we have strongly voiced our rejection of creating life in a laboratory. Mankind's belief is that a mother is far more than a vessel. She is the warmth, energy and love that allows a fetus to develop, be born and feel instantaneously accepted into the world. For a newborn, she represents its entire world for a short period of time. As such, our collective society sees her as irreplaceable even though technically it is possible to do so. But the bigger question may be, 'Why would you want to replace her?' Following the early stages of life, what you are asking about becomes more of a philosophical question. At that point, the biological father, a surrogate parent, a grandparent or a dedicated caregiver may all be equally capable of providing for the needs of an infant as it grows. Men may not be naturally as nurturing as women on average, but of course that assessment doesn't apply to all cases. Anyone who is motivated and willing to be a parent can certainly fulfill the role of caregiver, but it should be remembered that a child should never be born for the benefit of an adult. The parent should be there for the benefit of the child. This reality is paramount in the equation of growing our society and critical to the early needs of any child is his or her biological mother. You have to understand that from the viewpoint of the HRA we are looking at the big picture of propagating our species under the most ideal circumstances for the largest number of newborns. As socially unpopular as it may sound, the best-case scenario for any child is to have a nurturing biological mother supported by the biological father. To our agency the only thing that matters is the child's welfare and we will strive to support the ideal 'best-case scenario' above all others. Our mandate is to attempt to circumvent the most negative of family situations, which can often be achieved by such means as education, birth control and effective family planning. With these tools we can reduce the numbers of negative family situations and target the ideals."

"But what about loving single parents or gay couples. Why shouldn't they deserve to be parents like anyone else?" Claire pushed her concern.

"Because being parents is not merely a right for people to gain. A new life is far more than a bargaining chip or an achievement to be accomplished to make people feel good. We will always support any of those individual situations that arise because of the positive results which typically result but they should never be seen as the best case scenario for the child, because frankly they're not. It is not the ideal for any individual infant nor to the benefit of mankind as a whole. And that is what our mandate is based on as provided to us through COH. As I mentioned before, a birth is not about a deserving parent. It is about providing the best possible life for every child so it can grow up mentally and physically capable and able to contribute to humanity. I hope I have satisfactorily answered your question, Claire."

"I think so. It's so hard not to look at things from an individual point of view. I understand you have to maintain a broader perspective on behalf of the entire species. That may make it seem more clear cut, but we are a society of individuals, each with specific wants."

"You are right, Claire. But to respond to thats statement I will have to fall back on the words from a popular song written nearly ninety years ago which stated, 'You can't always get what you want, but if you try sometime, you just might find, you get what you need.'"

"Really, Mansoor, you are quoting the Rolling Stones as your argument?"

"How on earth do you know about them, Claire?" Jason interrupted.

"You can blame my grandfather for that."

****

"Hi, it's me again, Dan Wilson, and yes, I was a Stones fan. I've been sitting back and letting you work your way through all of the information and intrigue that has been coming

your way. However, I think the answer Mr. Rasheed gave to Claire about mothers and infants needs a bit of context. When I was a journalist, there became an increasing awareness of what was referred to as political correctness. People had to learn to choose their words very carefully to ensure they didn't offend anyone. Terms considered derogatory could not be used when describing individuals or groups of people and the number of terms and groups on the list kept growing. The cause of this reality was the negativity of our increasingly segmented societies. Each group of people, determined by such things as race, religion, gender, physical characteristic or social capability became labeled by various terms which ranged from descriptive to insulting. Over time, sensitivities to such terms or even subtle references became taboo and evoked increasingly severe social repercussions. The pendulum, had swung too far in the direction that created the use of negative labels, and had gradually swung back too far in the other direction. Hypersensitivity to the point of ridiculousness had become the norm as negativity and divisiveness escalated."

"Another social trend from the same general timeframe was the explosion of human rights and a focus on the needs and wants of the individual rather than the collective. Young people were raised to believe they were entitled to whatever they felt was in their best interest. The end result of these combined trends was the perceived need to treat everyone the same, independent of their differences. If you had read this book forty years ago, in 2018, you would have noticed insights and comments that would have seemed very unpopular with the current thinking of the time. Mr. Rasheed's comments about promoting the ideal of a biological mother and father as parents would have been completely unacceptable to many. It had become commonplace to offer up parenthood as a right rather than a responsibility and to treat infants as commodities. Many individuals and couples felt entitled to have anything they wanted, including their own children. The concept of

entitlement grew like weeds in the era of 'me first' conditioning. There were no prerequisites or boundaries when it came to determining someone's ability to raise, support and care for a child. The only segment of society not being considered, it seemed, were the helpless infants who weren't granted the backing of their own lobby group designed to protect their rights."

"As the insights and processes Dr. Stapleton promoted gradually transformed the human perspective, the trends of negativity, sensitivity and entitlement eventually began to disappear. The inclusive society that exists today is not burdened by the illogical and disruptive factors and feelings existing in the past. The funny thing is that individually, and as a society, we fought against the changes COI was promoting which have transformed our world in such a positive manner. All we could see was change and the unknown. The future can be a scary and negative prospect until you gain the proper perspective."

****

As Manuel Rosales continued to describe the approved Agency plans, Jason Wolfe headed back to his desk and prepared for his next guest. He was excited but a bit nervous about the upcoming segment. He always looked forward to this annual show where his guests were 'live and in person' rather than on a video screen from their location thousands of kilometres away. The experience was somehow more visceral and took him back to his early days in the business where most interviews were done live. It is far easier to read someone when you are face to face. From their body language, or the slight evidence of perspiration on their forehead, you could tell if they were uncomfortable or excited. Today he was expecting an abundance of perspiration, which would be a good thing. As the only show of the year with live guests, in front of a live audience, he was looking to make a big and memorable splash. 'Maybe it would be good if Claire was in my position,' Jason surmised, aware of his own human frailties. 'She probably wouldn't let her ego drive the direction of the show.'

Manuel was finishing off the details of his speech and Jason was ready and prepared to engage with him.

"Thank you, Manuel. You provided us with an excellent overview of your plans for the upcoming year. I am sure our viewers now have a clear idea of what to expect." Jason hadn't been paying attention and had no idea if that comment was true, but it seemed like the right thing to say to a person who, should he choose to, could influence the lives of every living creature on the planet. He shuddered at the concept of that kind of power in the hands of many of the past world leaders and conquerors. The history books are filled with narcissistic, ego-feeding individuals who would either dress up as the champion of the people or merely trample over them in the pursuit of notoriety, wealth and power. In contrast, Manuel and his associates at the Global Council and within the United Nations were problem-solvers and facilitators. They quietly and without fanfare, other than this one annual meeting, progressed the global human agenda with little in the way of compensation other than the satisfaction of making a positive difference. It truly had been a remarkable transformation.

"Coming up later in the show, we will have Señor Rosales back to review the projects that did not receive popular consent from the COH groups. We have a few minutes right now to discuss which of the unapproved projects you have the most concern about having to abandon."

Manuel thought for a moment, not immediately sure how to respond. "You know, Jason," he began slowly forming his thoughts, "it's not really about my concerns regarding whether or not a specific project is done in a certain time frame. My ideas and biases toward a specific agenda, although informed, are really inconsequential. It is when individuals, who are in positions like mine, push their own ideas that we get into trouble. It is especially true when those people have the power to get their way. We have come so far with respect to utilizing the will of the entire population in making decisions. It would be a huge mistake to go back to a system where my idea is more important than yours because of my position. The projects which were rejected in the recent process will get done whenever an educated population wants them. If the approval never happens, then clearly the project was not necessary."

"So you aren't going to lose sleep over any of them?" Jason tried again.

"My sleep patterns don't factor into this. By deferring projects, there will certainly be some people, in certain areas, who will not get what would be considered the most efficient delivery of services or living conditions for a period of time. However, if there is a valid reason for the broad population to not support those projects, then it is best overall to wait until they do."

"For the first time you are starting to sound like a politician, Manuel."

"I assume you are not saying that as a compliment."

"You assume correctly. The unsupported projects and strategies are not about the specific details of those plans. It was a protest vote created by a campaign of negativity through the leadership of Spencer Watt against the Global Council. Unfortunately, the people who will be victimized by the cancellation of those programs had nothing to do with this but are paying the price."

"You may be correct, Jason, but if the people don't trust us at the moment, then do we really have the authority to continue implementing programs on their behalf?"

"That is an interesting question, Manuel. Perhaps we can invite someone to join us in this discussion who can answer that question from his point of view. Ladies and gentlemen, please welcome to the stage, Spencer Watt."

The audience provided a modicum of polite applause interspersed with demonstrative cheering from a few obvious supporters or previous fans. As he walked across the stage and acknowledged the crowd, he appeared to be very pleased with himself.

"Welcome back to the show, Spencer," Jason spoke first. "Have you and Manuel Rosales met each other before?" he enquired.

Manuel rose from his seat to greet the man who had been openly critical of him and his colleagues.

"I'm pleased to meet you, Spencer," Manuel offered his hand.

"Mucho gusto Manuel," came the reply.

As soon as they were seated, Jason began the carefully scripted dialogue that was to follow.

"It has been about a month since we last spoke on this show, Spencer. Can you give us your thoughts on what has transpired since then."

"Firstly, I would like to thank you for inviting me today. It would be far more fitting to have invited the billions of people who I represent, but I suppose the logistics would be too much even for your show to handle."

It seemed clear Spencer Watt had come to the show to bask in his own glory, which was exactly what Jason was hoping for. His self-adulation should keep him distracted from what Jason hoped would unfold.

"I believe what has occurred over the past month is true democracy," Spencer continued. "The people have spoken and the Global Council has listened. All I have done is to facilitate the result. Mr. Morales and his colleagues have demonstrated their willingness to undertake the only true mandate which is to follow the voice of the people. Their pledge to respect the sanctity of life and guarantee that no more lives will be taken in the name of population control proves that the system works. All that was required was for the message of the people to be delivered to the Global Council in a way that it could not be ignored. I am pleased I could lend my assistance in making it happen."

"You said no more lives will be taken. Do you have absolute proof the Global Council knowingly authorized the clandestine execution of members of our society? Our previous guest, Mansoor Rasheed strongly denied any such occurrence," Jason stated.

"Do you really think they would admit doing such a terrible thing? Apparently, twenty percent of the people believe they may have done it," Spencer rebutted.

"Maybe, but what proof are they basing their opinions on?" Jason probed. "Do you have anything for us supporting your allegations? We have the Chairman of the Global Council sitting right beside me. It seems this would be the time to get to the bottom of this while the world is watching."

Spencer shifted his weight in his chair and looked directly at the camera. Thoughts were formulating but a little too slowly to be able to pull this off. As an actor, he was used to reading scripts not thinking quickly on his feet. He hadn't expected to be interrogated. He was here to be congratulated and honoured. "Look," he finally responded, "I'm not here to create negativity and drag this issue down into the mud. I don't think Señor Rosales deserves to be taken to task on a live show. The bottom line is, I helped them see the problems that existed and now we can all move forward together."

"Why do you think it was necessary for you to circumvent the system in place through Circles of Consensus and Braintrust? Do you believe the will of the people would not have occurred without the benefit of your actions?" Jason probed, not letting the issue drop.

"It's really hard to say," Spencer responded reluctantly, "all I know is that when I observed the tens of thousands of people who were willing to sacrifice their own safety during the numerous protests just to be heard, it moved me. These people were desperate to be taken seriously and now they have been."

"That's a good segue into what we have lined up for our audience. It really has been a historical couple of months, and we felt it would be prudent of us to document what has transpired. Does that sound like a good idea Spencer?"

"Absolutely, Jason," he replied smugly, enjoying his moment of regained fame and thankful they were moving on.

"Good. Our first video is from the period of time leading up to and during the initiation of the demonstration which was held in Hanoi. As we watch the video I will narrate what we are seeing. Has either of you gentlemen been to Hanoi?" Jason asked Manuel and Spencer. Both replied they had never physically been there so Jason continued his description.

"The Old Quarter, in the city centre, is where this man is setting a fire designed to be the focal point of the demonstration. It is just beside the Lake of the Returned Sword which is a beautiful and popular spot for locals to take an evening stroll. You can see the man is busy preparing the fire, and when he finishes he makes a phone call. Perhaps he is calling his wife to let her know he will be late for dinner, or maybe he is speaking with a collaborator about the proper time to light the fire. It probably doesn't matter but likely it was about the fire, because, as you will see, as soon as he ends the call he starts the blaze and kicks off the festivities. Then, ten minutes later, he casually leaves the scene. If we watched this for another four hours, we would see tens of thousands of people get involved and ultimately initiate violence. Police would be summoned and the situation would escalate. Sixty-three people would be either admitted to the hospital or treated and sent home. This appears to be a senseless occurrence created by what appears to be a single anarchist. However, if you watch closely, you will see five other people in the crowd with amplifiers who appear to be working with the fire starter. If you were to use facial recognition and identify the six individuals you would find that they are in fact acquaintances. As it turns out, the local police did exactly that and the perpetrators have been detained, interviewed and charged with criminal mischief causing bodily harm."

"These are the people you have provided your voice to, are they not, Mr. Watt?" Jason attacked his prey.

"Definitely not," he rebutted. "It is the tens of thousands of concerned citizens who were there peacefully voicing their concerns who I represent."

"That makes sense," Jason replied with a slight hint of sarcasm.

"Let's move forward in time about a week and we will go to the beautiful city of Buenos Aires. You live in that city, don't you, Mr. Rosales?" Jason asked the question, already knowing the answer.

"Yes I do. I was born there and have resided there for most of my life," Manuel replied proudly.

"Then perhaps you can describe the scene we are about to view."

"I will try, Jason. We are looking at the Plaza de Maya in the centre of the city near the waterfront. A man is building a fire next to the Piramide de Maya which was built in 1811 to commemorate the anniversary of the May Revolution. You can see the beautiful Casa Rosada in the background," Manuel described the scene, exhibiting his pride of the location and its history.

"Good, thank you, Manuel. We are now going to fast forward through this scene to the part where we see the man finishing his task of setting the fire, and then what does he do? You guessed it, he makes a phone call. Perhaps to tell his wife he will be late getting home for dinner," Jason teased.

"Probably not. He ends the phone call and then lights the fire, just like the man in Hanoi. Once again if we were to continue watching we would see him leave, and five accomplices begin working from within the crowd to get them worked up. The problem is, this time someone died. A woman was trampled to death when a section of scaffolding collapsed. Now perhaps there is a handbook you can buy called 'Demonstrations for Dummies' describing the optimum method for planning a riot and coincidently both of the gentlemen we have viewed purchased a copy. Step 1. Set a fire. Step 2. Phone your wife. Step 3. Light the fire. Step 4. Invite five friends along to incite the crowd which gathers while you take off."

The audience was enjoying his approach even though they had no idea where he was headed.

"If the show was part of a mini-series we could in fact show you eight other examples from the ten demonstrations suggesting that 'Demonstrations for Dummies' was in fact a best seller. In all cases the exact same recipe for disaster was followed and, in all cases, those responsible have been found and arrested."

Jason glanced at his two guests to see if they were enjoying his humorous take on this as much as he was. They didn't seem to be.

"So what do you make of all of this Manuel?" Jason asked.

"It looks like all of these demonstrations were part of a single orchestrated effort."

"Does that seem likely to you, Spencer?" Jason asked.

"Well, I suppose it's possible. Whatever group initiated this whole thing may have planned these unfortunate incidents as one," Spencer replied, suddenly becoming nervous. Thankfully he had only paid the ten groups a small deposit with the guarantee of a very substantial payday in six months when everything died down, assuming they did not implicate him in any way.

"But surely, after the one in Buenos Aires went sideways and someone was inadvertently killed, they would have stopped at that point. It is hard to believe they would have repeatedly started more demonstrations knowing what had happened," Manuel added his thoughts.

"Maybe they thought it was a freak incident and it wouldn't happen again," Spencer speculated.

"But it did happen again, ten days later in Madrid," Manuel refuted. "Two people died and still they staged more demonstrations. Whoever orchestrated these events clearly wasn't concerned about casualties, even though they were protesting to prevent fatalities."

"I think you're right, Manuel," Jason agreed. "There seems to be motivations here besides protecting humanity, but what could they possibly be? Any thoughts, Spencer?"

"I listened to their speeches and I was moved by them. They sounded very sincere to me. Otherwise, I would have never gotten involved. Anyway, thankfully this is all behind us. The Global Council has heard our pleas and has reacted accordingly."

"In essence, you are correct," Jason agreed, "but perhaps it isn't completely behind us. I have another video I believe will prove to be interesting." Projected on a giant screen was a picture of an old earthen building in need of repair. There were two small windows covered with wide wooden slats and a door that suddenly flew open. Four men exited into the early signs of dawn from the interior of the structure. Two of the men were in handcuffs and being escorted by military personnel to an enclosed vehicle. Then, a couple of minutes later, an elderly man was assisted gently through the door by two additional uniformed men and taken to a waiting ambulance.

"What are we looking at?" Spencer demanded.

"We thought you would be relieved to know that the man you thought was killed by the Global Council is alive and well. He was shaken and traumatized for sure, but he is still alive. His grandson, who works at COI, will be there tomorrow to help take care of him."

"I am very relieved," Spencer gasped, suddenly turning pale.

"You were so convinced he had been killed," Jason pushed further. "Who was your source of that information?"

"You know I can't reveal my sources."

"I do know you are neither a journalist nor a cop so telling us where you got your information from would be both legal and honourable, considering what you have put his family through," Jason continued, observing Spencer Watt closely. His early swagger had disappeared. His smile was barely hanging on below his nose and he was beginning to sweat.

"Look," Spencer took the offensive, "if you are going to accuse me of something then my part in this show is over."

"No one is accusing you of anything, Mr. Watt, other than perhaps being secretive. Speaking of, I have one more guest I would like to invite on stage. I am sure we will all be interested in what she has to tell us," Jason responded attempting to calm his guest.

"Fine, so who is this guest?" Spencer asked, looking forward to a distraction.

"Her name is Sasha Kovelov."

Jason turned to where she was standing in the wings. "Would you like to come out on stage and join us, Sasha. Please give her a warm welcome," Jason instructed the audience. She took a seat next to Manuel without a smile or acknowledging anyone in the room.

"Hello, Ms. Kovelov, welcome to our show. I would like to introduce you to our other guests. You are sitting next to Manuel Rosales, the Chairman of the Global Council and next to him is Spencer Watt, former movie star and current social activist."

She nodded politely at both men without saying a word.

"I understand you are a Technological Forensic Scientist. Can you explain to our audience what exactly that entails?" Jason enquired.

"I extract useful information from historical technical data," she answered succinctly.

"So you could find out if I bought my wife flowers for our anniversary five years ago."

"You didn't," she deadpanned a simple reply.

"How on earth do you know that?"

"You were not married five years ago. I like to research people who will be asking me questions."

"Wow, so what else did you discover about me?" Jason asked, genuinely curious what her response would be.

"Nothing very interesting."

"Ouch! Well, if you are interested, I can fill you in on some things after the show." Jason responded to the enjoyment of the audience, but seemingly not to Sasha.

"Did you also research our other two guests?"

"Of course."

"And are they more interesting than I am?"

"Actually, yes," came Sasha's response with a brief but perceptible smile.

"Really, would you mind telling us how that could possibly be true?" Jason requested.

"Well, Señor Rosales is a former judge who once presided over a case in Argentina where the daughter of the President was kidnapped and held ransom."

"Wow, I didn't know that and I always research my guests as well. Is Sasha correct, Manuel?"

"I guess it is safe to confirm it is the truth. The entire trial records were expunged to ensure confidentiality and the safety of all of the participants. I am shocked you were able to discover the information, Ms. Kovelov."

Her only response was another partial smile.

"And what, if anything, did you learn about Mr. Watt?" Jason asked, becoming more intrigued.

"He once won six academy awards, he has an interesting financial relationship with a man named Will Hamilton and he has recently had numerous private communications and wire transfers that normally could never have been traced or hacked."

"What do you mean by normally?" Jason sought clarification as he kept an eye on Spencer sitting beyond her.

"I mean that without a combination of clearance, tools and skills beyond virtually everyone on the planet, the conversations and money transfers would have been undetectable."

Spencer began to shift nervously in his chair.

"Virtually everyone except you, I expect," Jason clarified.

"Me and a handful of others at the ICPA."

"You're referring to the United Nations International Crime Prevention Agency?"

Spencer Watt's eyes began to shift from side to side as he seemingly began to examine his options in earnest.

"Yes," Sasha confirmed. "We were called in when it was reported that a Mr. Jeung Li was missing and reported as being deceased."

"Reported by Mr. Watt, in fact, to the entire world," Jason interrupted.

"Correct. The members of the Global Council knew they had not abducted or killed anyone, as was reported, so it begged the question as to who could be responsible," Sasha concluded her answer. "We began at the source and didn't need to go any further. At that point, investigators who you hired, Mr. Wolfe, tipped us off as to the whereabouts of Mr. Li who had not been killed but merely held captive."

"As we saw on the earlier video, he was rescued safely in a special-ops mission less than twenty-four hours ago," Manuel added to the detail. "His kidnappers are in custody."

"Who were they? Why did they abduct an old man?" Jason probed, already knowing the answers to his questions. A glance over at Spencer showed him staring down into his lap, completely motionless, seemingly frozen from fear.

"They were just hired thugs," Manuel answered, "but interestingly connected, as their orders came from the same source as did the people who orchestrated each of the demonstrations last month."

"That was where our forensics came in," Sasha reported, almost seeming human in her admiration of their clandestine work.

"This is fascinating, don't you think, Spencer," Jason placed the focus directly on his guest who still seemed to be in a hypnotic trance. Then, suddenly, he jumped up from his seat and bolted toward an exit, which two rather enormous uniformed officers immediately blockaded.

Realizing his fate, Spencer went limp and was immediately handcuffed and taken away. The audience applauded vigorously at the turn of events. Just like the end of an old-fashioned detective show, the villain had been cornered and trapped.

****

Well, it looks like we have come to the end of your adventure. Maybe it's my training

as a journalist, but I always felt the need to wrap up my reports with a synopsis of what I wanted the reader to walk away with. Because I lived through the entire span of the forty years leading up to this storyline and global society, I feel I am more than qualified to sum things up. Independent of where you lived in the world or when you were born over the past century, your life has been unique. The genetics, geography and timing of your birth pre-determined much of your life. The conditioning of the society you lived in determined how you would develop according to the changes that occurred in your lifetime. Change is an inevitable reality and with technological advancements it has become increasingly globalized.

Forty years ago, from my perspective in the media, it was clear to me our western society was deteriorating. Divisiveness was growing in most aspects of our mainstream society and there was little or no commonality of thought or feelings. Some people had good lives they wanted to preserve and others demanded change, away from their *existing plight. A common reality was for people to join segmented groups based on a specific commonality to promote and defend the rights of that group within the broader social structure. The media drove and facilitated much of the negativity and discontent that fostered this alienation and segmentation.*

Then Adam Stapleton became motivated to help people and a societal revolution began. The existing power structure became threatened and the general population found a means with which to connect. This book has described the result of a process leading to changes not even plausible forty years ago. The state of humanity had no way of understanding the realities awaiting them both individually and collectively. Centuries of war, fear and classism were slowly wiped away by the commonality of humanity we didn't even know existed. The emergence of technology provided a vehicle which allowed billions of people to interconnect, and Adam Stapleton and his colleagues facilitated the change.

I didn't see this coming. I don't think anyone did. Our current reality is what exists around us. Your future reality could be anything you can imagine.

The inconceivable is possible.

Chapter 40
December 24, 2058. Trenton, USA.

There was a light skiff of snow on the ground as Claire and Jermaine walked together from the train station to their mother's apartment. They each carried two presents.

"What did you get her?" Claire bugged her brother, never one to be able to wait until Christmas morning.

"If I tell you then you will feel bad about what you are giving her."

"What do you mean? I have a great gift for Mom!"

"Yeah, what is it?"

"I'll only tell you if you tell me what you got her."

"Fine. So what did you get her?"

"When we were home at Thanksgiving I took some of the old jewelry Dad had given her from her jewelry box and had a friend of mine re-form it into a cool broach. It's beautiful," Claire proclaimed.

"What a great gift. Well done!"

"So what did you get her?"

"I think it used to be called a mixed tape," Jermaine explained.

"You mean like a bunch of her favourite songs she can listen to?" she clarified, secretly pleased with the fact her mother would like her gift better.

"Something like that, but not songs."

"Then what?"

"Remember before Dad died and we used to have all of those family debates and philosophical discussions?"

"Yeah."

"Well, for some reason, at the time, I decided to record them all. I wanted to replay them so I could understand how Mom and Dad always seemed to win the debates by sounding so smart. I would study them for hours at night."

"I didn't know you did that," Claire responded in surprise.

"Yeah, well I never got rid of them so I decided to edit a highlight tape, keeping the best moments of the four of us sharing our intellectual and intimate ideas. I have kind of woven a story out of them."

"Wow, Mom is going to love it. She spends so much time alone I'm sure she will play it over and over."

"You are making her sound like a poor old woman with no life, knitting while she sits in a rocking chair with her cat."

"Of course not, but she must get lonely sometimes since we left home. I hope she is okay with us going skiing for a couple of days over the holidays. Do you think she would come with us?" Claire wondered aloud, worried about leaving her alone.

"And actually leave her rocking chair and knitting needles? Leave her apartment and talk to real people? That doesn't sound like the aging reclusive widow I know," Jermaine teased.

"But it's been five years since Dad died and two years since I left home."

"And now all she has is her cat. Other than the fact she is keeping the entire world from falling prey to psychos like Spencer Watt, like some sort of super hero."

"Does she even have a cape?" Claire asked.

"I don't know," Jermaine pondered, "but I know for sure she doesn't have knitting needles, or a cat." The two siblings laughed as they reached their mother's doorstep.

"Merry Christmas Mom!" they shouted out as they entered her apartment and saw her sitting in front of the fire reading.

"Oh my God, you're early," Cayley shrieked. "Can you believe we have five whole days together with no interruptions?"

Claire and Jermaine looked at each other and smiled.

"Just the three of us," they agreed, almost in unison.

Chapter 41
October 10, 2018: Washington State Corrections Centre for Women.

The slamming of a metal door startled Cayley out of what must have been a deep sleep. The dreary confines of her dungeon-like cell was a rude awakening from the idyllic dream state she had just been torn away from. She tried valiantly to remember the components of the fiction that had just unfolded from her subconscious. It was her future and it was remarkable, making her current incarceration that much more depressing. All she could hope for was that Matt would be true to his word and get her out of this hellhole. She couldn't wait to see her father, and to tell Julie all about her amazing dream.

****

This brings us full circle, back to the beginning, or perhaps, the middle. Did Cayley really conjure up a vision of her future while awaiting her release from prison. Did her version of what would lie ahead include the concepts of Circles of Humanity? I'm not a mind reader and she never said anything to me about it. She was in such a dark place, I can't even imagine what thoughts and feelings were controlling her existence. She had no way of knowing what would become of her life and I don't think it's anyone's place to tell her. Having our specific future revealed would ruin the experience of living it.

I have invited you along on this preview of our world forty years from now for the purpose of enlisting you to help make it a reality. These stories were created to help us all realize our true potential and to open our minds to a more favourable reality than we are often able to understand or imagine.

I began conceiving this storyline the day my baby girl was first incarcerated. It was three years ago and at the time, my career and my life in general had been demolished by grief and my incapacity to function. Writing became my personal therapy as I created a fictional path my daughter could follow in an attempt to return to society, and to me. I needed to hold onto that dream. I researched concepts of psychology to help me believe it was possible for Cayley to transform back to the person she deserved to be. She didn't ask for the life I dealt her.

As I created a scenario of success, I saw the need for a friend and mentor, since I hadn't fulfilled either of those roles for her. Within the concept of Book 1: Circles of Influence, I imagined Julie Peters and Adam Stapleton and allowed them to enter Cayley's life. In my imagination, and in the words on the pages I began to fill, her life began to change, just as I hoped she could do in her actual life. I placed her with a group of peers who I hoped she could relate to and grow with. Our society is full of youthful potential that isn't given the support it needs. The dramatic storyline was specifically fictional but far too relatable within our current society. The purpose of the story wasn't so much to create drama and tension, but rather to provide insights within a relatable sequence of events.

I also took the liberty of presenting a more flattering version of myself than I may deserve, but after all, this is my therapy and I needed to heal along with my daughter.

As I assembled the storyline, I gained societal and psychological insights. I began to see a future built on the promise of humanity. My therapeutic writing began to change me and positivity flourished within my hopes and dreams. Book II, Circles of Humanity describes the future I began to envision. For the sake of readability, I scraped together as much intrigue and conflict as could occur in a cohesive future global society.

In my mind, and in the books you have just read, I have created a future for my troubled daughter. I have given her everything she could wish to attain.

Admittedly, these stories began as a desperate fantasy designed to help me cope with my life. Now that you have travelled through my mind into what could be our collective future, I hope you will consider joining Cayley, and together, come to discover what is possible.

THE END

Please join me on my website:
www.circlesofhumanity.com
to continue your personal journey within a growing society of positivity,

Made in the USA
San Bernardino, CA
07 July 2018